ALSO BY A. S. KELLY

The 21-Day Boyfriend

LOVE AT LAST

Last Call
About Last Night
One Last Kiss
The Last One

FROM CONNEMARA WITH LOVE

The Best Man
The First Man
The Good Man
The Only Man
The Wrong Man
The Lost Man

O'CONNOR BROTHERS SERIES

Ian
Ryan
Nick

FOUR DAYS

Rainy Days
Sweet Days
Bad Days
Lost Days

IAN

O'CONNOR BROTHERS
BOOK 1

A. S. KELLY

Copyright © 2019 A. S. Kelly

IAN
O'Connor Brothers
Book 1

A. S. Kelly

English Edition

Literary and artistic property reserved.
All rights reserved. Unauthorised reproduction prohibited.

This novel is a work of fiction.
Names, characters, places and storyline are the fruit of the author's imagination or are used in a fictional sense. Any similarity to facts, places or people living or deceased is purely coincidental.

Photography by Wander Aguiar Photography

For more information, visit A.S. Kelly website:
www.ASKELLYWRITES.com

Follow A. S. Kelly:
Twitter @askellywrites
Instagram @askellywrites
Facebook @askellywrites

1
Ian

Three years earlier

The music is too loud, the voices too rowdy. The alcohol, my drunk friends, the overly-excited guests. The women are the same groupies as always, hoping to lure in a sports champion.

I hate these parties. I hate these people.

I hate my whole life.

I just want to play. Rugby is the only thing I know how to do, and the only thing that makes me feel good. It's what shapes my identity: without rugby, I wouldn't be anything.

"Hey, champ." A woman approaches the bar and takes the stool next to me. She touches my arm, and my nerves go rigid.

"We haven't met yet."

Maybe because I had no intention of meeting you.

"I'm Marilyn."

Oh, that's original.

"I'm here with some friends. Big supporters of the team."

Well, you don't say.

"This might seem silly to you, but I actually came here hoping to meet you." She squeezes my arm as I grip my glass tighter.

She raises her hand slowly, sensually, up to my shoulder.

"May I ask if this player is here with anybody tonight?" She whispers.

I take a deep breath and turn away, ready to put a stop to this before it can begin, when someone wraps their arms around my neck, practically choking me.

"Here I am! Sorry I'm late!"

She hugs me and pushes her lips against mine. "I couldn't find a taxi," she says, slowly pulling away from me.

I'm surprised and completely taken aback, but she smiles at me, winking. "Did you order me anything to drink?"

"Er, I…" I mutter like an absolute idiot.

Then she turns to the intruder and says dryly, "I think this is my seat."

I'm lucky I don't choke on my own saliva.

Embarrassed, the woman gets up and leaves the bar without a word, and this stranger, who appeared out of nowhere, sits down next to me.

"Vodka and lemonade, please," she tells the barman. "Heavy on the vodka, easy on the lemonade."

Then she turns to me and smiles.

Again.

The barman sets her drink down, and she immediately takes a few sips.

I stay there, frozen. Dumbstruck. Mute.

"So…" she begins, turning to face me, "it looks like you owe me a favour – an enormous one."

"Me? What?" I snap out of my daze.

"I saved your life."

"Are you joking?" I raise an eyebrow.

"I'm being completely serious." Her face is too.

"And how's that, exactly? Let's hear it."

"I've saved you from a boring night, first of all. From that leech trying to slide herself into your bed – maybe even your life! From a failed marriage spent buying shoes and clothes for your trophy wife."

I burst out laughing.

"You're not exaggerating there, are you?"

She laughs too.

"Perhaps, a bit, but you know, you never know how the night is going to turn out, what one meeting might lead to. Sometimes, a person can change your whole life, whether you want them to or not, and the results aren't always good."

"Seems to me like your imagination is running a bit wild. And I could've got rid of her without your help."

"Huh. Sure seemed to me like you were in trouble."

"Trust me, I know how to defend myself."

She looks me over for a few seconds.

"Yes, I imagine you do," she says rolling her eyes. "Anyway, it's too late now."

"For what?"

"You're tied to me forever."

"Really?"

"You better believe it. You're in big debt with me, my friend."

I look at her, amused.

"You could also pay up right away and consider yourself free."

"And what would that involve?"

"A dance. With me." She nods towards the dance floor at the end of the room.

"I'm sorry, I don't dance."

Her lip curls in disappointment.

"Oh, that's too bad for you," she says, putting down her drink and standing up. "I'll find someone else to dance with, and you'll still be in debt to me. And all debts must be repaid," she whispers in my ear before heading towards the dance floor in her red backless dress.

I watch her disappear into the crowd, still thrown off by the unlikely encounter, when my brother, Ryan, sits himself down next to me.

"Where'd she come from?"

I shrug.

"Same old gold digger looking for something exciting?"

"Probably," I say, unconvinced.

"You don't want to let her get away." Ryan elbows me and gestures across the room with his head. I see Jake, one of my teammates, approach her and another girl.

"You should do something."

"I have no intention of doing anything."

"She doesn't seem too bad."

"That's not what I'm talking about."

"Well then, what is it?"

I sigh. "That's not the kind of woman you can forget about after a night or two."

"And you picked up all of this insight by having a two-minute conversation with her?"

"I just know, that's all."

"And that's a bad thing?"

"A fucking disaster."

Ryan shakes his head in disapproval as I force myself to watch the scene playing out a few metres in front of me.

Jake approaches the girl and smiles at her.

I sit up straight on my stool.

Jake talks to her, unloading all of his charm, and she blushes.

I feel my stomach burst into flames.

Jake offers her his hand. She looks at her friend, who nods, then accepts it and follows him to the dance floor.

I jump to my feet instinctively.

Jake puts his hand on her bare back and lets it slide down slowly to her waist and she tilts her head to the side in surprise, perhaps a bit uncomfortable with the gesture.

I rest my elbow on the counter behind me.

Jake whispers in her ear, and she smiles again: mouth, eyes and face.
Everything.
Every part of her is smiling.
And my legs are shaking.

2
Ian

Present

I open the front door with my key and am immediately surrounded by the delicious aroma of my mother's baked ham. I smile to myself, knowing that she probably made it just for me; she always does when I come home. It's one of my favorite meals, and she spoils me like a little kid.

"Hey, I'm home," I say as I walk into the living room and find my father sitting on the sofa in front of the TV.

"Ian?" He turns towards me. "What are you doing here?"

I furrow my brow. "Mum invited me over for dinner."

"Yes, of course," he says distractedly, turning back to the screen.

I go to the kitchen where my mother has set the table for three. We haven't used the dining room for a long time. We're never all together in a big group like we used to be.

"Sweetheart," Mum says, hugging me a bit too tightly, and letting go slowly, rubbing my face where a beard has been growing undisturbed for a few weeks now.

"It's nice to have you home," she smiles tenderly, and a wave of sadness washes over me.

I know she's happy that I'm here just as I know she misses my brothers, but neither of them ever make an effort to come over.

"Everything's all ready. Can you tell your father it's time to eat, please?"

"Of course." I give her a kiss on the cheek and go back to the living room where the TV's still on, but my father isn't there anymore.

I knock on the bathroom door under the stairs, but he's not there either. I call to him from downstairs to see if he'd maybe gone upstairs to his room, but there's no answer.

I go to make my way back to the kitchen when I see the front door is slightly ajar, knowing I closed it when I came in.

I go over and look out the window: my father is standing on the pavement, looking out to the street. I go over to him, but he isn't aware of my presence. I touch his shoulder, and he jerks his head towards me, confused.

"What are you doing out here?"

He looks at me, but not really. His eyes are looking into mine, but his attention is elsewhere.

"Dad?"

"Ian? What are you doing here?" he asks, finally recognizing me.

"I'm..." the words die in my throat. And maybe something else too.

"Let's go inside, dinner's ready."

"It's already dinner time?" he asks innocently,

and I force a smile.

"Mum's made ham."

"Ham? That means Ian must be on his way. It's one of his favorite meals, you know, and Karen loves spoiling the kids." he laughs, shaking his head as he makes his way into the house. He stops at the doorway and turns to me.

"Will you stay for dinner with us?" he asks kindly.

"Why not – thank you," I manage, before the lump in my throat becomes too big to swallow.

"That's good, good."

My father heads into the house, leaving the door open and me standing outside alone, wondering what the future holds for the man who worked endlessly to give our family everything we needed.

Lost in my thoughts, I don't see Mum until she appears at my side. I open my arms, and she hides herself in them, resting her head on my chest. I wrap her up and kiss her head.

"Why didn't you tell me right away?"

"I didn't want to worry you. He didn't want me to."

I nod, pulling her closer to me.

"It's all happening so quickly, Ian. I'm not ready to lose him."

"I'm not ready either," I say into her hair.

"We still have so much to do together."

"I know," I agree, defeatedly.

Mum sighs before pulling away from me, attempting to compose herself. I dry her tears with my thumbs and give her my best forced smile.

"Let's go inside. Your father is waiting," she says as she slowly walks back to the front door.

"Mum?" I ask before she reaches the house. "Do you think we should call…"

"I don't know how long we'll have his full attention for," she says calmly. She's always calm. "But what I don't want is for them to come here and then start doing what they always do. So, let's wait a little while longer. If things get worse, we'll talk about it then."

She heads in, while I stay outside a few more minutes, breathing slowly, attempting to calm the storm of emotion battering against me. And it's something that I need to address right away, because I won't be able to do this on my own. I'm not strong enough.

Without overthinking it, I grab my phone from my pocket. Three rings later, a sleepy voice answers.

"Ian?"

"Were you asleep?" I ask, looking at my watch.

"No, I was watching a film on the sofa. I'm just chilling."

"You have to come back."

"What?"

"It's time for you to come home."

"What the hell…?"

"It's getting worse, Ryan."
"How much worse?" he asks in a whisper.
"Find a flight."

3
Ian

We're at the beginning of the second half, and we're up by ten, which is still not enough to consider this game a victory yet. We've got forty-two minutes of play left, and Connacht isn't showing any signs of giving up; we're first place in the league right now, which means we can't afford to lose this one.

"Let's kick their arses," our team captain, Jamie, says, slapping me on the back before taking his position.

I take a deep breath and follow him with my eyes, ready to run down the side as soon as these two dickheads stop trying to rip my pants off, as we wait for Jamie to work some of his magic. Alongside being our captain, he's also the smartest player I know, despite the fact that he's not particularly big.

As soon as I see Jamie run off with the ball, I break away from the opposition, who are breathing down my neck; but before I can receive his pass, he's tackled by three players who bring him down hard.

I throw myself into the scrum with the others, trying to wrangle the ball free, but the screaming from the bottom and the referee's whistle forces us all to stop.

The players get up, one by one, and I wait to see my captain emerge from the heap, but when the last giant is on his feet, Jamie is still laid out in the grass, with his face contracting in painful spasms, holding his right leg.

As I get closer to him, I gesture to the bench to send someone onto the field as I try to grasp what's happened.

"My knee, Ian."

"Take it easy, the paramedics are on their way."

"It's over."

"Don't be so melodramatic," I say, trying to joke around. "It's probably just bruised."

Jamie spreads himself out on the grass as the other team members circle around us.

"I'm screwed."

"You're crying like a little kid."

He covers his face with his hands while the paramedics lift him onto a stretcher and load him into the electric ambulance. I follow them, making sure Jamie gives the spectators a sign that he's okay.

"For the crowd, Jamie."

He shakes his head no.

"Come on, mate, you know the deal. Just a little thumbs-up, okay?"

"Fuck you and your thumbs-up."

I sigh and let my guard down.

"For *her*. Just do it for *her*."

Jamie moves his arm away from his face, and it's only then that I see his torment is the mirror image of my own.

He lifts his thumb into the air and fakes a smile that is broadcast onto the big screens, sending the fans into delirium.

I smile and accompany them to the changing room, but when they stop me from going in any further, Jamie grabs my arm. With his other hand, he takes off his captain's badge and hands it to me.

I squeeze it in my hand, and he lets go of it, laying back again, leaving me with an oppressive weight, too heavy for me to bear.

* * *

Two hours after the end of the game, I'm on my motorbike, racing towards the hospital where Jamie has been taken as a precaution. No one was able to say anything specific about his condition, although it's clear it has something to do with his knee. No one knows if it's a tear, a pull, or something worse. They wouldn't speculate without running some basic tests first.

After I park the motorbike, taking off my helmet, I go inside and ask the receptionist where I can find my teammate. After a few smiles and an autograph, the woman tells me where Jamie is, so I take the lift to the third floor. I find his room and walk right in.

"Well, have you found your balls or did you leave them on the field?" I ask, attempting to bring the drama down a few levels, but when she turns around on hearing my voice, my heart slides down my ribcage and slams onto the ground, right next to hers.

"Right now, all I want is some morphine," Jamie says, plunging the two of us into total embarrassment. "Anything not to be here with you."

If he hadn't just broken his knee on the field, I swear, I'd break it for him now.

"I wouldn't want there to be too much of a crowd here," I say, suffocating.

She and I in the same room.

There's not enough air for the both of us.

Riley gets off the bed without lifting her eyes to meet mine and explains, "I was just about to ask the doctor when they're finally going to take him for the CAT scan."

She passes right by me and walks out of the room.

"Wow, man," Jamie says, making fun of me.

"I see that you're doing better," I say, raising an eyebrow and ignoring his comment.

"And I see that you're the same old arsehole as always."

"How's it going?" I ask, changing the subject.

"I wanted to ask you the same thing."

"I'm not the one with the screwed-up knee."

"No, you're screwed-up in something else, Ian."

"Don't start."

"I'm not the one who started this thing. I just wish someone would say the word 'over' because I can't stand this anymore."

"There's nothing to end because we haven't started anything, Jamie, as you well know."

"What I know is that you're a fucking—"

"Here's my favorite patient," a cheerful nurse says, interrupting us. "Are we ready for a little trip?"

"With you, sweetheart, I'd go to the end of the world."

I shake my head in resignation as she helps him sit up straight in his wheelchair.

"Will you keep Riley company while I'm away?"

I look at him sideways.

"Don't screw anything else up before I get back," he adds before being wheeled out.

Well, at least he's in a better mood.

I pop my head out to see where Riley might be and after looking left and right, I find her at the end of the hallway. I gather up my courage and walk towards her, trying to swallow the beat of my heart pulsing in my throat and echoing all through my body.

When I get close to her, I clear my throat to get her attention, but she doesn't turn around. She's standing with her arms wrapped around her waist, small, vulnerable, and defeated.

"Everything's going to be alright," I tell her, trying to be kind.

She nods.

"Your brother never gives up."

"I know," she sighs. "Thanks for coming along."

"Maybe I could come by later to see how…"

"You don't have to."

"Jamie's my teammate, and we don't abandon one another."

She turns slowly, raising her eyes to mine, and I let myself be sucked into the emptiness I see there, and everything I've tried to keep together these past few months comes crashing down in an instant.

"Riley…" I try to speak, but when her name caresses my lips, painfully and with too much intimacy, something inside me snaps.

Her green eyes are hollow, veiled, and melancholy, her face is pale, drawn, and beaten, like she can't find peace and hasn't slept in days. It's that lost look that haunts me, that makes my legs shake, so much so that I have to steady my hand on the wall to hold myself up.

I watch her, small and defenseless. I notice her silence and feel her torment. I can see it distinctly, even if she tries to keep it hidden.

It's crushing me.

A few minutes of that silence is enough to leave

me feeling surrounded, backed up against the wall. Screwed. And those feelings force me to speak.

"I'd just like to help you out."

"There's really no need."

"Please, Riley. You're exhausted, let me take care of everything."

"I'm perfectly fine."

"You don't have to pretend with me, it's not necessary."

"I'm not pretending," she says, crossing her arms over her chest, closing me out.

"You can let yourself to fall apart, you know. I'm not going to tell anyone."

"Never, Ian O'Connor. Not in front of you."

And her words devour my heart, down to the last bite.

4
Ian

"Good thing I've only got one big bag, or how else would I have managed?" Ryan asks, appearing behind me as I get off my motorbike.

"Thanks for coming to get my scrawny arse, Ian," I mimic, making fun of him.

Ryan throws his bag to the ground and looks at me a few seconds before extending his hand.

"A hug would be appropriate here," I tell him, squeezing tightly.

"If we have to..." he says with fake distain, playing up his tough guy persona that no one, not even himself, believes.

I give him a pat on the back and let him go.

"So..." he says, delving his hands into the pockets of his leather coat.

"You're home."

He sighs heavily. "I'm home."

"Come on, I'll take you in to them."

"No," he stops me before I can get back on the bike. "Not yet. I'm not ready."

"Ryan, what's going on? Please try not to be an idiot."

"You can't tell me what to do."

"Of course I can. I'm your older brother, and I'm not a dickhead like you."

"First of all, you're not even—" he stops himself before going on. "Sorry."

"It's fine," I lie, locking my jaw.

"I just need a minute, okay? This isn't easy."

"I understand," I say, before handing him a helmet. He slings his bag over his shoulder and then puts the helmet on. "I'll take you over to mine."

"Thanks. Yours'd be great."

We both get on the bike and leave terminal car park, heading out onto Swords Road, then merging onto the M1, which brings us straight back into town. I ride in silence for about half an hour, weaving between cars. The night starts to fall, leaving us with a sense of oppression that threatens to crush us, prevents us from breathing.

I know he's noticed it too.

I can only imagine how Ryan feels right now; he left when his life got completely turned upside down about two years ago. He's kept his distance from this city, and I think he wanted to keep it that way for the rest of his life.

He moved to England to play on the London Irish team, but I know that he really moved to get away from Nick and everything that reminded him of his life here.

In the past two years, he's set foot in Dublin only once, when we found out about our father; he stayed as long as he could before leaving again, with no intention of coming back.

But now he's here. I knew he'd come home.

Ryan would never abandon his family in a situation like this; he just needed a push to make him see reason.

I park my motorbike in front of the gate, and we both get off. Ryan takes off his helmet and looks around.

"You still live here? With all that money they're paying you?"

I shrug.

I live in an area called Docklands, south of the Grand Canal. It's not too bad; granted, it's not the trendiest place in Dublin and at one point, nobody really looked in this area, thanks to the never-ending construction projects and the squatters. But in recent years, it's had a bit of a makeover, and has become a neighbourhood just like any other.

A place to live. That's all I need.

Ryan enters my apartment a bit confused, running his hand through his hair. Then he turns to look at me.

"Why, Ian?"

"Make yourself at home," I say, ignoring the question.

"You could have everything you want."

"I already have everything I need."

"Really?" he asks, looking at me with an eyebrow raised. "Everything?"

"I could choke you in your sleep, you know."

"You wouldn't dare," he challenges.

He's still got the same arrogant look that he

had as a young man although really, he's grown up now.

Kind of.

"Try me."

He shakes his head, smiling half-heartedly.

"Am I going to have to share a bed with you?"

"I have a sofa."

"Okay, that's fine for a few days…" He heads over to it and drops down onto it, a dead weight.

I go to the kitchen to turn on the kettle.

"A beer would be better," he calls, picking up on my intention to make coffee.

I open the fridge and take out two bottles, sitting down next to him.

"I don't have a lot of time. There's somewhere I need to be, and I don't know how long it's going to take me."

"Don't worry about me."

"You sure?"

He looks at me sideways.

"So… we're in the shitter."

"Yep."

"Does anyone know I'm here yet?"

"I thought it would be a nice surprise for Mum. Let her think you just decided to drop by."

"You don't feel like telling her that you forced me to come back?"

"Did I?" I look at him quizzically.

"I asked to be taken off the team."

"Jesus, Ryan!"

"What the fuck was I supposed to do?"

"I didn't ask you to give up your career."

"What career, Ian? The only one of us who has a career is you."

Here we go. I knew it. He's always ready to backhand me with his resentment.

"That's bullshit."

"That's the way it is. I'm certainly not the champion in the family and neither is that arsehole Nick."

"Please don't start with the same old drama." I get up from the sofa and take a few steps away.

"Have you called him?"

"I wanted to do it together."

"I hope you're kidding."

I turn to him. "I couldn't be more serious."

"What the hell is wrong with you? Why would you think that's a good idea?"

"I just want this family to be united."

"You realise that's not going to happen, right?"

"Yes, it will. You're not two little fucking kids, Ryan. It's time to act like adults and to do the right thing. Stay here, together."

"Easy for you," he says standing, approaching me. "You're not the one who had to give up everything."

Myself. And my life. That's what I've had to give up.

"No one forced you."

"Oh, really?" he says, raising his voice. "And what should I have done then? Go on, let's hear it…"

"You could have stayed, found a solution."

He bursts out laughing, bitterly. "You don't know what you're talking about."

I don't know what I'm talking about?

I swear to God, I'll strangle him.

"You had a bad experience, and you reacted the best way you knew how to under the circumstances, but it's all water under the bridge now and your family needs you."

"Well, here I am."

I sigh and pat him on the back again.

"Alright, let's call that arsehole."

"If it's really necessary…"

"It is."

He lifts up his hands in a sign of acceptance. I hand him the telephone while he stares at me incredulously.

"No, no! Not a chance in hell!"

"You're the only one who can make him come home."

* * *

I slowly and quietly approach the room, and push open the door gently without knocking – I don't know if Jamie's asleep yet.

The night shift nurses were very helpful, as if they had known I would be coming. I imagine Jamie has won them all over with his charm.

I pop my head inside, and Jamie notices me right away. He gestures me to come in quietly, nodding towards the chair in the corner of the room where his sister is sleeping.

I enter with a painful sigh, closing the door behind me.

"Hey," I whisper, moving towards the bed. "What's the latest?"

"Seems it's just a sprain. No surgery."

"Oh, that's great news."

"Yeah."

"You'll be back on your feet in a few weeks."

"Hope so."

I sit down next to him.

"She ran right over. It was on the news," he says, reading my thoughts. "She was scared." He smiles sadly. "Same old Riley."

"She worries about you."

"I'm the one who's worried about her."

I shoot her a glance full of remorse and then return my eyes to Jamie.

"I wish there was something I could do, but I don't know how to help her. She won't let anyone get close to her; she doesn't want me around. Seems like sometimes she doesn't even want me in her life. She's so stubborn…"

"You did it on purpose, didn't you?"

"What's that?"

"This accident wasn't an accident."

"Are you shitting me?"

"It wouldn't surprise me."

"Even I wouldn't go that far."

"I don't know about that."

"Let's just say the right time has come. Maybe it was fate."

"I don't believe in crap like that."

"Maybe you should."

"Destiny would have you risk your career so that she and I would run into each other?"

"Well, I wasn't really hoping for that outcome, but now that we're all here…"

"You're a damn manipulator."

"Maybe, just a bit."

"You can't control our lives."

"I'm only protecting what I love, and my sister is what I love most in my life."

"And sport?"

"It's only because of her that I have all this. Life gave me just one sister, and Riley gave me the rest."

"You're a great player, Jamie. You deserve what you've earned."

"Not without her giving me every possibility in the world," he sighs pensively, then continues, "you have to do something."

"What?"

"I've watched the little games you've both played for too long, and I've wanted to stay out of it. I thought at least one of you was a bit brighter than that."

"Stay out of it, Jamie. You don't know what you're talking about."

"I don't know what I'm talking about? Oh Jesus, I know it off by heart. You're *both* the problem. You drive me mad."

"We aren't doing anything. We haven't seen each other in…"

"A year. I know."

One year, two months, twenty days and three hours.

"I can't even bring up the subject with her. You know you've become the unnamable bastard?"

"Okay. Well, she's hit it on the head."

"So, I decided to work on you."

"On me?" I look at him.

"I can't let her to go into hiding again."

"Isn't she sitting right here?"

"I don't want her to run away from herself. And you, my friend, you're going to help me."

"Me? What the fuck do you want me to do?"

"This time, you're going to do the right thing."

"I didn't force her to go into hiding."

"You hurt her."

Huh. Sounds like he knows a lot more detail than I thought she'd be willing to share. It's useless for me to tiptoe around it. I should cut him off now before he gets carried away.

"I'd do it again."

"Well, you're not going to."

"What makes you so sure?"

"Because I've seen how you look at her, mate."

Shit.

"How could you want that for your sister? Someone like me?"

"I wasn't the one who chose you."

Jamie pulls himself up to a sitting position. He looks at her for a few seconds and then starts speaking again.

"I just want to see her happy. She gave up on her own life for me, and I'd do the same for her."

I clench my jaw at what Jamie is implying.

"And what about you?"

I jerk up to look at him.

"What about me?"

"What would you be willing to do?"

My gaze goes back to her, curled up on a chair in her brother's hospital room.

"I've already let her go once."

"Would you do it again?"

"What do you want from me, Jamie?" I ask in frustration.

"I want you to be honest, with me and with yourself."

I look at her again, and I feel my heart tighten in my chest.

"I don't think I can to do it again," I say honestly.

"Well then, at least just try not to send her off running again."

"And how the hell am I supposed to do that?"

Jamie looks at me, serious.

"Sometimes, if you want someone to stay, all you have to do is ask them not to leave."

5
Ian

This morning, all I wanted to do was take my time, wake up without an alarm, have a shower, drink a coffee, and take a long ride to keep out of Ryan's hair – who has apparently decided to vegetate at my house – but as soon as I tried to push off, it became clear that something was wrong with my motorbike, and I had to tinker around with it until early afternoon. I could have waited until Monday to take it into the garage, but I hoped that it might be something insignificant, so I could deal with it myself. I like getting my hands greasy, lying on the ground and touching all of its most intimate parts as if it were a woman, because that's how I treat it.

I pull myself off the ground and grab a rag to clean my hands as I look at my bike in satisfaction, pleased with myself for having fixed it on my own.

"Wow, you've got your future nailed down," Ryan says, trying to wind me up.

"Sure do, how about you?"

"Fuck off."

Always in a good mood.

I open the gate to my apartment, which used to be in the garage, but when the area was remodelled the place was changed into a loft and, all things considered, it makes sense. I could have put a door in, but I don't mind keeping part of the original design, and it's pretty ideal for my bike.

I go outside to get some air and have a smoke, after being closed inside almost all day, but as soon as the gate is halfway up, I see someone standing on the other side of the road.

I crouch down to go out, and as I am on my way up, the cigarette that I had just put in my mouth falls to the tarmac.

Crap.

She looks around with the air of someone who mistakenly ended up in a bad neighbourhood, afraid and nervous. She's wearing a pair of jeans, gym shoes, and a huge sweatshirt, her hair completely windswept.

A strange sensation grapples my stomach as if someone had bitten me from the inside.

I step out on the pavement at the same moment she notices me; she crosses the street slowly, looking in both directions while my heart beats arrogantly in my chest.

She stops and keeps her eyes on her shoes, biting her lip nervously and trying to fix her hair.

I stand still with my arms hanging at my sides, attempting to control my breathing, resigned to her invasion and the disaster that is about to storm through my life again; I'd like to push away from myself with all of my might, but I know that I don't have the strength.

I decide to put an end to my agony, and to hers,

and get right to the point.

"Why are you here?" I ask her, taking out another cigarette and nervously lighting it, trying to mask the need to send her away immediately.

"I need to speak to you."

Send her away. Send her away. Send her away.

I throw the cigarette onto the ground and invite her to follow me inside, holding the gate open for her to pass. As soon as we enter my living room, Ryan jumps to his feet from the sofa.

"Holy shit!"

"Get out of my house right now!" I point to the door.

"Where the hell am I supposed to go?"

"Not my problem."

Ryan stands there, frozen with his hands on his hips. He looks at me questioningly and then shakes his head in disapproval.

He grabs his jacket and walks over to me, whispering in my ear.

"I see a shitstorm on the horizon."

"Out!"

He raises his hands in a defensive gesture and waves to Riley before finally leaving my apartment.

I go to the kitchenette to put on the kettle and make some coffee. I pour two cups and walk back to her, still stuck in the doorway. I hand one to her, and after looking at it for a few seconds, she decides to accept it, thanking me with a nod of her head.

I point to the sofa, and she takes a minute to determine if it's safe. She sits on the edge as if she's preparing to make a run for it at the first opportunity.

"I'll get right to the point," she begins, her voice highly controlled and overly confident, but her shaky hands holding the cup betray her.

I rest my hips against the counter behind me because I don't think my legs are able to hold me up.

She's been here for two minutes, and I already feel like I'm suffocating.

"Try to stay away from me."

"What the hell…?"

"I don't want to see you. I don't want to deal with you, and I don't want to have you around."

"And what should I do?"

"I certainly can't stop you from seeing Jamie, but when you're both out of the centre…"

"You're telling me not to come round?"

She nods.

"You're… you're… you're pathetic, Riley."

My pride and my stupidity speak for me.

"Of course." She stands up and comes closer, resting her cup on the counter next to me. "I should have expected it."

"What?"

"That you'd react like a bastard," she says, showering me with her resentment, which triggers mine as well.

She goes over to the door, but I can't let her just show up here like nothing happened, insult me, and then walk away.

She can't do whatever the hell she pleases with me.

I follow her and grab her arm to stop her from leaving.

I squeeze it.

My fingers make an impression on her skin. I make her turn to me and hold my face right up to hers.

I'm angry, furious.

Hurt.

"I am a fucking bastard," I enunciate each word with rage, looking her in the eyes, but when I recognise the terror in hers, I release my grip on her arm, realising what I was doing.

She takes advantage of my confusion to back away in fear towards the door, massaging the spot where I grabbed her with her fingers. Before she's able to lift it, my hand slams down on the metal.

"You shouldn't have come here. It was a mistake. It's always a mistake when I'm involved. You should know that."

I slowly let my hand slide down and take a few steps backwards to allow her breathe.

And to let myself breathe.

"If you don't want to see me, you can start by not showing up at my house," I tell her through my teeth, trying to erase the last memory I have of her. "You should leave now."

She turns and lifts her chin.

"I'll go right away, don't worry."

"I'll take you home."

The words come directly from my stomach.

"There's no need."

"I wasn't offering."

She glares at me as anger colours her face.

"You're a real piece of work, you know that? First, you say I'm pathetic, that I have to get out of here, and now, you want to take me home? You've got a real problem, Ian."

"It's you, Riley. You're the only problem I have, and you know I don't like having problems," I tell her, looking her right in the eyes, where the reflection of everything we weren't hits me forcefully, smashing into my heart in an instant.

God help me. I'm still there.

"Well then, I'll just go myself."

She turns again, lifts the door, and disappears onto the street.

I stand there, incapable of moving, of speaking, of thinking.

I can't even breathe.

God. She's still here.

6
Ian

I knock on the door while opening it, and stick my head around to see Jamie putting on his jacket.

"Ready to go home?"

"Hell, yes. I can't stand being here anymore, even if the staff are great."

"Oh, I imagine they are," I say shaking my head. "Where's your stuff?"

"It's all in that bag there," he says, pointing over to it. "We're just waiting on Riley. She went downstairs to get my folder."

"Riley?"

He looks at me, pleased with himself.

"What the fuck are you trying to do here?"

"Me? Nothing."

"Okay then. I have everything we need. I asked them to call us a cab so..." Riley lifts her eyes from a bunch of papers she's holding in her hand and stops in the middle of the room.

"Do all of your meetings have to be like this?" Jamie asks looking first at me and then at his sister.

"Sometimes, it's even worse," she says bitterly, crossing her arms over her chest. "What are you doing here?"

"I came to bring Jamie home."

"That's why I'm here."

"I called him." Jamie intervenes. "I asked him to stop by and pick up my car."

"I wish you would have thought of that before, I could've avoided taking a day off work."

"I forgot to tell you."

"Of course," she says, looking at him in annoyance.

"Well, we're all here now, shall we go?" He starts out of the room.

Riley sighs in frustration and bends over to pick up Jamie's bag.

"Leave it. I'll take it."

"I can do it," she says proudly, before hoisting Jamie's big bag and following him into the hall.

Fair enough. This is what I get.

In the car park, Riley puts the bag in the boot while Jamie gets into the back seat.

"What are you doing?" she asks him.

"I can't sit in the front. I need to extend my leg. You can sit next to Ian," he says with fake innocence.

Nothing about what he just did is innocent. He's a dirty, no-good manipulator, that's what he is, and he's definitely not helping this awkward situation at all.

Riley huffs and takes her place in front as I take mine behind the wheel and drive us out of the car park.

I try to avoid breathing in the car, and I'm pretty sure Riley's doing the same. Jamie talks and talks without a break, trying to engage us in conversation but neither of us have any intention of joining in.

Detachment. Indifference. That's what the situation calls for.

In almost total silence, I leave the city and head towards Ballsbridge, hoping that this nearness doesn't kill either of us.

* * *

"Thanks a million, Ian," Jamie says, sitting on the sofa. "God, how can I already be this worn out? I haven't done anything."

"It's been tough on you," Riley says, setting the bag down. "And you need to take it easy, okay? Try not to do too much for a few days. Do you need anything? Do you want me to stay?"

"Nah, I'm fine. I might be getting a visitor later."

Riley shakes her head and looks at her watch.

"Alright then, I'll leave you in the hands of your visitor. I'm going home. If you need something, call me, alright?" she tells him, lowering down to give him a kiss on the cheek.

"Ian can give you a ride," Jamie announces.

"That's not necessary."

"But Ian insists on it," he continues, raising an eyebrow, daring me to contradict him.

Bastard.

"Of course. It's no problem."

Say no, say no, say no.

"Really?" Riley asks, finally looking me in the eyes, "There's no problem? I thought I was the problem you needed to free yourself from, Ian."

I deserved that, too.

"What are you talking about?" Jamie asks, curious.

"Oh, a nice conversation we had—"

"It's not a problem for me to drive you home," I interrupt her.

"It's a problem for me. I'd rather call a cab," she concludes before taking her bag and walking out.

"Move it, you arsehole." Jamie motions for me to follow her.

I sigh in frustration and go outside.

"Riley," I call to her. "I'll take you, come on."

She turns to me, tilting her head. "I'm not going anywhere with you."

I get on the motorbike and hand her the helmet.

"Get on," I order her.

"You can't tell me what to do, and you won't convince me to get on that damn bike."

"I'm not going to repeat myself."

"Don't try to intimidate me. Your 'tough guy'

act doesn't work on me."

Completely frustrated by her presence, I lean the bike on its stand and approach her threateningly. She takes two steps backwards, but I don't let her move away more than that as I grab her arm and squeeze it tightly.

Her fragile body is completely dominated by mine and the sensation of having this much control over her sends my senses into overdrive.

Riley pushes her hands against my chest to keep me away from her, and it provokes a strange response in me; it's a mix of resentment, because she feels the need to put this useless distance between us, and something that burns my stomach.

"I said I'm going to take you home."

She holds my gaze with the same hardness that I showed her, before shaking off my arm and grabbing the helmet.

"Don't ever try to touch me again," she threatens, putting the helmet on her head.

Her words don't hurt me.

No.

Her words explode inside me, empty me out. Destroy me.

"I live in town, just outside the centre. 537 North Circular Road."

I get back on the bike and extend my hand to her, but she refuses it and gets on without my help. I hit the pedal and we're off, forcing her to hold on to me, right over my belt. I can feel her nails scratching through the fabric, at my skin, and a shiver runs through my entire body. I'm sure it's just the cold morning air and the speed of the motorbike.

There's no other reason.

Absolutely not.

I ride along the street that faces the sea. The hazy winter sun unexpectedly rises slowly over a slice of water and the saltwater scent mixes in the wind with the smell of coffee and pastries from the cafés with their already gathering crowds.

I watch the city wake up before my eyes, the sky in soft shades. I'm aware of her arms around my waist, her body so close to mine, and I find myself enjoying this ride after spending so much time alone, and this silent company. Her hands slowly soften their grip, resting looser around my waist.

For the first time in my life, I find myself wanting something that I never believed in, and that desire for more reminds me just how truly alone I am.

* * *

When we get to Riley's place, she points out her door, and I park on the pavement. She gets off the motorbike and takes off her helmet, letting her dark, damp hair wave down her back.

And my heart skips about five, maybe ten beats.

Holy crap.

"Thanks for the ride," she says briskly, before digging into her jeans. "Shit!" she yells, kicking the gate. "I must have forgotten my keys."

Perfect.

Getting off my bike, I take a look at the street and the houses on it. There's an aged cottage, with a wooden door and shutters, the kind of place you rarely see anymore – the kind that would probably fall down if you gave it a good push.

It's a subtle, still memory – one that shadows over the present.

I shake my head vigorously, hoping to drive it off, but the memory remains, suspended between the need to push it away and the need to remember what I am.

"Don't you have a spare key hidden under a plant somewhere?" I ask her, forcing myself back into the present. "Do you see any plants around here? I have to find a locksmith or someone that can..."

"Nah. Leave it to me."

She looks at me skeptically, crossing her arms.

"I'm sure it's an old lock."

"I have no idea."

I give the handle a shake before going to my motorbike to grab some tools from under the seat.

"What are you doing?"

"Make sure no one's watching us."

"What?"

"Relax." I wink at her before getting to work. I clear my throat and make an attempt at conversation. "Do you live by yourself?" I ask, not knowing why.

"What are you implying?" She goes right to the defensive.

"It's just a question," I justify, even though I shouldn't have to.

"We don't have to make conversation."

"I was just trying to be polite."

"No one is asking you to," she responds bitterly.

And the same bitterness that I hear in her voice invades my stomach, as if someone had set fire to it.

I close my eyes and inhale deeply, trying to rid the sensation of being a complete idiot.

It doesn't make any sense to keep getting angry with Riley. It doesn't help me feel any better, it won't bring back all that I've lost.

It won't bring her back to me.

"Well, you know… what do you do?"

"I work at Gate Theatre on Parnell Street," she says, helping me out of my embarrassment.

"That's a nice place," I comment, even if I have no idea what I'm talking about.

"Have you ever been there? To see a show, I mean?" Her voice takes back a shade of colour.

I smile instinctively before looking at her over my shoulder. "Do I look like the theatre-going type?"

She smiles too, lowering her head, and I can luckily still hide the effect it has on me.

"Done. That was easier than I thought," I say, opening the lock.

"I don't want to know where you learned how to do that," she says, raising her hands, and walking into the apartment.

"You're welcome," I reply through gritted teeth.

"I would invite you in…"

I don't let her finish as I hurry inside.

"Make yourself at home," she says sarcastically.

I take a quick look around and am left speechless. I don't know how long she's been living alone here, but this place is barren; it's completely bare, cold and impersonal. It's a small, oppressive apartment with an odour of mould that fuses together with loneliness, and I'm not sure which one is harder to take.

It's a scent that's been imprinted in my memory – one that continues to torment me at night, forcefully taking control of my soul.

A table, a chair, a sink, a counter full of glasses, with empty wine bottles covering every inch of available space. A second-hand sofa takes up almost the entire space dedicated to the living room area. There's a bed, a night stand. Nothing personal, no photos.

There's no light. There's no life.

She isn't here.

I turn to look at her and something inside me breaks. My toughness crumbles in her eyes, so wide and lost, plummeting me into an endless vortex I'd like to remain in forever, to avoid being spit out into the sunlight again.

She tries to escape, heading towards her bedroom, but I grab her arm before she can make her getaway. I don't squeeze hard this time.

My touch is delicate. It's a strange sensation, touching her again. It makes my head spin, and for a second, my sense of balance feels off, like I've been hurled into another dimension where feeling something for myself and for someone else is not a sign of weakness or something to be avoided at all costs.

"It's just a house," she says, reading between the lines of my silence. "A place to live, that's all."

"But why…"

"I needed a place for myself that wasn't in Jamie's shadow."

A place of her own is understandable, but this: the neighbourhood, the apartment, the emptiness. All things that, I'm afraid to admit, I have an intimate knowledge of myself. I try to shoo away the thought, that indelible mark on my soul that I've tried to shake off for years with no result, because what you are and where you come from cannot be changed, no matter how hard you try. One moment is all it takes, a brief encounter with the past, and everything comes rushing back, catapulting you into a memory of something you never wanted to be – and yet, here you are, unchanged.

"This is not who you are."

"This is exactly who I am, Ian."

"That's not true."

"There are a lot of things you don't know about me," she says in a tone that tells me I will probably never know.

"You can't live like this," I tell her, hearing my voice soften.

"Why do you care how I live? I'm not your problem," she says with an edge, freeing herself from my grip.

"Riley…"

"Don't look at me like that."

"Like what?"

"Like you pity me," she says, and I feel a stab in my chest.

I breathe deeply to numb the pain that has come back to haunt me and to break my heart.

"I don't."

I move to touch her face gently. My fingers run along her features, which relax under my caress, as if they were being moulded by a tenderness I didn't know I had. The warmth of her skin fuses with mine, and I almost find myself holding my breath in an attempt to control my emotions, which threaten to betray me.

I let my hand slide down, and ask her something I don't want to know the answer to.

"Do you really hate me so much?"

"Yes."

One syllable, three letters.

The fucking truth.

"Even though I understand, it doesn't make sense. It's not fair."

No, Riley. The thing that isn't fair is that you came into my life and stayed there just long enough for me to see you leaving. That I waited too long, like a damn idiot, continuing to hurt myself. That I wasn't man enough to keep you. That I'm not able to feel anything that isn't unhealthy and destructive.

And then Riley speaks again, ripping my heart out and setting it on fire.

"It's just... I miss what we had and I know we can't have it anymore." She lifts her eyes to me. "I miss you."

Our eyes lock for a few seconds, and I simply let myself be taken in, closing the door behind me.

I stop to distinguish the line where the green of her eyes fades into blue, setting off a battle with no clear colour winner. I realise I've been holding my breath the moment her eyes soften and some almost imperceptible dimples appear at the corners of her mouth. And I can no longer control my heart rate; I've been staring at her like an idiot.

I lower my gaze, breaking the contact, but I'm

still inside her.

    And she's still trying to survive inside me.

7
Ian

I leave another voicemail message. It's the fourth one, but he's still not picking up. I can understand him not answering Ryan's calls, even though I was hoping that hearing his voice would make him reason, but he's not answering me either. *God Nick! How much of a dick are you?*

Before putting away my cell phone, I check for new messages. I left her my number. She said she had erased it from her memory and from her phone book.

I made note of that too.

She wasn't too convinced, but in the end, she took it down. Obviously, she hasn't written, called. Nothing.

It's better this way. One less problem to think about. I've got enough on my mind these days.

Better this way, I repeat through clenched teeth.

I stayed with her for as long as I could before realising in her eyes that she needed me to leave: and then I granted her wish. I would have stayed longer, talked about things, tried to understand, but she didn't feel the same.

I have to confess that, as a first meeting, it didn't go too badly.

Actually, it was a complete disaster.

The truth is that I didn't want to leave her, a part of me felt that if I did, I wouldn't see her again. And maybe that would have been a good thing, stopping everything before I self-destructed, but it would appear we've gone past that point, and I know where it leads.

Because I've already seen this play out, and I know how it ends.

She'll disappear just as suddenly as she appeared a year ago. I'll make her run away because I won't be able to keep her here. And I'll be left alone again, drowning in a sea of regret, unspoken words, and suffocating sighs.

She'll take everything with her. She'll slide under my skin, she'll suck my blood dry and she'll leave me for dead on the sand, and the tide will wash up my empty, useless body.

That's what I've been, and what I still am.

That's what she's done to me.

I ask myself what the hell is going on, what has happened to her life. I can't help but wondering why I wasn't there. Why I have denied myself of her. Why I stood back when all I should have done was ask her to stay.

Two simple words: *Please stay.*

It's not so hard.

"Hey, Ian." John sticks his head out. "Coach is looking for you."

I head back to the gym where the team is going through their morning workout. I walk through the room where the guys are lifting weights, dividing into groups with their trainers, who push them to their limits. As I approach the coach's office, he gestures me inside.

I sit down in front of him as he finishes up a phone call, drumming his fingers nervously on the desk. When he hangs up, he sighs heavily, before looking at me with a serious expression.

"Well, kid," he says, resting his back on the seat and folding his hands. "Is there something you want to talk to me about?"

I look at him doubtfully. "We're ready, just like always."

"I'm not talking about the team."

"I don't understand."

"You're distracted. You're tired. It's clear that your head is somewhere else."

"I didn't sleep very well last night, but I'm still focused on what needs to be done."

"And that's why you got tackled three times today?"

I shrug. "It was just practice," I justify, miserably.

"Just practice...?"

"That didn't come out right."

"If something's bothering you, we can talk about, you know."

I shake my head.

"Is there a woman?"

"No."

"Mmm."

"There's no woman."

"Okay."

"I just have some family issues at the moment."

He sighs. "Your father."

My head snaps up.

"I was just on the phone with McCall, Ryan's coach."

I look at him and raise my brow.

"Your brother gave up everything without any explanation. The coach is furious, and the president wants his head. If Ryan doesn't go back immediately, they could nullify his contract."

What a fucker.

"Before making a final decision, he called me to see if I knew anything about it."

I let myself fall back into the chair.

"I asked Ryan to come back, but I didn't think he'd create all this fuss."

"I'm sorry, kid."

I tighten my jaw.

"And what about that idiot, Nick?"

"I'm trying to get in contact with him."

The coach huffs. "He's probably busy on a tropical island photo shoot with his arse hanging out."

I laugh, shaking my head.

He gets up and walks around his desk before stopping in front of me.

"Everything's all on your shoulders, right?"

"Not exactly, it's just that, I'm... alone."

"You know that you're not alone. We're a team, on and off the field."

"They're personal problems."

"We're a family. Personal problems don't exist here."

"This one is, it doesn't concern the boys...or you," I say, shooting him a quick glance.

The coach doesn't say anything for a few seconds. Then he turns to the glass door and watches the guys training.

"We're counting a lot on you. Jamie's off the team for a bit."

"I know," I say, crushed by the pressure.

He turns to me.

"Will you be alright?"

"I'm fine."

"Remember that if you need anything, I'm here. We're all here. And if you don't feel like..."

"Playing? It's the only thing I do feel like doing."

"That's what I wanted to hear."

"If that's it, I'd like to leave."

"That's all."

I nod before leaving his office and going back to the gym where I attempt to drown my problems in hard, physical work and sweat like I always have.

To dedicate myself to the only thing I know

how to do – rugby. It's the only thing I've got left.

* * *

Three years earlier

I go into the gym and head towards the changing rooms, when a familiar laugh stops me. I turn slowly to see a waterfall of hair, waving over someone's shoulders.

I squeeze the door handle and walk through, pretending nothing happened, but my legs don't move and neither do my eyes. And then she turns slightly, allowing me the pleasure of seeing her profile, and my stomach goes up in flames.

"Hey, what are you doing? In or out?" Jake says behind me.

"Huh?" I look at him, confused.

"You're blocking the door, mate."

I shake my head and let him pass.

"What's so interesting?" he asks, following my gaze. "Ah, got it."

"What?" I snap out of it. "No, it's not…"

"I can't blame you."

I lock my jaw instinctively.

"Hey Ian!" Jamie comes over to us holding her hand.

"Hello again, you," she says smiling at me.

I try to smile too.

"How's it going?"

"Fine," I reply dryly.

"I'm Jake," he sticks out his hand, introducing himself and flashing a smile that looks like an invitation to a knuckle sandwich.

"I know," she replies. "You made a move on me at the party a few nights ago."

"I... er..."

Jamie bursts out laughing.

"Forget about it, mate, you don't have a chance. My sister is too much for you. She's really too much for anyone," he says smiling, but inside, I know he's right.

Jake acts like her rebuff is no big deal, shrugging it off like nothing happened, but also shooting her a glance that lasts a little too long.

"I brought Riley to see the centre. I wanted to show her where we train."

"He practically forced me," she interrupts.

"That's true." Jamie says looking at her. "She's never shown any interest in rugby, doesn't even come to the stadium. I'm not even sure she actually watches the games on TV like she claims she does."

"You'll never know for sure," she jokes.

"It's just because you're my sister that my charm doesn't work on you."

"Leave it to me," Jake tries again shamelessly.

"No one can convince her. She hates rugby, and most of all, she hates the players."

"Except you," she adds affectionately.

"You just haven't met the right player yet," Jake persists.

I have to hand it to him, the guy never gives up.

"Maybe you're right... Who knows, I might change my mind for the right player," she says smiling before laying her eyes on me, invoking a fit in my chest that crawls down my left arm.

Here it is, my first heart attack at thirty years old.

The end of my career.

"We'd better get out of here before she starts taking Jake seriously. Another pass at my sister in front of me or behind my back, and I'll skin you, is that clear?" Jamie isn't joking around. "I promised Riley a full tour including the gym, pool and field. And if I can convince her, she'll stick around for practice today."

"Can't wait," she says sarcastically.

"I'll see you in a bit," Jamie concludes, before heading back to the gym, Riley waving at us.

I watch them walk out and something in me stirs, something strong and dangerous. Something that could lead me to give up what I believe in, just for one smile that could knock me out and two eyes that I have memorised in my mind; ever since that night that I let her slide into my thoughts, flipping my heart, that I thought I had thrown to the bottom of the ocean, and that has now found a way to free itself and take in a breath of oxygen, stealing it from me.

8
Ian

Present

I leave the gym, totally knackered. The only thing I want to do is collapse on the sofa, but it's still taken by that idiot brother of mine – the one who still hasn't got off his arse to make an appearance at home. What the hell did he even come back for if he's never going to go over and visit them?

I take out my phone and decide to try again - maybe today I'll be able to convince him, but it rings through with no reply. I now have two brothers who have decided to ignore me.

I should just kick him out.

I get on my bike and head towards the city for dinner with my parents. We always tried to have dinner together at home, even as adults whenever we could, and I try to keep up the tradition.

It never felt like a chore to me. I enjoy spending time at home, but the emptiness that my brothers left when they went away can be oppressive at times. It's hard not to let it get you down.

Nick and Ryan abandoned their family, their city and their country just to get enough distance between them to stop them from killing each other, and at first, I applauded the effort to keep them apart, to help them reflect on their mistakes and then get over it. But too much time has passed, and they haven't spoken to each other since they both left Dublin, and I'm starting to think that things will never change.

I guess I'm not helping the situation either; in a way, I'm an enabler. I act as a go-between for them. I take care of the family, I make sure no one gets hurt, that everything is okay and that my parents are fine.

I'll confess, all these worries can be suffocating.

I breathe in the cold winter air that freezes my face; it relaxes me, helping me feel free even though I'm on edge, finding it more and more difficult to stay in control.

Despite the fact that I've not had a moment of peace all day, between training, the problems at home, and Ryan, there's another thought that's been running through my mind.

A thought that I have to get rid of, right now.

I wanted to call her, but it seemed excessive to me. So, I sent her a message. To be honest, I sent three, all with no response.

I understood from her silence that my interest is not appreciated, nor is my company. I should have expected that: it's what I deserve. I have to accept it and move on. After all, I'm the one who wanted it this way.

I chose the easier way, the safer way. I made my decision a year ago, and I don't intend to go back on it now. I did the right thing for her and for me.

I can't pay any attention to the shivers that run

through me when she looks at me, to my heart that tries to bust out of its cage when I touch her. It's only a weakness, something to be nipped in the bud.

I bury the thought of her to the furthest corner of my mind as I park my bike in the alley behind my parents' house. I dismount and take off my helmet and go over to my father who's outside pruning the hedges.

"Hey Ian," he says with a smile. "These plants really needed some work. Your mother was complaining she couldn't see the flowers out the window anymore."

"You could've called me, I'd have come earlier to give you a hand."

"I can do it myself, I'm not that old," he jokes, going back to his bushes.

"Well of course you aren't, that's not the point. I'd be happy to help."

"You have your own life," he says without looking at me. "You need to live it and stop worrying about us... about me," he finishes, lowering his voice.

My life. He has no idea.

I put a hand on his shoulder, and he sighs before looking at me.

"I know things aren't going well..." he begins, turning away from the shrubs. "I am aware of it, you know. Not always, but on certain days, when I'm...myself, I have the feeling that I've lost something. I don't know if I'm explaining myself very well."

"Dad..."

"I'd like you to promise me something."

"Sure, whatever you want."

"I'm asking you because your brothers, well, they have their own things to do..."

"No, don't even think about it," I interrupt him immediately.

"Your mother has the right to live her life. I don't want her to spend years taking care of me, washing me, dressing me and worrying that I might set the house on fire."

"Mum loves you."

"Do you think I don't know that?" He smiles tenderly. "And I love her. That's the reason I don't want her to be a part of everything that's coming my way. You have to promise me."

"I don't know if I can do that."

"For her. You can do it for her." He looks at me very seriously for a few seconds before I force myself to nod. "All right then, let's go inside." He wraps up, taking off his gloves and heading towards the house.

I watch him go in, and after a few seconds, he appears behind the living room window. My mother joins him, says something that makes him smile and then gives him a gentle kiss on the lips.

I watch them in their happiness, so tender and in love, and I can't help wondering how many more moments like this there will be for them.

When the worst will hit, taking away the best part of them. And of me.

This family is the most precious gift life could grant me, and I would do anything to keep it going.

* * *

Fifteen years earlier

I get back from school and throw my backpack on the kitchen table, covering my face with my arm because the odour of cigarette smoke in a confined space makes me nauseous. I open the window, even though it's freezing outside, to let a little air and light in.

I look around, and I realise the kitchen is exactly how I left it: full of dishes waiting to be washed and dirty, sticky ashtrays everywhere, full to the brim.

I pick up the letters that have been lying on the floor, and relief floods through me when I see an envelope I was anxiously waiting for – our welfare cheque.

I hide it before Mum can find it and decide to spend it as she pleases. I go to look for her, even though I know I'm going to find her in the same position where I left her this morning. I poke my head into her room and find a figure lying on the bed, wrapped up in the dark.

"Mum?"

"Mmm..." She turns to me.

I sigh in relief.

"Didn't you even get out of bed today?"

"Sure I did," she says, confused, as she tries to set her feet on the ground, knocking over a bottle as she does so.

I clench my jaw trying to control the anger as I move towards her.

"Don't look at me like that," she says. "Don't pity me."

"I don't."

"I'm just tired. It'll pass."

"Have you eaten anything?"

She shrugs. "I don't think there's anything to eat in the house."

"I'm going shopping. I'll make you something, alright?"

"Since when did you start cooking?" she asks, unaware of the significance of her question.

I don't answer her, but instead go back to get the cheque, which I'll cash in at the corner shop at the end of the road, allowing us to make it through until the end of the week, but making no promises for the one after that - or any that follow.

* * *

Present

I get out of bed dazed, even more tired than when I went to sleep. I can hear a racket coming from the kitchen. I sit up and look around to see Ryan trying to pull something out of the cupboard. I get up, putting my bare feet on the floor and march in the direction of the chaos that is currently invading my life, which I would have preferred to avoid.

"What the hell are you doing?" I ask, resting my hands on the counter.

"Jesus, Ian!" Ryan turns to me with his hand on his chest. "You're as quiet as a mouse!"

"Can't say the same about you."

"I was just trying to make some coffee,"

I look at the clock. "It's seven a.m."

"I'm used to getting up early."

I sit on the stool in front of him.

"Aren't you cold?" he asks, alluding to the fact that I'm not wearing a t-shirt.

"Not at all."

He sets a cup of coffee down in front of me.

"Wow. I'm touched."

"Piss off!"

I take a sip, and I'm lucky I don't bring it back up.

"A bit of sugar, maybe?"

"I like it bitter." He crosses his arms over his chest.

"I don't." I get up and walk around the counter to get some sugar.

"Holy shit, you're... you're..."

I lower my gaze and shrug.

"I like to sleep naked."

"Jesus Christ, Ian! Do you mind putting some pants on? You're not alone here!"

"You're in my house."

"Okay, but come on!"

"I don't have any problem walking around my house in the nude, Ryan. If you're getting an inferiority complex, you can always go jump off a…"

"Okay, okay, I got it!" He says, raising his hands and backing away.

I laugh under my breath and add a little milk to my coffee, mixing it slowly.

"What's that?"

I turn to see him pointing at the tattoos I have on my hip and abs that disappear right above my groin.

"I didn't know those birds went that far down."

"I'd be worried if you did know."

"You're in a particularly good mood today."

"Must be the good company."

Ryan walks off towards the bedroom, and when he comes back, he's got my jogging bottoms in his hands, which he throws at me.

"I can't talk to you like this."

"No one asked you to," I reply dryly, but slip on the trousers all the same. Then, I grab my cup, place two pieces of bread in the toaster, and sit down to wait for them.

"Aren't you supposed to be training today?" Ryan asks, completely comfortable with my life's schedule.

"On Mondays, we train in the afternoon."

He nods and purses his lips. I think he's starting to miss it.

"Well, I'm going to have a shower," he says, going in the bathroom before I can press the issue.

I look at the clock again. It's ten past seven, and I'm already exhausted.

I have to wait half a day before hitting the gym to release some of this pent-up tension. I can't go running because we're not allowed to overdo it.

What other options do I have?

I could break Ryan's face, but maybe I shouldn't. I'm starting to think he might not have many career options other than underwear model.

I look at the phone sitting on the counter and anxiety pulses through me. I grab it and flip through the messages.

A full 24 hours have passed. No reply.

A big, fat nothing.

Ryan walks back into the living room with a towel around his waist, dripping onto the floor that I'm going to have to wipe up.

He stands in front of me with his hands on his hips as if I was thirteen years old and he was my big brother.

"Is that what I think it is?"

I ignore him.

"Don't do it, Ian. Don't call her."

Shit.

Our roles really have been reversed.

9
Ian

Two years earlier

She opens the door, just sticking her head in, and is visibly surprised by my visit.

"Hi," I greet her.

"Hi… Jamie isn't home," she cuts to the chase.

"Yeah, I realised that when I noticed his car was missing," I lie shamelessly. I know full well that Jamie isn't here. "I was in the area, and I thought I'd stop by."

"Come in," she opens the door to let me in. "It appears that Jamie's got a new flame."

"I imagine," I say smirking. Jamie always has a new flame. "Am I disturbing you?"

"No, not at all."

"No hot date tonight? It's Saturday evening, you know…"

"Nope," she says blushing. "What about you? No love-life news?" She asks, biting her lip.

"Not at the moment," I reply steadily. "What were you watching?" I change the subject before I throw up on her coffee table.

"Captain America."

"Oh, come on…" I tease.

"What can I do? I've got a crush on Chris Evans."

"Well, if I was a woman, I probably would too."

She laughs.

The sound of it fills my ears, my soul, the entire room.

"Have you eaten?"

"Not yet."

"Do you mind some company?"

"Not at all. We can order something."

"Nah," I say standing up and heading towards the kitchen. "I can make something. I just need a few basic ingredients," I say opening the fridge. "Like these." I pull out some chicken breasts. "And these…" I say grabbing some vegetables. "And if you've got some pasta…"

"I think there's some in the cupboard."

I move around in her kitchen, opening cabinets, and drawers. I pull out pots and pans, chop up vegetables, and turn on the hobs, mixing and tasting as I prepare our meal.

"If you want, turn on some music," I say, adding a few more herbs to the chicken.

"Ah-ha," She heads into the living room and comes back with her phone, which she promptly hooks up to a set of speakers under the TV. I watch her work, enjoying these stolen moments from her daily life – ones where I am nothing more than a useless extra.

* * *

Riley sets her plate down on the table in front of us and rubs her stomach.

"God, I ate so much. I didn't know you were such a good cook. Who taught you, your mother?"

"I'm self-taught."

"You could open a restaurant."

"That's a stretch. But I make do."

"Well, if things don't go the way you hope with rugby, you've got a backup plan already."

"Rugby's everything to me."

She looks at me, tilting her head.

"Even though I know I don't have many years left in me."

"What are you talking about?" She asks, taking a sip of wine and stretching her legs out on the sofa just enough to graze my thigh.

We're both on our third glass, and I'm starting to feel warm.

But maybe it's not the wine.

"I'm getting to a certain age. I'm not as young as Jamie," I comment, trying to ignore the alarms going off in my head. "In a few years, I'll need to quit."

"You're not that old," she quips.

"For the level I'm playing at, it's different."

"What do you want to do afterwards?"

"I still haven't figured that out. I'll cross that bridge when I come to it. How about you?"

"Me? I'm good."

"Isn't there anything you'd like to do?"

"There are loads of things, but I've never thought too seriously about doing them."

"We all have the right to want something more."

"I have a good job, and all things considered, I like it – it would be hard to ask for more."

I look at her, hoping she'll go on.

"I started working when I was sixteen years old. I hadn't even finished school."

"Why?" I ask cautiously.

"I couldn't afford not to."

"Your family couldn't afford it?" I ask with discretion.

"We don't have a family."

"What does that mean?"

"Jamie is all I have."

"Your parents are dead?"

She shakes her head. "My mother left when we were little, Jamie can't even remember her face. We were left with our father. We lived in a small apartment in Rathmines. Dirty, damp, and dark. We didn't have a lot of money," she continues, embarrassed.

"He wasn't a hard worker... and not much of a father. He wasn't much of anything," she concludes bitterly.

"Riley, I..."

"You didn't know."

I shake my head.

"We don't like talking about it. It's not a time in our lives we want to remember."

"I'm sorry, I didn't mean to be pushy."

"You weren't," she says shrugging. "You didn't know and you asked."

"Questions you shouldn't feel obligated to answer."

"I don't feel that way. I'm fine. It's been a long time since then. Jamie and I have muddled through."

"Did you take care of him?"

She nods. "You know, Jamie wasn't like he is now. He was a sensitive boy; he needed to come out of his shell, to learn to be strong and face the world with his head held high, and he didn't stand much chance in that house. I tried to be strong enough for both of us, to give him the security he needed and the support that he deserved but that no one ever gave him. I promised him that he could be anything he wanted, and that I'd help him. I did everything I could to keep my promise. We had some dark, difficult years but we were together, and, in the end, it all worked out for the best. I'd do it again a thousand times. Nothing is more satisfying than seeing the man he's become."

I take her hand spontaneously.

"It's all in the past."

"You don't have to hide what you are, Riley. Not when you're with me."

She smiles timidly.

"You don't always have to be strong."

"Oh, I'm not, believe me."

"Yes, you are."

"There were loads of times I didn't think I'd make it... I was exhausted, alone, I'd given up. But just looking at Jamie gave me the energy to go on. I finished school a few years later by going to evening classes. That meant I could leave my old jobs and find a better one. I used to work in retail during the day and in a pizzeria in the evenings. I started off at the bottom in a better job, and I worked hard to get ahead. I'm still not exactly high up, sure, but I created an opportunity for myself which meant we could live decently, and most importantly, allowed Jamie to study, train, and become the champion that he is now."

"You must be very proud of yourself."

"Well, I didn't have a lot of choice. I had to either roll up my sleeves or..." She doesn't finish the phrase and looks elsewhere. "When Jamie first started becoming successful, I was happy for him, even if I knew it meant that sooner or later, I'd be left alone."

"What does that mean?"

"Well, Jamie is all I have."

"But you have your own life."

"My life," she whispers, "I'm starting to think that there isn't anything more out there for me. I don't know if you can understand, but I don't think I'd be able to trust another person, to have a family." She shakes her head. "Maybe this is all there is for me," she sighs.

She sits in silence for a few minutes, and I'm scared she'll be able to hear the loud, dangerous beat of my heart, pumping like crazy, risking irreparable damage.

Right now. In her house.

A house I stupidly talked my way into, if only to hurt us both in the process.

"You deserve everything, Riley," I tell her, even though I recognise I'm getting into dangerous territory

She looks at me in that way that she has. Jesus, that look makes me hope and dream, longing for something that doesn't belong to me... something that I'll never have in my hands.

Something that will never be mine.

And then, Riley kills me simply and swiftly, burying me six feet under.

"I have everything I need. I have my adorable brother, my work, a few good friends, like you."

Despite her words, her voice is melancholy, full of solitude.

Hers.

And mine.

"I'm sorry, I didn't want to bring you down like this. Don't feel like you have to tell me these things," I tell her because I would prefer to suffer in silence rather than see her in pieces.

"I have to tell someone and... I wanted to tell you."

"Me? Why?"

"Because you're the only person I trust."

She says it looking me in the eyes. She says it without hiding, without distraction, and without making it easier on herself.

In this moment, sitting on the sofa, Riley is speaking to me with her lips, her eyes, and her soul. She's giving me a part of her that she doesn't show to the rest of the world.

And she steals my heart.

I know this is probably the most painful part of her life, the part that she keeps locked up. The part you would never want to share with anyone. But she shared it with me.

Her story is something that opens old wounds and forces me to remember, It's the thing that doesn't let you close your eyes at night, that gives you nightmares of free-falling from the 78th floor of a skyscraper in one of those never-ending flights where you are screaming but you can't hear your own cries; where you try to react but you can't move a muscle. Then you wake up in agony, drenched in a cold sweat. And you understand that you never want to feel that pain again, even if it was worth all of the love in the world.

I let her talk, in a voice that is barely audible, but that seems to be screaming in my ears. She speaks calmly, having already accepted what life has given her. She hasn't shed one tear, and I know that in her place I would be sobbing under the table, hugging my knees to my chest.

She speaks and invades my world, seeking out my every piece.

And she finds them all. One by one.

The most absurd thing is that she isn't aware of what's happening. She couldn't imagine that by opening this door today about her past, she's also opened the same door into mine. She doesn't know that her suffering has already become a part of mine, that I can't think about anything but her. I'd like to find a way to erase what she's gone through and colour myself into her world.

I'd like to tell her that not all men are like her father. That she can have everything, she just needs to open her arms to the right man. That I wouldn't ask for anything more than to live in her eyes. That I wouldn't ask for more than the chance to stay next to her every day of my life. That she never has to hide who she is, but that she has to let herself be discovered because there's someone before her now who understands and feels all of the same things she does.

That I would be willing to do anything to be able to love her and be loved in return.

But I don't tell her any of that, I keep it to myself, like I always do. I bury it, hiding it deep down, where all my fear and rage reside.

"Can I ask you something?"

"Y-yeah, sure."

"Why do you worry about me so much?" She asks, barley looking at me with those big eyes from beneath her long eyelashes.

I could list her thousands of reasons.

I could tell her that from the first time I saw her at that damn party, something in me stirred, something I thought I'd buried deep enough.

I could tell her that when she smiled at me for the first time, I felt the floor give way under my feet, and I realised that trembling isn't just something that people do when they're scared; it's something that shakes you from within and makes you understand that you're still alive.

I could tell her it's because I'm a fucking bastard through and through, and I'd like to find a way between her legs and find my name on her lips in the moment that I make her mine.

I could tell her that it's because I'm an empty man who's experienced abandonment first-hand, always hoping that there might be something else out there for me. Something that wouldn't hurt me, break me, or destroy me.

I could tell her it's because her hair was made to be brushed by my fingers, that her eyes were made to be adored by mine, that her lips were made to be bitten by me, that her body was perfectly formed to be under, over, and next to mine.

I could tell her that the desire to kiss her, to have her, to write her name on my skin is killing me and if she keeps looking at me like that, I won't be able to control myself. I'll jump on top of her right here on this sofa, marking each centimetre of her skin with my teeth.

I could tell her that her nearness drives me crazy

and tears me apart because I know I can't have her, but I'd prefer to die slowly from her gentle sighs rather than to deny myself the sound of her voice, of her heartbeat.

I could tell her it's because this stupid arsehole wants her all for himself, because he's never had anything in his life that was more beautiful, and he can't help but want to relish in her beauty. But I don't say any of those things. I don't expose myself to her, like she did.

I simply say, "I'm in debt with you."

10
Riley

Two years earlier

Ian loads the dishes into the dishwasher. He cooked for me, and we ate on the sofa. I told him a bit about my life, and I don't know where the words came from.

I never talk to anyone about the past; Jamie and I keep it secret. We don't want any little part of our life with him to become public knowledge.

Jamie has his career, has made a name for himself in the world of sports, and the last thing I want is for the past to come back and screw everything up. It's something we need to protect ourselves from, and it's my responsibility to do so for as long as I can.

And that's the reason I try to stay on the sidelines and not interfere in Jamie's world, even though he so desperately wants me to be a part of it. I know it's better for both of us this way.

The best thing would be for me not to be associated with him as Jamie Murray's sister and for just a few trusted people to know who I am. You never know when an extra ear, someone a little too interested in other people's business, could be lurking around the corner.

And yet tonight, instead of locking that door, I left it ajar to let him make his way in. It seemed like the natural thing for me to do, maybe because Ian isn't just what he shows people; he's much more than that, I'm sure of it. And I'd like to be the one granted permission to discover everything that Ian hides from everyone else. Ian is discreet and loyal: Jamie trusts him unquestionably, which means I do too.

I don't know what he saw, how he processed what I told him, or how he feels about it, but he's still here.

I'm sitting on the counter in the kitchen, watching him, completely mesmerised, unable to do or say anything. His sure, purposeful way of moving has consumed all of my attention.

"Another glass?" he asks, suddenly waving a bottle in front of me.

"Why not." I turn to grab two glasses from the cupboard behind me. He opens the bottle and comes towards me. I set the glasses on the counter, and he pours for both of us. He offers me one and draws his hand in to clink his glass against mine in a toast.

"What are we toasting?" I ask, looking him in the eyes.

"To friendship," he says.

And my heart starts bleeding.

"To friendship," I repeat.

It's a lie.

Enormous. Dangerous. Senseless.

His.

Mine too.

When did this happen? When did we become friends? Who drew this stupid boundary between us, prohibiting us from thinking of something more than that? To understand, to hope that for us, there could be something more?

When did I become aware that my heart had stopped crying and started trembling?

When did I realise that he's the only one who knows where and how to look for me?

When did I start seeing him as the only man I could trust?

When did I realise that my life would always be unhappy and incomplete?

I take a sip of my wine, but I can't stop looking at him. His deep blue eyes pass over me.

They heat everything up. They set everything alight.

They set me alight.

Why, Ian? Why are we friends?

Why didn't you dance with me that night?

Why didn't you stop me that morning when I ran away from your house in a hysterical fury?

Why didn't you tell me that we could fill the missing space in each other's lives?

And why do you keep showing up in my life when I least expect it, filling it with your voice, your scent, your silences, your smiles?

Why do I keep leading myself on, knowing full well that there's nothing more for me than what I already have? Nothing else exists. Because a man like you, Ian O'Connor, could never really be interested in me, in what I was and what I still am.

And why do you continue to look at me that way, as if you can read my mind or worse yet, are thinking the same things and keeping them to yourself?

Why, Ian?

Why aren't you the one I share all my moments with?

"What do you think, shall we watch another film?" he asks, interrupting my stupid fantasy.

"Sure."

Anything to get him to stay a little longer.

"I'll bring the glasses into the living room," I say, hopping down from the table and picking them up. I need to distance myself from him so that I can regroup, regain control of my emotions so that Ian can't see my need – my desire – to be more than just his friend.

Wrong, painful.

Heavy.

I head into the living room, set the glasses on the table in front of the sofa, and then turn around to hurt myself a little more.

Because all of this hurts me. His presence. His interest. His friendship.

He hurts me.

He who makes me hope and believe.

Something that makes me desire.

I'm starting to want something. For myself.
Him. I want him.
But this is nothing but a doomed romance – and I'd rather not know how it ends.

11
Ian

Present

"So, the rumours were true." I enter the rehabilitation room where Jamie is taking his first steps at getting himself back into shape.

"You've really decided to stop your whining and move your arse?"

"Good one…" Jamie says with a grin, while Steve, one of our physical therapists, laughs quietly.

"How's the progress?"

"He'll survive," Steve says, playing down the situation. "Two weeks, maximum three, then he'll be back to training."

"Fantastic news."

"Sure is for you."

Good to see that Jamie has already got back his God complex.

I shake my head and grab a stool near them.

"Hey, don't you have anything better to do than sit here and watch my physio session?"

"I'm taking a ten-minute break before heading to the pool for some laps."

Jamie sighs heavily, then asks, "Steve, would you mind giving us five minutes, please?"

"No problem." Steve dries his hands on a towel

and leaves the room.

"What's up, are you worried about something?" I ask Jamie who has an uncharacteristically serious expression on his face.

"My one and only worry. My Sister."

"Jamie..."

"Were you at her house?"

"Yes, I took her home the other day."

"And she let you in?"

"Not exactly, I kind of invited myself."

Jamie nods. "I haven't been able to set foot in there for three months. Last time I did, I made some comments she didn't appreciate."

"I understand."

"I didn't want to invade her privacy, I just wanted to help out."

"Have you ever considered that maybe she doesn't want your help?"

"She doesn't want anyone's help," he says, getting off his stomach and walking around the room before stopping in front of the main glass doorway where the other guys are doing their weightlifting. "Have you *seen* that shithole she lives in? I understand she doesn't want to live with me, we're adults, we have our own lives, but Jesus!" he says, raising his voice. "I don't want her to get worse again."

"Worse?"

"You see, my sister puts on this facade that she's strong and independent, but I recognise it for what it is."

I wait in silence for him to continue.

"She doesn't break down, doesn't cry, she doesn't take things lying down and doesn't wallow in things."

"That's not a bad thing."

"She's a ticking time bomb, Ian. Sooner or later, she's going to explode, and when she does… I'm afraid there won't be anything left of her."

"I don't understand."

"She keeps everything inside. Her feelings. She hides things, buries them. She throws her smile in your face and you think everything is fine. But behind all that, Ian, there's a world that no one knows about and it'll suck her in when she isn't expecting it. Sooner or later, all that tension will come out, and I'm afraid it won't be pretty."

"Do you think you might be a little over-the-top here?"

"Do you… know?" he asks cautiously.

"What are we talking about?"

"Has she ever told you about our life, our childhood, our family?" he asks, clenching his jaw on the last word, while I go back in time to dust off that memory.

"She mentioned something, once. She told me that you're alone and that you lived on your own."

"Did she tell you why?"

"Er, yeah…"

"Did she tell you all of it? The unedited version?"

"I don't know." I stand up agitated. "She told me a few things, but I don't know if there's anything else, if she hid some part of the story from me, or if she lied to me... Why are you asking me all this?"

Jamie sighs and goes to sit back down, inviting me to take the spot in front of him. I do, grabbing the stool and pulling it closer.

"I don't want to do this, believe me. Opening Pandora's box isn't going to be good for any of the three of us."

"The three of us?"

"Trust me, it's not going to be good for you, either."

I look at him, worried.

"But maybe it's time that someone knew about it, someone who could understand and maybe help out."

"You're pissing me off now. Just say it, for Christ's sake!"

"First, let me ask you something."

"Let's have it."

"What's the deal with you guys?"

"Are you serious?"

"I've never been more serious about anything, and it's really hard for me."

"Nothing's going on, Jamie. There never has been. We were friends, you know that, and then things got out of hand. She thought that there could be more between us, and I let her know that wasn't possible. I hurt her and now she hates me."

"Let me rephrase the question. Are you in love with her?"

"You're crazy." I jump to my feet.

"I'll take that as your answer."

"Don't take it as a fucking thing!"

"Sit down and try to calm yourself."

"You're really pushing my buttons with all this. Why didn't I mind my own business this morning? Why the hell did I come here to see how you were doing? I should've left you to suffer under Steve's magical hands."

"I'm going to ask you again, and this is the last time, because I want you to be honest with me."

I sit down again, shaking my head nervously. It feels like I'm being interrogated here. I rest my elbows on my knees and drop my head into my hands.

"You want to know the truth, Jamie? The truth is that I don't have any idea what the hell love is."

Jamie leans in towards me, mimicking my position.

"Well then, let me tell you a story, and maybe, after you've heard it, you'll understand what it means to love someone more than anything else in the world."

12
Riley

Ray comes to the door. "Er, Riley?"

I lift my head from my computer and push up my glasses just in time to see Jamie behind Ray's back.

"What are you doing here?"

Jamie comes into my office, leaving Ray in the hallway. He comes over to my desk and rests his hands on it.

"We have to go, there's a taxi outside."

"Go? Where?"

"To *The Bridge*."

"Are you kidding?"

"They're waiting on us, let's go."

I look at him, confused.

"You've forgotten."

"What?"

"My birthday!" He crosses his arms and flashes me a fake look of disapproval.

"Your birthday is tomorrow."

"The guys organised me an all-nighter; don't worry, we won't blow out the candles until it's midnight."

"Jamie…"

"I won't take no for an answer."

"I'm not coming to the party."

"I'll go..." Ray interrupts, still standing in the door staring. "If they're all like him..."

"This is my brother, Jamie."

"Oh, shit." Ray walks into my office and extends his hand to Jamie. "I'm Riley's best friend. I don't understand how we haven't run into each other before."

"Simple: Jamie doesn't set foot into my life and vice versa," I respond.

"Well, it's time to change that."

"Are you doing what I think you're doing?"

"I'm trying to go celebrate my birthday, and I want my sister to be there."

"We can celebrate it, just the two of us, tomorrow."

"Riley..." Jamie sighs. "Please? I want you to be there."

"I don't want to see him," I say under my breath.

"Him... who?" Ray butts in.

"He won't be there. He had other plans."

"Are you positive?"

"Absolutely. Family plans."

"I'm sorry, who are we talking about here?" Ray tries again.

"No one." I give in and stand up, ending the conversation. I turn off my computer and gather my things.

"He can come too," Jamie says, nodding over

at Ray.

"Obviously I'm coming," Ray answers without a shadow of embarrassment before popping his head out the door and yelling, "Kate, move your arse. We're going to a party tonight."

I shake my head and smile. Ray is always ready to go looking for a wild night. He has a passion for guys who are too tall, too busy, and most of all, dickheads. I'm concerned that my brother has at least two of those qualities.

We leave the building where a taxi is waiting for us, and after all the necessary introductions, we get in the car, ready for the evening, which will surely be a disaster.

Kate, Ray, and I work together at the Gate Theatre. It's a job I'm crazy about. Okay, I'm just a secretary and to be more specific, I'm Kate's secretary. She manages the organisation of the shows, and Ray is her part-time assistant.

When I applied for this job, I didn't think I had a chance. I had a bit of experience, working for a few years in an events agency, but nothing to do with managing shows as professional as these. Kate brushed away all of my doubts; she's a fantastic person and an excellent boss who's always believed in me. After a three-month trial period, I signed a contract for a full-time job, which was lucky for me because I don't know what I would have done otherwise.

I lost my old job to redundancy, but it's not a sob story; now, I'm working in this fantastic place with great co-workers.

A bonus of working at the theatre is that I can see the shows for free. Since working here, I've discovered I love Jane Austen's work and have a real passion for Shakespeare. I haven't read many books, and I never finished high school, so at the beginning, I felt intimidated by my own ignorance. I wasn't able to follow them, to understand word choices or vocabulary, but after seeing a show at least five times, I started to feel more comfortable with it, making me feel like I wasn't in the wrong place and that it's never too late to learn.

I lose myself in my thoughts, looking out the window as the taxi leaves the city centre and makes off south towards Ballsbridge where Jamie and most of his teammates live.

It's one of the coolest areas in Dublin, right on the sea where the UCD campus is located, and where Leinster has their general headquarters.

I lived there for a while too when I was at my brother's house, but I decided it was time for me to get a place of my own and leave Jamie to his life. He's a grown man and he doesn't need me.

I can't deny it's an attractive location, but too luxurious for my taste. I prefer having a tiny, private apartment, where I can crawl into my own den and hibernate there in peace, hiding if necessary. Somewhere no one comes looking for me.

I try not to let myself get weighed down too much in thinking about the past, keeping my nails dug into the present, just hoping that this night will fly by, and I can go home quickly because I'm exhausted, in pain, and not really present.

I'm completely out of sorts and out of my head.

Maybe I'm coming down with something. Or maybe it's something else.

Ian was at my house, my little safe space. He invaded my privacy, he judged my lifestyle; even if he didn't say so explicitly, I read his thoughts, his eyes, and his embarrassed silence.

He sent me a few messages that I decided not to answer. I don't want to let him throw off my balance and lead me down a one-way street that can only end up hurting me.

I won't be fooled again.

He hasn't changed and neither have I.

We're what we always have been.

Alone and dangerous.

Messed-up.

"Hey, smile, it's my birthday," Jamie says, turning around from the front seat to smile at me.

He's right. I'm a terrible sister.

"Ready to celebrate!" I try to sound convincing and pull myself together for him.

The taxi pulls over, and Ray is the first one out, coming around the other side to open the door for me.

"This is paradise. I've dreamt of coming here for months. You know I've got a weak spot for big athletes, especially when they're tattooed."

I laugh despite myself.

"This place is owned by four guys from Leinster," Jamie says, taking me under his arm and limping because of his knee injury. "The team meets up here after every game, but we also use it for things like parties, celebrations…so basically, we're always here. Now you've been here too." Jamie winks at him, and I roll my eyes. I stiffen myself at the entrance, blocking his way too.

"Riley," Jamie says in my ear, "everything's going to be fine. I promise you. I'm your brother, and I want you to have fun tonight."

"You're not trying to manipulate my life, are you?"

"Absolutely not."

I sigh and walk through the door before him, sincerely hoping that Ian won't be here. I don't want him to think I'm going after him or that I'm here for some other reason. This little dive into the past was more than enough for me, and I don't feel like swimming right now.

We greet the bouncers at the entrance, and they open the doors for us. We walk down the stairs, which are narrow and increasingly dark, leading us to the basement where the place is located. It feels like a cave down here, but it's actually pretty inviting. I haven't been here much, maybe two or three times, but the team, the staff, and the fans keep it full around the clock.

We take a seat at a free table, and Ray doesn't waste any time searching for someone to ogle as I fix my eyes downward on the table, trying to make myself as small as possible and hoping that no one will notice me.

"I'm going to go say hi to the guys, okay? Be back in a bit. Order whatever you want. It's on them tonight," Jamie says, smiling and walking away but not before passing under Ray's x-ray vision.

"You want to stop that?" I threaten him.

"Did you know your brother...?"

"Yes, I know full well."

Ray huffs and gets up to order us some drinks.

"Wow, it's really quite something, isn't it? Lot of people here tonight," Kate interrupts. "What else are you hiding from us, Riley?"

I flash her a forced smile and discreetly raise my gaze. I check out the room, and thankfully, Ian's not here. It's highly likely he won't even find out I came. Another sigh escapes my lips; this time, it isn't relief.

Damn it.

We get our drinks and the first round disappears in no time. I get it, we're at a party and the idea is to enjoy it. The second round goes down as quickly as the first, and by the third, I start to feel lighter, less weighed down. I take my jacket off and open my blouse a bit to get some relief from the heat building up in there, and Ray lets out with a whistle of approval.

"Go on, girl," he hoots, making fun of me, as if he really appreciated what he saw.

We chat, laugh, and relax – I even begin to calm down almost enough to wish there was music playing that we could dance to. My wish comes true after a few minutes and the place comes alive with a song I love.

Kate must have read my mind, because she stands up, pulls me from my seat, brings me to the dance floor, and starts moving next to me. I cover my face with my hands, shaking my head because I feel embarrassed; no one around us is dancing, but her drive is contagious and after a few beats, I'm right there with her. It's the perfect song for two people to dance to.

Our spontaneous gesture attracts some attention, and the dance floor fills up in a hurry.

Ray joins us with a guy he just met, where they start to whisper into each other's ear, smiling and dancing next to us, happy and carefree. I can't help but feel a little jealousy pierce my stomach.

Jamie raises a glass in our direction to let me know he likes the fact that I'm letting myself go, at least tonight, and I blow him a kiss from a distance, to thank him for having brought me.

Kate squeezes herself against me, grabbing my hips, and rubbing against me seductively. She's undoubtedly drunk, but in the end, who cares? She just wants to have fun, so, I play along and grab her by the waist, and move my body against hers.

We let ourselves go to the music, to the alcohol flowing inside us, and to life itself, and for a few minutes, I really feel good, like I haven't felt in a really long time. My muscles loosen up, my head is light, and my thoughts have flown somewhere else.

A group of guys approaches us, persistent. Apparently, the show has caused an uproar, and they want to get involved. Kate and I try to step away – we weren't on the hunt tonight – but a guy, about thirty and visibly drunk, doesn't seem to pick up on our signals.

He makes his way in between me and Kate and takes control of the situation. He grabs me by the hips and tries to pull me towards him as I push my hands against his chest, trying to break away from him.

His breath stinks of alcohol, making me nauseous, and his insistence becomes oppressive, but I'm not strong enough to push him away – and he doesn't have any intention of letting me go.

Before I can turn my head to look for my brother, someone puts his hands on the drunk guy's shoulders and slams him to the ground.

And my heart stops beating.

13
Ian

I pace back and forth at the back of the club with my phone against my ear. I've been trying to get hold of Nick all afternoon, but he won't answer or call me back. I've left at least ten messages and I'm starting to get pissed off talking to his answering machine.

I make one last try before going in to celebrate Jamie's birthday. I told him I wasn't going to make it, that I wanted to spend the night at home with my family, but then I thought a distraction might be exactly what I need. We're a team, on and off the field, and being with my friends will help me keep my mind off what I now know and wish I didn't. I'm about ready to throw my phone against the wall when that arsehole finally has the decency to pick up.

"Where the fuck have you been?" I accuse him, not even saying hello. "I've been trying to get hold of you for days!"

"I was busy."

"Have you listened to my messages by chance?"

"Yours and that other dickhead's."

"Don't start."

"Did you tell him to call me?"

"He's your brother."

"That doesn't mean he's not an arsehole."

"Jesus, Nick, when are you going to grow up?"

"Listen, Ian, I understand I haven't come home much..."

"How long has it been since you've set foot in Dublin?"

"You know why I can't."

"It's time now."

"You don't get to make that decision."

"You have to."

"Excuse me, are you giving me orders? You?"

"Don't be an idiot."

"I've got things to do."

"Things to do?" I laugh, making fun of him. "Photo shoots with your arse hanging out?"

"I'm still on the team."

"As what, the mascot?"

"Fuck you, Ian."

"Try not to piss me off, Nick. Move your arse and get back here."

"What's the big rush?"

"I don't know how much time's left."

"What the hell are you getting at?" he asks raising his voice.

"I can't talk about it on the phone."

"No, sorry. Now you're just going to have to tell me what the hell is going on here."

"He's getting worse. He doesn't recognise me, Nick. Not most of the time."

"I don't understand – you told me it was all

under control, that there was still time."

"That time is up."

"Christ..." I hear him panting on the other end and I realise I may have been too harsh.

It's true that Nick's an idiot, but that doesn't mean he has no feelings, especially when it comes to his family.

"How serious is it?" he asks after a few seconds of silence.

"He's getting worse quickly."

He sighs. "I'll see what I can do."

"I'll expect you here by this weekend. No later."

I hang up feeling a little bit lighter. That was progress, wasn't it? Trying to reason with a big stubborn ox, nothing to it.

"Hey Ian. What are you doing here?" John joins me outside. "You better get in there."

"What's happening?"

"Two girls were putting on a little show and they've attracted a bit of a crowd... I don't know if I've explained that very well."

"A little show?"

"In the middle of the dance floor."

I raise an eyebrow.

"Two women, you know. It looked like they were about to get to it right in front of everyone."

"What are you, thirteen?"

Jesus, who am I talking to?

"You don't want to miss it."

"I wouldn't dream of it," I respond sarcastically, opening the door and leading him inside.

I head down the stairs and glance around. There's a group of people on the dance floor and everything seems to be fine, but then my eye lands on a corner of the floor aside from the main area, where a man is trying to get with a girl.

"Don't you think they're making a big deal out of it?" I say, observing the scene, which isn't a big deal per se, but I just hate these kinds of things.

"Should we go break it up?" Scott says, joining our group.

Someone has to.

Dodging around a table, I approach the couple with determined steps, hoping that a talk and a drink might help calm things down without any spilled blood. We've already had too many fights this month and it'd be better to keep it out of the press.

I get to the guy's shoulders with the intention of politely asking him to knock it off, but then my eyes fall on her.

And my heart explodes in my chest.

I grab him by the shoulders and throw him to the ground with all of my might, then I sit on top of him, preparing to pummel his face into a mass of blood and dust.

I throw the first punch and it's loud enough to hear bones crunching, but I don't give a fuck about the pain in my hand – it's nothing in comparison with what's going on in my heart.

When I pull my fist back for another, John and Scott grab me by the shoulders.

"Mate, what the hell is wrong with you?!"

What the hell is wrong with me?

I get off him, rubbing my fist while his friends pick him up and drag him away. John grabs my arm, asking me for an explanation that I can't give him.

"What the hell is going on?" Jamie comes over in a fury, wanting to have a go at the guy too, but Scott blocks him off. "Did he have his hands on my sister?"

"Your... oh shit," Scott says, lifting his hands to his face.

In the corner of my eye I see Riley hunched over in a corner with her arms wrapped around her chest and her eyes glued to the ground. Jamie goes to her, making sure she's alright. She gives a small nod, and I free myself from John's grasp and join them.

And when she lifts her eyes to mine, everything stops breathing.

Including me.

Because all I want is to feel her. On top of me. Just one time.

Feel her sighs in my ears, her warmth around me, her hands sliding over my body. Have her eyes, her caresses, her mouth. For me. Just for me.

Forgetting about her entire world and creating a new one together, made up of just the two of us.

And when she tears her gaze away, turning her back to me and walking quickly in the other direction, I understand that I've lost.

I've lost everything.

I've lost her.

Riley gathers her things, speaks animatedly with a woman and a man, then kisses Jamie and leaves the building, leaving them speechless and confused.

Everything's happening too fast, but the moment she heads towards the stairs I know it's time to make a decision. One that could change the course of things forever, could lead me to make a mistake. Huge and irreparable. The kind that destroys your life and someone else's too.

And yet, I go for it all the same. Head and heart agree.

"Move your arse!" Jamie yells above the noise of the crowd, pointing towards the stairway.

I run up the stairs and out of the door, where I find her on the pavement. She snaps her head up and stares at me, swallowing what remains of my intentions, and the rest of my fucking life.

Because she's got it all right there in her hand.

"Riley," I whisper, touching her face with the back of my hand.

Her breathing tickles my lips and my entire body stops with the heat of her body.

Riley takes two steps backwards, away from my hand, taking my pride and my hope along with her.

"What the hell got into you?" she yells furiously. "Why did you punch that guy? What were you trying to do, kill him?"

"He was…"

"He was dancing with me!"

"How much have you drunk tonight?"

"What?!"

"He had his hands all over you!" I yell back, feeling the rage creep in. "Good Lord, Riley, are you so far gone you didn't even notice?"

She looks at me narrowing her eyes as I get closer again and wrap an arm around her, drawing her to me. She instinctively puts her hands on my chest and I stop in that moment and feel the cold, because her touch sets off a fire in me.

Her chest rises and falls quickly, revealed by a shirt that is too open and shows off too much of her. I let my eyes fall down to her chest, along her neck, up to her mouth.

I swallow hard, pushing back the instinct to put my hands in her hair and pull her to me.

"He had his hands all over you," I repeat more calmly this time.

"That's not your problem," she says and her voice has gone down a full tone as well. "You can't go around trying to kill everyone."

"I can't let someone touch you like that, Riley,"

I growl, dying from the desire to bite her lips and make them mine. "I couldn't stand it."

"I don't belong to you."

There it is. I heard it. My heart crumbling to dust in her hands.

Riley isn't mine. She never was.

I didn't allow her to be.

And even though I feel her slowing abandoning herself in my arms now, putting away the armour and taking off the mask; even though I could kiss her and feel her on my skin, I can't.

I can't have her like this.

Not if I can't hold her with me.

I let her go instantly.

Her nearness makes me suffer, and I can't control it. Not now. Not when the pain is coming back to swallow me up and ruin my life.

Her eyes are asking me to stay, to talk, to clear the air, but instead I turn and go back inside to avoid this thing getting out of hand for both of us.

To avoid letting her stay here, in my arms. To avoid losing my head again for a woman I'll never be able to love as well as she deserves.

14
Ian

I'm nearly at the end of a long run along the Grand Canal when my phone starts vibrating on my arm band, forcing me to stop and turn off the music.

"Ian?"

"Mum?" I say, huffing. "Everything okay?"

"Your dad has gone out."

"Okay."

"We had just come back from the supermarket and while I was putting things away in the fridge, he must have walked off without saying anything."

"Maybe he just went for a walk down the road." I turn around and start off towards home, ready to jump on my motorbike and race to their house.

"He's never done anything like this before," her voice creeps up.

"I'll be right there. I just need to go home and get my bike. Have you spoken to the neighbours? Have you asked around at all?"

"I'll do that now."

"Good."

"Ian?"

"Yes?"

"I'm scared."

"I'm on my way."

Back at my apartment, I grab the keys and force Ryan off the sofa.

"Dad is missing! Mum's in a panic. Get up, for God's sake!"

Ryan grabs his jacket and slips on his shoes quickly, following me outside.

* * *

As we pull up to my parents' house, we find Mum sitting on the front step. As soon as she sees the car, she jumps up and her hands fly to her mouth.

"Ryan... I can't believe it... when..."

"I'm sorry it took so long, Mum." I hear him say as I go towards them.

"We're here. Any news?"

She slowly looks away from Ryan and shakes her head no.

"I'll take a drive around the neighbourhood. You go inside and stay calm. I'm sure he'll come back on his own."

"I'll stay with her," Ryan says.

I nod in agreement: Mum is upset, Ryan being there can only comfort her. I'm confident that Dad's somewhere close by, probably confused, or maybe he can't find the way back.

I decide to go on foot, so I can stop and check

out any places he may have gone to. I pass the bakery on the corner and ask if they've seen him but they haven't. Same thing at the dry cleaners, pub and supermarket. Nothing.

I go back with a growing fear that something might have happened. I cut through the park on Northwood a few hundred metres from home, when I see him on a park bench watching the swings.

I let my breath out and reach for my phone, letting Ryan know that I found him, before going to the bench and sitting next to him.

After a few seconds of silence, he lifts his eyes to me.

"Out for a run?" he asks with a smile.

"Yep."

"It's a nice neighbourhood. Great place to raise kids."

"Have you got any children?"

"Two."

"Do you bring them here much?"

He laughs. "Oh no, they're too old for that now. But I did, yes. It wasn't like it is now though, with all these games. It used to be all dirt and they could play around on their bicycles while I sat here on this bench, just like I am now, and watched them from a distance."

"Sounds like a good time in your life."

"It was."

"What are your children's names?"

"Nick and Ryan."

I rest my back against the bench and extend my legs. I close my eyes and lift my face to the sky, enjoying this mild sun marking the beginning of winter.

"I'm going home now," he says getting up.

"I'll walk you," I say, getting up too.

"Do you know where I live by any chance? I'm a bit confused at the moment."

"No problem, I'll show you where it is."

"Thanks a million…"

"Ian."

"Ian. You're a good boy, Ian. Your parents must be very proud of you."

"I hope so," my voice cracks, but he doesn't seem to notice.

I walk him home in silence and when we get to the door, Mum runs out to hug him.

"Hey, I wasn't gone long. Did you really miss me?" he asks laughing.

"You know I can't be without you even for a half an hour," she responds with tears in her eyes before hugging him tightly.

In that moment, Ryan comes to the door. My father stops in his tracks an instant just looking at him in confusion.

"Dad…" Ryan tries.

"Ryan?" he asks and even at this distance I can see the tears swelling in my brother's eyes.

"I wanted to surprise you," he says, moving

towards him.

"You've come back," Dad whispers, incredulously.

"I'm home, Dad," he hugs him, completely engulfing him. He lifts his eyes and meets mine. "I'm home," he repeats before miming a 'thank you' to me, choking me up.

My father breaks away from him and invites him to come inside, happy to have his son with him, but before disappearing behind the door, he turns to me again.

"Thanks, Ian."

"You're welcome."

Dad goes into the house with Ryan while my mother comes over to me.

"Where was he? What happened?"

"He doesn't remember me," I reply, ignoring her questions.

"Oh, honey..."

"He told me that he has two children," I go on, swallowing down the tears.

"You know that he—"

"Yes, I know."

"Please, Ian..."

"I'll take care of it. I'll make Nick come back."

"You always take care of everything. What would we do without you?"

I don't answer. What can I say?

"You know that we love you, Ian, we always have."

I sigh. "Will you be alright now?"

"He's quietened down. He'll take his medicine and hopefully rest a bit."

"Well then, I'm going to go. I still need to take a shower and get back to Nick and tonight there's a pregame meeting I have to be at, but if you want…"

"No, we'll be fine. Ryan's here now."

Right. Ryan's here. I know she didn't mean it like that, that she's not trying to hurt me, but it does.

I hug her and head towards my motorbike.

"Ian?"

"Yeah?"

"Your dad is so confused at the moment, and I was distracted for a second. It won't happen again."

"You can't be everywhere at once."

"Neither can you."

I force a smile. She's right, we're similar in that, even if it seems hard to believe.

"I'm off."

"Take care of yourself, Ian. Please, live your life."

And my thoughts can only go in one direction.

I get on my bike and head home, going over what Mum said about who I am, what I feel and try to push down, to the image that comes to mind.

Her eyes. Her emptiness.

Something I'd like to rip apart with my hands so that she can't feel the darkness tearing at my heart.

* * *

The images from the other night keep tormenting me: Riley on the dance floor, Riley pushed up against that guy. His slimy hands on her hips. Me punching him, attempting to murder him, the guys pulling me away from him, Riley hunched over in a corner.

And then her, just a breath away from me. Her chest against mine. Her lips calling out to me. Her heat mixing with mine. The desire to feel her under my skin.

I fought against myself trying to quieten the longing with training, the team, my family but it was useless. Nothing helps.

I was outside the theatre for a while, maybe a half an hour, undecided if I wanted to go in or not. I just couldn't separate the present from the past, push it aside. I couldn't ignore that feeling, of being sucked into her eyes and all that's hidden there. To forget these years, that night and the sensation of having something in my hands that was worth risking everything for.

I know that it's wrong, that letting her get close to me is dangerous, that she'll drag me into a downward spiral of remorse and bad decisions, but I need to do something. I need to make sure that she's really okay and not playing hide and seek with her emotions, because that's what it feels like.

Despite the fact that I've tried whole-heartedly to avoid getting involved, I'm up to my neck in it. Again.

I see her everywhere. She is everywhere, or maybe she's in the place she's always been. From the first night I made the wrong decision in my life, setting off a series of other equally bad decisions, to where I am now, who I am and who she is today.

What we've become.

She opens the door, walking down the stairs distractedly, trying to get her jacket on without watching her feet and her heel trips up on the last step. I run to help her and she lands in my arms. It looks like something from a film, a real-life romcom where the main character is a bit clumsy and the hero is always on standby, ready to save the day; but this isn't a film.

This is my fucking life – and I'm about to dive head-first into a disaster with no way out.

She stands up and for a second, we make eye contact.

"Are you alright?" I ask her, when she lowers her gaze and I start breathing again.

"It's nothing."

"Does it hurt?" I point to her ankle which she doesn't appear to be putting any weight on.

"What are you doing here?" she changes the

subject.

"About the other night... I'm sorry. I shouldn't have reacted like I did."

"I overreacted too."

"I saw you there with that guy. I thought that he..."

"It doesn't matter."

We close off in a moment of silence, the embarrassing kind where it feels like you've gone through everything you had to say too quickly and you look around for some kind of emergency exit.

"Were you just going somewhere?" I say first.

"I'm on my break. I was going to get some coffee."

"Can I come with you?"

Thrown off by my request, she hesitates for a moment but then shrugs. We start walking in silence, shoulder to shoulder up Parnell Street. At the first traffic light, we stop and she lets out a little groan of pain.

"Does it hurt?" I ask pointing to her foot.

"A little, yeah."

My pride yells at me not to do it. My reason instructs me not to touch her. My heart begs me not to go on. But I'm not listening.

I extend my arm to her which moves on its own as if it were controlled by an external force. She looks at it for a second, considering it before accepting it, but when she does... God, I feel all of my muscles contract and the bite in my heart clamps down a bit harder.

All I did was touch her damn arm.

Do I have any idea what the hell I'm getting myself into? What it means to look at her, feel her, touch her and not be able to have her?

She's only been back in my life for a few days and we're already at this point?

How could I even imagine having thoughts like this about her? Why don't I just let myself be eaten by my own guilt? Why don't I give up and stop torturing myself like this?

Because I already know how it's going to end. I've seen this one.

She'll slip into every thought and every breath.

She'll dig greedily into my heart with her nails and after having scratched every surface, when the scars are too vast to be sewn together again, she'll turn her back on me and walk away with the blood still on her hands.

And I'll let her go. I'll stand there frozen in my puddle of blood while she walks away with everything, leaving me to my agonising desperation. Because that's what happens when you let your heart decide for you, when you let yourself open up to someone, when you believe in them.

You end up alone.

Abandoned.

And yet, here I am.

When we get to O'Connell Street she nods for

me to go into Starbucks. I order two coffees at the counter while she grabs a place on the sofa.

I look over at the window and imagine she hasn't had anything to eat. Not knowing what she might like, I ask the girl behind the counter to add two muffins – one blueberry, one chocolate chip. I get everything onto two trays and make my way to the sofa. "I thought you might be hungry" I say.

Riley rests her back on the sofa and I don't know why, but she seems smaller than usual to me now. As if she were trying to become one with the fabric.

"Is everything alright?" I ask, worried.

She nods.

"Riley... don't lie."

"It's okay."

"'Okay' my arse. Did I do something wrong? Did I say...?"

She looks up slowly and my breath hitches.

"Why are you here, Ian? What do you want?"

"I don't know." I answer honestly. "I wanted to... I had to see you."

"It's not a good idea. It's never a good idea when it comes to you."

I take the blow and remain standing.

"Don't do it again."

"What?"

"Come into my life and then disappear."

Her words open a gash in my heart capable of sucking everything around us into it. Every table, chair, sofa; every person and every damn sigh that escapes her mouth.

I'd like to take all of it and make it more luminous and more perfect for her, because Riley is simply perfect and everything else is tarnished by comparison.

I am nothing in comparison.

"Riley…" I breathe hard and let out the strangling thought that has always been within me – and it's time to tell her. "I'm the one who wants you to come back into my life," I say, without considering the consequences of what I'm saying, the effect they could have on her.

The moment my words make contact with the air, her eyes find mine, penetrating so deeply that I'm afraid she may have hit my soul and may now understand how worked up I am for her.

"I'm not what you want. We both know that."

I swallow, trying once again to send away this feeling that's trying to make its way up to my lips, transform into words and fly to her. Trying to diminish all of her insecurities, and to show her that she's perfect, that she hasn't done anything wrong, that I was the one who screwed up.

"You don't know what you are."

I'm panting. My heart is going crazy. It's like you're falling off a cliff, and no one hears you screaming, no one reaches out to help you. I'm going to shout as loud as I can for her to hear me.

"Give me a chance."

"You had your chance."

"I was an idiot."

"You still are."

"You're right, I know."

"I'm not going to let my heart be broken by someone like you."

"But what if I wanted to put it all back together?"

"That'd be rich, seeing as you're the one who crushed it in the first place."

"Just one chance. That's all I'm asking for."

She looks at me doubtfully.

"You're a bastard, O'Connor."

"I know what I am and I know that I'm not going to change but I want to be *your* bastard."

She shakes her head but can't hide a little grin.

"One chance," she says, stirring her coffee. "But you'll have to earn it," she says, serious.

"Damn right, I will."

She smiles slightly and I feel something building in me: hope.

Salvation.

She doesn't know me, doesn't know what lengths I'll go to, to get what I want. And right now, there is only one thing I want, and she's sitting right in front of me.

"You're very confident," she smirks.

"You have no idea."

Okay, I fucked this up a year ago. Actually, my messing it up has lasted a lot longer than that: it started when I met her, when she set down her roots, the kind you can't get rid of even if you dig up the earth. And I thought I could just pull them out with my bare hands.

I thought I could ignore the signs, the acid in my stomach, the heart beating too fast and the sighs. I thought I could spare myself. But that doesn't work for anyone, not even the biggest arseholes.

Because the people that destiny sets in front of you are there to be loved. You have to take everything good about them and safeguard it, like a precious treasure you've been searching for your whole life. You have to love them for all their flaws, their fears and insecurities because that's what makes them real, vulnerable, unique. You can't renounce all that, throw it away or hold it against them just because you're a hard-headed idiot.

You just need to love people and try to make them happy, do your best. And give yourself to them completely, let them see you as you really are and let them decide if they want to stay or not. You can't lock them out just because you're afraid that they'll wake up one day and realise they've made a mistake.

"I know I'm going to regret this," she says shaking her head and taking a blueberry muffin. "I love these," she says, starting to relax.

"I love them too," I smile at her.

She's set down her battle axe. Her walls are

starting to crack. I can already see the first brick falling to the ground and turning into dust at my feet. I just need a tiny something to work with, something I can grab onto that allows me to slip back into her life and convince her that she was made only for me.

I made the biggest mistake a person could make, but now I'm here to make it right.

* * *

One year earlier

We're lying side by side on my bed. Our skin is touching, our breathing mixes together, my heart is going nuts and my body is trembling.

I'm not going to make it. I can't hold out much longer. I can't go on ignoring what I feel, what has taken residence in my mind and my body for years now.

My obsession. My downfall.

Two years of imagined kisses, caresses and unfulfilled fantasies. Two years of repressed desire and insanity. Two years where I sat witness to my own destruction – and to hers too.

Every glance, every word, every damn breath has been agony. Every night I've spent away from her has been enormously and uncontrollably painful to me.

And I don't plan on doing it again.

I want to touch her. Right now. I want to feel her with my fingers, with my lips, with my eyes and my entire body. I want to feel everything.

I want to feel her.

I know I won't be able to go back once we cross this line and that our lives will self destruct with no chance of survival, but the desire to have her clouds over all of my logic and disables any efforts I've made to keep my distance from her.

I let my hand slide down along her skin.

She shivers. She wants me.

I let myself enjoy that madness.

I taste her, slowly, scared and almost breathless, on the brink of giving in.

I stop.

I'm almost suffocating under my own breath.

I brush one of her nipples gently with my thumb and it goes hard immediately, a rush of excitement flowing through my veins.

She leans in, her mouth on mine. And then, I feel the bitter taste of tears on her lips and I understand that we're taking too big a step here, that under our feet is a never-ending abyss. Eternal.

"I can't do this," I tell her, with my heart in pieces and my soul in desperation.

But I do it all the same.

I tell her that I'm a man who is unable of giving. That I only know how to take. That I want her body but that I don't want her.

I tell her that this thing between us is a problem, a big, dangerous one and that I don't like having problems, especially when it involves a woman.

I tell her that she needs everything and that I'm a bastard who wants to get between her legs, for a night or two, but who will never be able to give her more than that.

I tell her she'll have none of me.

Even if the truth were to be told, she's already got everything there was to take, she keeps it tight in her hands, imprisoned, and I know that it'll never be returned to its rightful owner.

I hurt her. I rejected her.

I push her away from me, from what we can never share, because I know that she needs someone and that I'm not that person.

She doesn't really want me and soon she's going to realise that for herself. I don't want to be left here with nothing.

I can't let her leave me.

I get up from the bed, get dressed and grab my keys. I leave the house letting the door slam behind me, confident that when I come back, I won't find her waiting for me.

15
Ian

Present

I open the door and the sound of Mum's laughter lifts my mood immediately. A night at home with the family is just what I need. I close the door behind me and peek into the kitchen where Mum is crying with laughter over something Ryan has said.

"Hey, what's going on here?" I ask, grabbing a carrot from the salad on the counter.

"Oh nothing, your brother was just telling me about the last time he got pantsed on the field."

"What a show," I tease and he punches my shoulder.

"Where's Dad?"

"He's setting the table in the dining room. Today's a good day," she smiles and my heart fills with hope.

Maybe all isn't lost.

"I'll go and see if he needs a hand, seeing as Ryan doesn't look like he'll be off his arse anytime soon."

I grab some glasses from the counter and take them through to the next room. My father is setting down the napkins and cutlery, in seemingly good spirits.

"Oh, Ian!" He looks up at me. "I didn't hear you come in."

"I just got here." I put the glasses down and notice immediately that my father has set the table for five. Maybe it's not the awesome day Mum expected after all.

"Er, Dad?"

"Yeah, son?"

"You've set too many places."

He looks at me for a second before looking back at the table. "There are five place settings," he says looking at me again. "There are five of us."

"No, Dad, there are only four of us here tonight." I try to be delicate, not knowing how this conversation is going to end.

He shakes his head and goes back to what he was doing and I decide to let it go: there's no point upsetting him over this.

"I'm going to the kitchen to get drinks. What would you like?"

"Half a glass of wine'd be great."

I go back into the kitchen just as the front door opens in front of me.

"What the fuck?"

"That's how you welcome me back?" Nick says, throwing his bag to the ground.

"Nick…"

"Oh, I see you still remember my name."

"You ugly son of a—"

"Nick!" my mother appears behind me. "Oh my God, you're here!"

He opens his arms and she runs to him and dives in. Nick squeezes her tightly and lifts her off the floor, making her squeal in delight.

"I told you there were five of us," my father says calmly behind my back as he goes over to my brother and my mum.

"Dad," Nick's voice comes out distorted.

"I knew you'd come back."

My father joins the hug and all three of them remain that way for a few seconds, still in the doorway.

"You did it," Ryan whispers in my ear. "You reunited the family."

I nod emotionally.

"And now you've got to deal with this shit," he adds before emptying his glass and going back in the other room.

* * *

We all sit at the table in the living room, much to Mum's delight. Nick tells us about his most recent photo shoots, given that his days of talking about the actual sport have dwindled significantly.

He's too cool and too much of an arsehole to be satisfied with just being a player, he prefers to be the public face of ten different brands of underwear, sports lines, watches and who knows what else. He's forgotten that he's first and foremost a rugby player and then – maybe – something good to look at.

Ryan sits in silence, keeping his eyes on his plate and his glass in his hand. He didn't even say hello to Nick, which has not escaped my mother's attention.

For the moment, everything is calm: no fighting, no knives to anyone's throat.

Maybe we've grown up, able to have a civil conversation and potentially go back to being a normal family, before someone's terrible decision threw us all up to our necks in a pile of shit.

"So, little Ryan got booted off the team, huh?"

I spoke too soon.

I kick Nick under the table, but he dodges it.

"Fuck you, Nick."

"Please, boys." Mum tries to come between them.

"What did I say?" Nick's stupid face could be a punching bag. "Did I get it wrong?" he challenges, looking at Ryan in invitation.

"I took a break."

"A break... huh. I guess you're not that important to them."

"As if *you* were. You're a model now, right?"

"Just for the fun and the money. At least I still have a place on the team."

"Right. When they're desperate for someone to send onto the field. What's the matter, you're not afraid of ruining your pretty face, are you?" Ryan slams down another glass and I can feel my head already exploding.

"Kids," my father stands up and I choke on my water, afraid he's having one of his moments. "Take your arguments elsewhere, not in front of your mother. I want you all in the garden, right now!"

Nick and Ryan get up huffing.

"You too, Ian."

I stand up and follow them outside. My father closes the door and signals us to take a few steps away from the house so Mum can't hear.

"I'm going to tell you this just once. I don't want to repeat myself because I don't know if I'll be able to."

"Dad," I try to interrupt him, but he cuts me off, raising his hand.

"I'm happy you're all here. Thank you, Ian, for bringing them home."

"I had nothing to do with this," I try to justify.

"I'm sick, not stupid," he shuts me up. "It's okay. You're here now, and Karen is much happier than she's been in a very long time. She's been so worried about me, I can't let you give her any more stress. If you want to stay here, you'll have to get along as civilised human beings, like brothers. You need to bury the hatchet, at least as long as you're in this house. You can do what you please once you leave, but not in front of your mother, is that clear?"

My brothers nod.

"I can't hear you."

"Yes, Dad," they reply in unison.

"Do it for her, she deserves it with everything she's going through."

"Dad," Ryan says, putting his arms around my father's neck. "I'm sorry, it won't happen again, I promise."

"That's fine."

"I'm sorry," Nick says, sticking his hands in his pockets. "I'll try my best."

Dad nods.

"Let's go back inside and try to act like a family."

Nick and Ryan go back into the house with their heads hung low, but carrying on their idiotic routine, pushing each other to race through the door first.

I shake my head and follow them, but my father takes me by the arm.

"I'm sorry about the other day," he says in a whisper. "You're my son, Ian, as much as they are."

"No, Dad, you don't have to—"

"I want you to know that I loved you from the first day you came through this door. When you showed up on this doorstep with all of your rage, needing to be loved. I loved you instantly. For me, you became an O'Connor in that moment, and always will be."

I can barely hold the emotions.

"Now come here and give your dad a hug. Don't squeeze me too much though, go slow."

I laugh as the first tear falls down my face. "You're the pillar of this family, Ian. I don't know what we'd have done without you."

"That's not true."

"Yes, it is. You're strong and giving and we were very lucky. Thanks for letting us in to your heart."

"It was you guys who gave me this home."

"And you're the one holding it together. You're the one who continues to be there even if not everyone deserves it. You're the one who stopped your brothers from killing each other. You're the one who brought them all home. You, Ian, are this family. And I'll never thank you enough for that."

16
Ian

"Well, closing yourself up in a bar doesn't seem like the best way to get some air."

Ryan asked me to take him out of the house for a while. He's been here a few days and already seems exhausted. He finds Dublin suffocating. I don't know if it's because of the situation with my parents, if it's because he can't deal with what he left behind or if he and Nick have already come to blows, and I almost hope it's the latter – at least I'd be able to get rid of one of them for a while.

I nod to the barman to bring us two beers.

"This is a nice place."

"They opened it a while ago. A few guys from the team were looking to invest in something and this is the result – *The Bridge*."

"Right next to the stadium and the training centre. Very strategic."

"Exactly. It's always full of die-hard fans and women out on the pull."

"Sounds fun," he says sarcastically.

"Not for me."

"Sure. We're always there."

I swallow down the mouthful I've got and avoid looking at him.

"Ah, Ian."

"Shut your mouth."

We both drink in silence, waiting for the alcohol to calm our nerves; mine, because I'm feeling antsy, and his, which I sense are probably tenser than mine, even if I can't help hoping he chokes on his pint – just for one less thing to deal with.

I take out my phone and set it on the bar. I look at it constantly, I can't help it.

What am I hoping for?

"Still glued to your phone?"

Ryan's got a death wish. He wants to die, tonight, in this bar.

"Mind your own damn business," I growl.

"There's only one person that gets you like this."

I don't bother looking at him.

"See, we're talking about her again. It's always about her."

"Piss off, Ryan!"

"You can take it out on me if it makes you feel better."

"Not as much as I'd like."

He stands up, grabbing his beer.

"I'm going to say hi to the guys. Make a fucking decision. I can't stand you like this for much longer."

He can't stand me much longer?

I turn to face the room and rest my back against the bench behind me. Ryan goes to a table where a few of the guys from the team are hanging out. He sits down and starts chatting with them. I try not to choke on my own heart, which seems to now have taken up residence in my throat.

I look at my phone again.

I grab it and walk briskly out of the pub.

* * *

I'm already on my way to her house when I hit the green button, because my stupid heart always leads me to her street. I know I should ignore it, push it down, tape it up and throw it in a secret underground location, but it just doesn't want to be kept hostage any longer.

"H-hey..." she stammers in surprise.

"I just wanted to hear your voice," I tell her honestly.

She sighs on the other end of the line.

It's useless to make up a story, that's not what she wants. She's looking for the truth and I'm going to have to give it to her.

"How was work today? Was it a rough day?" I ask because I really want to know.

What she does. How she lives. When she breathes.

"It was pretty intense. I just got home."

"I bet you haven't eaten yet."

"Well, no, I haven't had time. I was just going to see what my fridge has on offer," she jokes.

Riley joking around. How long has it been since I've heard that?

"Can I stop by? If you're not too tired."

"Stop by? What do you mean?"

"I'd like to spend some time with you."

"Oh…"

"Would that be alright?"

"I guess so."

Hope courses through my veins. For once, it hasn't landed me in a ditch instead.

"I'll bring dinner. Is pizza okay?"

"Perfect."

"Tell me how you like it."

"W-what?!" she stammers.

"The pizza, Riley. How do you like your pizza?"

"Oh…" her voice drops. "The pizza… I don't mind, you choose."

"Riley…"

"Yeah?"

"I want to know what you like."

I really do.

"I don't know, maybe pepperoni and mushroom?"

"I'll be there in twenty minutes."

* * *

I park outside her house and jump off my bike. I go to the door but before I can knock, she opens it.

I don't think I'm prepared for it at all.

The sight of her is something painful yet necessary. It's a cocktail of fear and hope. It's my worst nightmare come to visit me when I least expect it, and my most beautiful dream coming true. It's an enormous mistake, but the best decision in the world.

She stands there in the doorway, smiling innocently with some terrible striped socks and a tracksuit that would be big enough for me to get in there with her.

Raw, vulnerable, beautiful.

I'm sure she has no idea the effect she's having on me, the fire that is starting from all corners of my body and growing more dangerous with every damn minute I spend with her.

"How did you get that pizza here on your motorbike?"

"Huh?" I get my thoughts together.

"I was saying... oh, it doesn't matter," she smiles again. "Er... I've only got one chair."

I shrug, "We can eat on the bed."

When I say the word bed her cheeks go aflame.

"If that's alright with you..."

Everything, Riley. All of it's alright. I'd take anything, as long as you're the one giving it to me.

"Did you say something?"

Did I just say that out loud?

I shake my head. She smiles again.

Fuck, this is killing me. If she keeps this up, everything'll go up in flames. My respect, my guilt and my fear that someone will rip me to shreds.

We sit on the bed, careful not to touch, but that's fine. It's understandable. It's probably too intimate a situation for both of us. It's going too quickly.

"Would you like some wine?"

"Water's fine, I've got to drive."

"Oh yeah, of course. I'll get you a bottle, I didn't think of that."

"I'll get it," I say, standing up and going to the kitchen. I act like it's my place, as if I were a regular presence here, when actually I've only been here once before.

But I still feel at *home*. She's the only place I feel at home.

I take a deep breath and take a few sips of water to calm the tension. When I go back, I find her with a piece of pizza in her mouth and my heart starts hammering again.

"What?" she says with her mouth full.

Jesus, Riley.

If only I'd danced with you that damn night.

If only I hadn't let you go.

If only I weren't terrified out of my mind.

If only someone hadn't taken everything from me.

I would've given you every part of me; unconditionally.

17
Riley

Ray gave me a ride home in his car. We finished late tonight and no one felt like walking home. We had a show at eight that I was working on, and after closing and everything, when I got out of his car it was already eleven.

I threw myself onto the bed, my hands over my face, attempting to keep away the thoughts that have engulfed my mind since I saw him at the hospital that day.

I tried to keep some distance between us, to be indifferent and show him his charm had no effect on me. I even tried treating him badly.

Nothing worked.

I've learned to fake it through the years, to mask all of my emotions and to let people only see what they wanted to see in me – to give off what they were willing to accept or understand. But it's useless to do it with him. It's useless to pretend I don't tremble when he talks to me, or try not to blush when he looks at me, or lose my breath when he gets too close.

Ian O'Connor is everywhere. He invades your life and takes control of it. He's all over me, covering me like a second skin. It's as if he can feel all of my emotions. He's dangerous. He's something I should avoid if I want to stay on my feet because he hears everything, even if he says nothing.

Even if you try to hide yourself, he finds you; and I'm not sure I want him to.

But when I heard his voice on the phone, something in me flickered. All the memories, the wounds, the fear turned around. All I thought about were our nights curled up on the sofa, close, relaxed. Of our chats, and the laughing. Of all of those looks full of meaning. Of what I felt when I was in his arms. Of what I still feel, what I always do if I close my eyes and let my heart speak freely.

I let my feelings run free just for a second and something invaded me, something stronger than fear, stronger than the past, disappointment and refusal. Stronger even than the solitude I've carried around with me my entire life. It's something I've been forced to live with, something I've become used to. A gap that only he can fill. He feels it, exactly like I do.

Because loneliness isn't something you can see or touch, but you feel it. You feel it in your head, in your body and your veins. You feel it in your heart. It sleeps with you, eats with you, accompanies you to work.

It lives with you.

And you feed off of it. You give it space, let it take control of you. You simply let it be. You can't fight it.

And as much as you can surround yourself with people, you still feel it because it becomes a part of you. It almost becomes comforting, because you can count on it being there and in some way it's your only loyal companion.

And yet, with him, I don't feel it. For once in my life it's loneliness that is excluded, not me – and I think that's only possible with one person in this world. The only other person who shares your loneliness in his heart and is afraid to let it go.

That person has found his way back into my house, and into my life.

He asked me for a chance and I'm giving him one – well, my heart is. I'm giving him my trust.

I'm letting him into my little hideaway.

I'm giving him a part of myself.

A year ago, Ian O'Connor broke my heart. A year later, I'm ready to let him do it again.

Ian comes back from the kitchen with two bottles of water in his hands but as soon as I look at him, he stops still in the doorway.

"What?" I ask him with my mouth full.

I'm not able to spit out an entire phrase because the way the looks at me makes my stomach flutter, a sensation I thought I'd left in the past.

His face opens into a big smile, showing off his perfect teeth. I realise he's got a chipped tooth and a busted lip that give him a sexy, mischievous look, that his body is filling in the doorway like it were a picture frame – and here I am staring at him, as my stomach does a double flip.

I feel my cheeks burning and a strange sensation

threatens my body, unable to respond to the alarm signals.

He smiles cheekily as he goes to sit down and I swallow my pizza. I shake my head a little, causing my glasses to slip down my nose. He lifts a hand and with one finger, pushes them back into place. I could faint from the emotion that overwhelms me.

He sighs and runs a hand through his hair before nailing me with his eyes again.

"Are you free on Sunday? At about three o'clock? There's a game and I've got tickets, you know, for friends, relatives... I thought that maybe... you know, if you felt like it..."

"Are you asking me to come to the stadium to watch a game?"

"Am I going too fast?"

"I don't know," I reply honestly. "Maybe."

"I just don't like wasting time," he says, raising the corner of his mouth in a grin. "I don't want to miss out on anything else. I know you don't care much about rugby, but I'd be happy if you came."

"Why is it so important to you?"

"One time you made a comment that maybe, for the right player, you might change your mind about rugby. I think I could be your player." He comes dangerously close to me. "I want to be your player."

"I can't believe you remember that stupid conversation."

"It was the first time you came to visit the training centre a few nights after that infamous party. I remember a lot of things, Riley." His voice drops a tone.

"That almost sounds like a challenge."

"It is. I'm very competitive."

"You might lose," I provoke him.

"I have no intention of losing," he says confidently. "I'm an O'Connor and the O'Connors never lose."

"There's a first time for everything."

"I'll risk it," his voice lowers again and I feel my legs trembling.

"So... S-Sunday."

"Aviva Stadium at three."

"I could drop by."

"Seriously?" he asks, suddenly excited.

"I'd like to."

He tries to mask a smile by touching his nose with his hand and I try to mask my embarrassment attempting to bury myself four feet under the ground.

"I hope Jamie won't be upset, he's been asking me to come for years, but he's never convinced me."

"I'm not Jamie," he says, so certain. "So, see you there?"

"You'll see me there, even if you'll never even notice me with all those adoring fans," I joke, but he doesn't smile.

His face becomes serious and his eyes darken slightly. He closes the distance between us and slowly his hand drops to mine, brushing it slightly, giving me goosebumps.

His fingers intertwine with mine, perfectly, even though his hand is double the size of mine. His is hot and strong and mine is cold and weak. His is covered in calluses and mine is smooth and delicate. His squeezes mine from need and mine is squeezed in necessity.

There is no more perfect union, and my heart starts to regain its faith.

"I would be aware of your presence, Riley. I would always feel it, anywhere, even if I don't see you. I'll know."

18
Riley

One year earlier

"What's wrong?" he asks me, out of the blue.

I'm on the sofa, distractedly watching the TV next to him but he's not interested.

"You're acting strange. Are you alright?"

"Uh-huh," I respond vaguely.

"You didn't eat tonight."

"I wasn't hungry."

"You haven't been eating much recently."

"You're not checking up on me, are you?"

I stand up, annoyed, and turn off the TV. I shouldn't have come to his house tonight, just like I shouldn't have done for the past five nights. The fact is, I need to be here. This is the only place where breathing doesn't seem so painful.

"I shouldn't have just showed up at your house like this. You must have your things to do, your... meetings," I say, feeling jealousy fill my lungs.

"What are you talking about?"

"I drop in at your house with no warning, I make myself at home, eat your food," I sputter, almost hysterically. "Maybe you'd like to go out with someone or... take her to bed, not hang out with your friend's sister." The words come out blunt and angry.

"What the hell are you on about? Did I ever give you the impression that I didn't want you here?"

"No, but—"

"What's the problem, then?"

I shake my head, slip on my shoes and grab my jacket.

"What are you doing?"

"It's late, I'm going."

"Have I said something wrong? You seem upset."

"I'm not."

"You are. I don't want you to leave like this."

"Everything's fine, I'm just tired."

"Then stay."

I snap my head up and look him in the eye.

"You said it yourself, it's late, it doesn't make sense for you to leave. I'll sleep on the sofa."

I feel my cheeks go red, my whole body too.

"Oh, go on, what's the big deal?" he says, playing it down.

"I don't know."

"Let's go," he reaches his hand out to me. "I can lend you one of my shirts."

I follow him, speechless, towards the bed. I stand there watching while he digs around in his drawer, pulling out a t-shirt for me. He hands it to me and I accept it, digging up a little smile.

"I'll give you some privacy," he says, heading

towards the bathroom.

I sit there motionless for a few seconds, confused and scared by the situation. I slip my shoes back off and slide out of my jeans. I pull off my jumper and throw it on the floor. I put his t-shirt on, which comes down to my knees. It's huge, just like him. I grab the collar and bring it to my nose.

I inhale. Sharply. I fill my lungs and my heart with his scent. I sigh like an idiot and then snap my head up as I sense his presence behind me.

Ian overshadows me completely with his body, pushing me with his shoulders against a wall. He looks down at me, my legs shaking.

It's not from fear. He could never frighten me.

"Something's not right here."

I try to avoid eye contact.

"Riley."

"I don't—"

"You're hiding something from me, and I'm aware of it, you know that?"

"That's not true." I stammer unconvincingly.

"Don't hide from me."

"I'm… not."

"I want to see you."

All of my muscles go rigid.

"You might not like it," I whisper, barely audible.

"You'll never know if you don't give it a try."

The problem is that I like what I see. His large,

defined shoulders. The muscles in his arms as his hand rests on the wall behind me. His smile, a little crooked, a little sexy and a little cheeky. His enigmatic blue eyes that hide a world that no one can see, but one which I dream about; it's a secret world, made of hope, desire and infinite security.

I like being here, in this apartment which at first glance could seem cold and bare, but which actually emits a warmth that wraps you up. I like the feeling that I get every time he touches me, running from my mouth to my stomach, when he talks to me a bit too intensely and lowers his voice.

I like all of it, dangerously so.

"Come on," he says, moving away. He holds out his hand for me. "Let's go to bed."

I let myself be pulled along towards his bed, I sit down and he gently pushes me to the mattress. I lay my head on the pillow and inhale his scent which feels like home to me now.

Then he stands up like he's about to leave me and I grab onto his hand and squeeze it tightly. He jerks his head round to look at me in search of an explanation I'm not able to provide. I don't know how to explain in words how I feel right now, what I need almost as much as I need air to breathe.

He looks at me for a few seconds before exhaling deeply and lets his hand drop.

Disappointment fills me immediately.

I feel small, cast aside into a corner.

I hear his steps walking away from me as I close my eyes and swallow my dignity, but then the mattress sinks and I can feel his heat next to me. I open my eyes, begging my heart to take it easy because I don't want him to realise it's going nuts. Then his arms are around me.

Ian is hugging me.

And what I feel is life. Real life. It's a life to be shared, out in the open without secret hiding places, without nightmares, without fear.

It's a life worth living.

His grip isn't forced, he's not doing it because I asked him to. He's doing it because he wants to.

His arms squeeze my hips and his lips brush against my hair and I feel his breath on my neck. He breaks my barriers making them crumble down dangerously.

My entire body trembles at this new emotion.

"You're shaking," he whispers, moving in closer; I feel all of my muscles relaxing, and it's strange because I'm in Ian's bed, my body is touching his and I've never felt so safe in my life.

We stay in bed, intertwined. Nothing else happens. There are no other words or explanations. There's only our breathing that fills the space and an intimacy which I've never felt before. I'm in Ian's arms and everything is out of place and so wrong, but in my eyes, it couldn't be more right.

"Riley," he whispers, making me shiver. "You can trust me."

I close my eyes and do as he says, sinking into the tenderness of his voice.

* * *

I wake up in a fog, feeling a strange weight on my chest and stomach. I lift my head and it takes me a few seconds to understand what's happening. Ian's head is on my chest and his hand is on my hips. Panic assails me.

I move just slightly and he pulls away from me and turns on his back. The apartment is dark but from the light creeping in from outside the curtains, I can see his hard profile, his tensed jaw and his lips pursed subtlety.

He doesn't seem relaxed or comfortable here with me and I don't know what the hell I had in mind. What was my head telling me when I asked him to get into bed with me?

I get up, moved by anger.

I can't do it. I can't let myself get caught up in him, his nearness, his warmth. I can't run here and hide in this space just to avoid being forced to face myself.

He can't bury everything with him or I won't be able to handle it, because something's coming. I can feel its hot breath on my collar, and as much as I try to keep it away, it'll be back to drag me down into the darkness.

It'll come and take everything away with it.

It'll take me too.

19
Ian

Present

I get off the bus, thrusting my gym bag over my shoulder, and head down towards the changing rooms with my headphones plugged in, trying in vain to calm my nerves with music. I go in and sit down on the bench, resting my elbows on my knees and let my head fall into my hands.

Someone shakes my arm. I lift my head just enough to see who it is and find the coach standing in front of me, his arms crossed. I remove my headphones and stand up, in respect.

"You're worked up. You're never like this before a game."

"I'm not."

He raises an eyebrow and cocks his head.

"Everything's fine, I'm ready."

"Not judging by your face. You look like you're facing your first Pro12, like you're ready to run to the toilet and heave your guts up."

"Well, that's not the case, I can assure you."

"I hope not, boy, because you're the captain now, and you'll be on the field from the first minute of the game. Don't make me regret my decision."

"You won't, Sir."

"I hope so. For your sake."

He looks at me for a few more seconds before turning to Scott and John who are pissing around, as usual.

I hear him raise his voice and get them back in line before I stick my earphones back in and let the music relax me, helping me to concentrate on heading outside with the others. I'm one of them, a *Lion*, ready to get on the field and wreak havoc – but my thoughts are elsewhere.

I've let someone come into my life and mess with my emotions, my moods and my thoughts. I'm playing a game, about to lay down my hand, aware of what I have to lose.

Everything.

I could lose her too.

For once in my life, I'm taking a risk.

I jump to my feet and take out my headphones, throwing them onto the bench.

"Hey, mate," Jamie walks up to me with his hands on his hips. "Anything wrong?"

"Absolutely not."

"Huh. Doesn't seem that way," he comments, nodding towards my phone on the bench.

"Just a shitty song, that's all."

"A song, huh?" I shrug and start getting undressed.

"If you have a problem or don't feel like your head's in the right place right now…"

"I'm great, Jamie." I say raising my voice a

tone.

"It's my job to make sure you are."

"Everything's fine," I add, softer.

"Okay," he says doubtfully and starts to walk away, but he speaks again. "I almost forgot... One of the security guys says he let someone in under your name."

I snap my around head to look at him.

"I see we're making progress," he comments with a look on his face that is just waiting to confirm what he's already assumed.

"What? No, it's not what you think."

"Uh-huh."

"We're friends."

"Puh-lease."

"Piss off."

He lifts his hands. "I'm not doing anything."

"Well, go and keep doing it somewhere else."

"Reserved seats, eh?" Scott says, butting into the conversation.

"You ever mind your own fucking business?"

"There are no secrets between us. Come on, spit it out," John adds, joining in too.

"Shouldn't we be concentrating right now?"

"Nah. Actually, a minute of distraction is just what you need to calm those nerves," Jamie intervenes.

I huff and start to put on my kit.

"So?" Scott urges.

"You don't really think I'm going to talk about it with you all?"

"Why not?"

"Because you're all arseholes, that's why. With big mouths and no brains."

"All this fuss over a woman? Come on, like we couldn't relate?"

I shoot Scott a hard stare.

"Oh, Jesus, good thing she's just a 'friend'," he says, winding me up and elbowing Jamie who smiles, in on the joke.

"I'll kick your arse, Scott."

"Try it. I'll have you on the ground in twenty seconds."

"Sure about that?" I move in closer to him, threatening.

"That's enough now!" Jamie returns to his usual role as captain. "Both of you. And Ian, calm down, okay? They were just kidding."

I nod, taking a step backwards.

"Now, move your arse, Scott. Warm-up is starting in a few minutes."

Scott walks away without another word as I sit on the bench to tie my shoes.

"I haven't finished with you," Jamie says, pointing his finger at me. "I want to know everything, got it?"

"Shouldn't you be at home resting, or off on the bench watching the game?"

"I can't leave you all alone. You'll fuck it all

up."

"You're really hating not being captain right now, aren't you?"

"I can afford the break," he bounces back with a smile. "You – not so much. Anyway, no use trying to change the subject."

"We weren't talking about anything else."

"There's always something more important."

"Please don't start with one of your lectures now, alright? All I did was invite her to the stadium, seeing as you weren't about to do it."

"You've never invited any women to your games."

"What's the point?"

"I know how you think, O'Connor."

"You think you know everything, don't you?"

"Obviously. You can bet your arse I know more about sports than you do, more about women and men too."

I laugh, shaking my head. Incredible.

"Are we going to make a move this time?"

"It's not what you think."

"Mmm hmm."

"I told you, we're just friends."

"I have friends too, Ian, but they don't have this effect on me."

I scoff. "She's just—"

"Riley," he concludes, resting a hand on my shoulder. "Try not to fuck it up this time, okay?"

"Fuck off, Jamie."

"I will, don't worry. For now, let's just give them a show out there," he says, one last quip before heading out the door.

"Two minutes, boys!" The assistant coach calls us out. I stand up and take a big breath before going out there and doing the only thing I know how to.

Win.

20
Riley

Three years earlier

After searching for Leslie for more than a half an hour, I give up and decide to go home. I never should have come to this stupid party, but Jamie wouldn't let me wriggle out of it. It's an important night for him: he was just nominated captain of the team and he really wanted me to be here. I think it's the first time I've ever set foot in the blue room. I was so nervous that I asked my friend from work to come along, and she jumped at the chance. She loves rugby; well, she loves the players, my brother in particular, and the thought of meeting some brought about an uncontainable reaction in her. I'm sure she's already off in a corner somewhere trying to bag herself one.

I leave the building, hugging my coat across my chest, and dig around in my bag for my purse.

Mission Impossibile.

The bloody clasp won't open.

I can't stand Leslie's bags. They're too small, too blingy and too technological.

I huff, leaning my back against the wall, planning to slide down it and take a quick nap on the pavement until I sober up, or Leslie comes back and teaches me how to open this damn bag, when a warm voice speaks in my ear.

"Hey, I was looking for you."

Shit.

"You're leaving already?"

"Yes, exactly: it's late and I have work tomorrow." I try to get him away from me.

"I can give you a lift if you like, my car's parked over there."

He brushes my face with his hand, and I feel like I might throw up.

I try to push him away and get back to my senses a bit, to politely tell him to piss off, but it's even more difficult than opening this damn bag.

"I was just about to call a cab, actually," I say flatly, going back to digging through my bag.

"The night doesn't have to end here," he insists.

Jesus Christ, what idiots these sports freaks are.

"No, thank you. Really, I have to get home."

Who let me drink so much?

"Something wrong?"

A voice from behind us makes us both jump a little.

"Hey Ian. I was just leaving with…"

"Riley!"

What an idiot.

"Of course, Riley, I was just about to drive her home."

"That's not true." I feel the need to justify myself.

Ian crosses his arms over his chest and looks at me sternly.

"She's actually coming with me," he says decisively.

Seriously? I must've missed something.

"I was just looking for her actually," he says, moving in closer towards us.

"I didn't know you two were together," he tries one more time; I feel like I'm caught in a testosterone-fuelled tug-of-war.

Athletes. Muscles beat the brains ten to one.

"Now you know."

He raises his hands and shoots me a look I can't discern and then makes off towards the car park.

"Everything okay?"

"I could have held him off by myself."

"Sure."

Even drunk I pick up on the ridicule in his voice.

"But you know, I owe you, so…"

I smile, instinctively.

"Come on, I'll take you home."

"Oh, no," I suddenly wake up a little. "No one's taking me anywhere tonight."

"You're drunk."

"Not too drunk to understand that you're trying to…"

"I'm not trying anything, Riley."

Did my name always sound this beautiful?

"I just want to make sure you get home. Alright? Give me the address and I'll call a cab for you."

He looks at me as he waits for an answer, his phone in his hand.

"Well?"

Address. Yep, got it. That shouldn't be too hard.

"You don't remember?" he presses.

"I'm trying to. Just give me a second."

"Take two," he says, teasing me again.

Okay, they're all arseholes.

I step away from the wall and take a few paces along the pavement, tapping my finger against my temple.

Think, Riley, think. This is not difficult.

I turn my head towards him, starting to see stars; maybe I'm moving too quickly, because the next thing I feel after I close my eyes is two strong arms grabbing me, stopping my fall.

I hear his voice, I feel someone lightly slapping my face. I feel his heat but I'm too tired and I can't open my eyes to tell him I don't need his help.

I don't need anybody's help.

I can do it, I just need to rest for a bit. I need a two-minute time-out.

Then I'll tell him to piss off.

21
Ian

Three years earlier

"Oh, my God!"

My coffee almost spills right over my hand.

"I can't believe it!"

I hear her slide out of bed and move around the apartment.

"You!"

I turn to see her pointing her finger at me.

"You're a… you're…"

I sit on a stool, looking at her in amusement.

"How could you?!"

I let her vent. I understood right away that all the bolts are tight on this one.

"Jesus Christ! How did I end up in your bed?"

She storms towards me, clutching the sheet to her chest.

"It's useless."

"What is?" she yells.

"You covering yourself with that sheet. You're fully dressed under there."

She stops in front of me and peeks under the sheet.

"Oh," she says in amazement, but still without letting it drop.

"Would you like some coffee?"

"Do you think that would be appropriate?" she paces around the counter and sits down opposite me. "One sugar and some milk please."

I pour her a cup and hand it to her. She takes it and gulps it down.

"Thank God."

"Er, my name is Ian."

She looks at me sideways.

"And we…"

"If we'd had sex, I assure you that you'd remember it."

Her eyes widen to better catch my expression.

"You're right. We didn't do it. If we had, you wouldn't be so bitter."

"Bitter? Me?" I say, pointing to myself.

"Uh-huh," she grunts, nodding and taking another sip of her coffee. "You'd be all happy, dancing around the house singing."

I throw my head back in laughter.

"How did I end up here?"

"You couldn't remember your address."

"That's true," she says putting her hand to her head. "That open bar was a terrible idea."

"That's usually how it works."

"And you? What were you doing there?"

Is she serious?

"I could ask you the same thing."

"My brother," she shrugs. "He convinced me to

come."

"Your brother?"

"Jamie Murray?" she says uncertainly.

She takes another sip of her drink and my throat constricts.

Fuck.

"Jamie Murray is your brother?"

I just brought my new captain's sister home.

Perfect. They'll kick me off the team for an entire season. Or he'll break my leg at the first chance he gets.

"Yeah," she responds distractedly. "I don't even follow rugby. Jamie's always trying to get me to go to the games but I can't stand the idea that he gets hurt. I know it's just sport but I prefer not to watch. I haven't seen a game since he was a kid playing in the second division, but please don't tell him that. He's convinced I watch them all." She says, shaking her head. "I hate the sport. All of it, honestly."

"You can't mean that…"

"And the players! So perfect, so arrogant, so dumb…" she says without considering her present company, and then looks up and bites her lip.

A few of my heart beats drop to the floor.

Shit.

"Don't tell me," she closes her eyes and her face goes bright red.

I shrug, trying to hide a smile.

"You're probably famous, too."

"Not really."

"I'm sorry."

"It doesn't matter."

"Really, I—"

"I don't like those parties either. Too many people, too many 'heroes', too many hormonal women."

She smiles too.

Fuck.

She looks around to study the apartment and my mood changes on the spot. I should have guessed. Now she's going to ask the usual question: why do I live in a place like this? She'll dig into my life and try to keep a foot in the door. I knew I shouldn't have brought her here.

"This place is amazing."

"Mmm," I comment, already annoyed.

"It was a garage, wasn't it?"

"Still is," I say flatly.

"I like it," she takes another sip of her drink and I choke on mine. "It's unique," she looks at me with nothing but sincerity in her eyes. "You did well to leave the door like it was. Leaving it like it was originally is a bit like keeping hold of your roots."

Breathe, Ian, breathe, for crying out loud!

"Oh my God!" She jumps to her feet. "What time is it?"

I look at my watch. "Seven thirty."

"I have to go, I'm late." She starts moving

frantically around the apartment.

I get up too.

"I have to call a cab."

I grab my phone from the counter and hand it to her.

"Thanks," she says, but before ringing the taxi company, she looks up at me. "Where are we?" she asks putting a hand over the microphone.

At my house.

A woman is in my house.

And my heart is completely fucked.

22
Riley

Present

Arriving at the gate, I give my name as a guest just like Ian instructed me to. The security guard checks his tablet, calls someone on his walkie talkie and after a few minutes, another man in uniform joins us.

"Ms. Murray?" he asks me.

I nod.

"Please follow me."

I do as instructed, and I can hear Ray snickering behind me. "We're VIPs," he says mockingly, earning himself an elbow to the ribs.

The man leads us to an area, indicating our seats with his hand. We take our places and thank him as Ray starts looking around, just waiting to find someone up to his standards.

"Your life is more interesting than I imagined."

"I'm starting to regret asking you to come with me."

"You invited me because you knew you'd have fun with me – and you know my weakness."

I laugh, shaking my head.

"I'm going to get something to drink. Be back soon."

Ray walks off and I try to relax in my

uncomfortable seat, looking across the field at the perfectly cut grass, ready to welcome a bunch of huge guys who are all arms and legs and who don't know how to do anything except constantly show off their muscles.

I've never been a big fan of rugby, even though Jamie's been playing his whole life. I've always supported him from a distance. It never felt like my world or my place, and I didn't want to interfere with his life.

I love my brother and I love what he does, I'm proud of him, but seeing him on the field being beaten up in public doesn't help me. It reminds me of ugly things I'd rather to forget and it just brings me down.

I understand that it's different for him. In his eyes, it's a chance to show himself that he's strong now, almost invincible and that no one scares him anymore. I admire him for that, but I don't want to be a part of it.

Ray comes back with two beers just as the two teams are making their way onto the field. He gets to his feet, all worked up and I stay right where I am, in calm silence, listening to the crazy beat of my heart. It seems to be drumming out an unknown rhythm, making me shiver.

"Which number?" Ray shouts into my ear.

I scrutinise the teams while they prepare for kick-off, scanning every face, when I see him standing tall and proud in his blue kit. I think my heart could just fall all the way down the stairs and plop out onto the field.

Good Lord.

Ian is breathtaking. He's tall and muscular like the rest of them, but there's a pride in his eyes, in the way he stands and a concentration on his face that makes him dangerous and damn sexy.

I take a few sips of beer and Ray urges, "Well?"

"Number 11," I mutter without pulling myself away from the glass.

"Holy shit!" Ray exclaims, coming to his feet again. "That's your friend? Ian O'Connor?" He raises his voice to the point of embarrassing me. "The one from the club? How did I not recognise him? Well, all dressed as he is..."

I try to disappear into my chair.

"Oh, Riley, you hide too much from me. We need a little chat."

Ray sits down with his eyes still wide.

"You realise, of course, that he's one of the sexiest rugby players on the face of the Earth? Next to your brother, obviously."

Are you serious?

"God, Riley. Please, tell me you're sleeping together. I need to know what he's like below the belt!"

"Ray!" I cut him off before he can keep going.

"Okay, I get it, it's private."

"It's nonexistent. He and I are friends, more or less."

"Well, at least tell me if you're friends with

benefits."

I look at him sideways.

He puts a hand on his forehead and crosses his legs blatantly. "You're a lost cause, Riley."

The game begins and luckily Ray leaves me alone, too busy watching the most minute details out on the field; every tackle, every time someone gets pantsed.

I have to be honest, I'm not following the game at all. The only thing I'm able to keep my eye on is number 11. When he moves, when he stops, when he dries his sweat with his shirt, when he spits, when he breathes. His tensed muscles, the mud on his thighs, his messed-up hair, covered in sweat. His body, tense and ready to pounce on the ball at his first opportunity.

I can't believe what I'm looking at, what is going through my mind and what I feel. Through my entire body.

Fire, adrenaline... desire.

Thank God, the first half ends and I am able to go back to breathing normally. I don't think I've exhaled for the last 45 minutes and I don't know if it's possible to survive being underwater for this long.

"Wow," Ray interrupts my train of thought. "Honey, tell me the reason you're not sleeping with him is because he's gay. Give me at least this little dash of hope."

"I don't think he's gay," I tell him apologetically.

Not in the farthest regions of my mind.

The players slowly make their way off the field, giving each other slaps on the back or the arse. Ian goes into the changing rooms, his back to me, and I can't help feeling disappointed that he didn't look this way even once.

After half time in which Ray and I go down to the concession stands to grab another beer, the players come back onto the field.

I sit back down and take a few more sips of my beer as my eyes watch the players going this way and that on the field, throwing themselves down, showing off, scoring and cheering, and internally, the image makes me smile – even though being here makes me nervous, I can't deny how it makes me feel.

About fifteen minutes into the second half, Ian charges down the right-hand side of the field with the ball under his arm, running towards the goal. He doesn't notice the pair of giants about two metres behind him, ready to tackle.

I stand up, spilling my beer all over Ray the moment they grab him and throw him to the ground. I hold back a scream, putting my hands in front of my mouth as more players pile up on top of him, maybe all of the other players, I don't know. I can't distinguish anything anymore, it's all a mass of solid color.

Ray stands up too and wraps me under his arm and squeezes me tenderly to give me courage. After a few minutes of pandemonium, the players start to peel off one by one, but Ian is still laid out on the ground.

My heart is lodged in my throat and my anxiety tries to choke me. I feel like my legs can't hold me up.

Ian isn't moving.

His teammates all gather around him. The paramedics come out too, kneeling down next to him. Then, slowly, he starts to get up and I let out a sigh so heavy that Ray pulls me in even closer.

Ian looks around, dazed. The minute I see him scanning the crowd, I understand what it is he's looking for. And when his eyes meet mine, I realise I won't be able to let him go.

Because he's inside of me. He always has been.

He's *my* player.

"Just a friend, huh?" Ray says in my ear, but I ignore him.

I can't give him an explanation when I don't even know what to tell my own heart, which has reassembled itself as if by magic.

The pieces fit together perfectly with no help. Of course, there are fault lines, and it may never go back to how it used to be, but it's whole.

And it's beating again, for him.

I pace, torn between the urge to run away from what scares me and sprinting down to the field and throwing myself in his arms.

"I know it's hard, honey," Ray says sweetly, dragging me away from my thoughts. "It's difficult to trust someone, to trust what you're feeling and to let yourself go. It's hard to understand and even harder to accept. It's damn hard letting yourself fall into the emptiness. And you can say what you want, tell me the same lies you tell yourself, but Riley, your heart isn't capable of lying. Your heart's wearing a number 11 jersey, and it's already rooting for him."

23
Ian

I get up slowly, assisted by the paramedics who are asking me if everything's alright. I nod repeatedly and try to take some nice deep breaths to store away as much air as possible and calm my stupid heart.

It's not about the hit, or the fact that I blacked out, it's not about the fear or the game. It's none of that.

"Christ, Ian, you really scared me," John says, taking me by the arm. "Are you alright? Do you need to get off the field?"

I shake my head trying not to make the stabbing pain worse.

"You took a nasty hit, mate. And you're bleeding," he says pointing to my forehead. "You have to go off. We need the points," he says, nodding to the bench.

"No." I stop him. "I can't."

"You have to."

I shake off his grip and look around, confused. Jamie storms onto the field, coming towards us.

"Jesus, Ian!" he yells as the others catch up with him. "Get off this field right now, do you hear me? That's an order! Or I'll have you off the team until January!"

"You can do whatever you want… later." I

walk away and look at the crowd, who are all on their feet watching the scene unfold on the field. I scan the bleachers, the reserved seating with that annoying pang in my stomach that takes possession of my body.

Where are you...?

I know she's out there somewhere. I felt her eyes on me the whole first half and I felt her desperation when I got tackled. I felt her fear.

I felt her. Coursing through me.

I look once more, desperately, through the crowd when I finally spot her, standing there with her hands in front of her mouth. It's a force as strong as a hurricane that pulls me in, dragging me towards the unknown.

Because I'm aware of the damage I'm causing her and what she'll do to me. But I can't help it.

I want this fucking disaster.

I want her to ruin my life. I want those damn eyes on me, I want that stunning smile aimed at me, and I want to see her tears the first time she lets in her pain. I want to be the one to dry those tears and hold her, to comfort her when it doesn't seem possible to start over.

I want her to be my torment, my punishment and my salvation.

I want her to be the one to turn my world upside-down before helping me put everything back in place.

I want her to be there for every game, watching

me and suffering with me and cheering me on. For her to be the one waiting for me at home when I get back.

I want her to be me and I to be her.

I have always and only wanted her.

Riley is upset, speaking to someone standing next to her. Then she shakes her head and it looks like she's ready to make a run for it.

Even though I know that the emergency exits are closed by this point, she isn't ready to let go, to let me into her life again and allow me to take care of her like no one in her life ever has.

Riley isn't ready and no matter what I say or do, I won't be able to convince her to trust me.

Riley isn't ready to be my cheerleader.

I'm not her player.

I've lost.

This time, I really have lost it all.

As I allow the guys to accompany me off the field, as the paramedics escort me to the changing room, as they sit me down and dress my wounds, I realise that I've got one wound that no one can heal; because the only one who could help me is the same person who injured me.

There are certain hits we don't recover from – not by resting, not with time, not with medicine. Not even with a miracle. They're the ones that mark your soul and prevent you from ever going back to what you were before.

* * *

I get dressed slowly, still in a daze from the pain. They dressed my external wounds, but the internal wounds bleed through my chest.

The guys come to see me one by one to ask how I'm doing and I limit myself to simple nods of the head, because if I even tried to say one word, I'd probably start bawling like a baby. A baby who's abandoned by his mother, hidden near the bleachers of a rugby field.

I look at my phone again. I close my eyes and take a deep breath before deciding to put it away, along with this insane desire to have something that's just mine.

I zip up my bag and sling it over my shoulder, heading towards the changing room exit, when I see a figure I'd really rather not see right now standing there leaning against the frame.

"Everything alright?" Nick asks.

"What are you doing here?"

"I came to watch the game. How do you feel?"

"They just threw me to the ground and stomped on me like a herd of mad bulls."

"Nothing we're not used to."

I smile bitterly.

"Can I drive you home?"

"The bus is waiting for me."

"I don't think the coach will mind if you leave with me."

I shrug.

"Come on," he says taking my bag and hauling it over his shoulder. "Let me be the big brother."

Getting back home, I throw myself on the sofa.

"Want a beer?" Nick offers, opening the fridge.

I nod, covering my eyes with my arm.

I hear him moving around, and after a few seconds he joins me. He passes me the beer and I accept it, sitting up with a little difficulty.

"We're only going to get older," he says, taking a jab at me.

"I just had a bad day."

"At least you guys won."

"Did you ever think we wouldn't?"

"It's exciting watching your games," a trace of bitterness in his voice. "I've always envied the team spirit you have here."

"Well, we *are* a team, on and off the field."

He takes a few more pulls on his beer. "You're the best, bro, the best in the family."

"Don't start up with me."

"I'm being serious. Sometimes I think if I'd worked harder instead of being an idiot…"

"It's not too late to turn it around."

"I don't play anymore, Ian. I haven't set foot on the field for six months."

"I know that."

"It's too late to play that card. At least in the

world of sports."

"You could do something else, I don't know, be a trainer, a coach."

He busts out laughing.

"I'm not even qualified to do that. Can you see me giving orders to others? Make them respect the rules, the training…Me? I don't listen to anyone else."

"That's true."

We lose ourselves in the silence for a few minutes.

"I was thinking maybe I could stay," he says in all seriousness. "Not, like, forever, but you know… give it a go."

"Sounds like a good idea."

"I don't think Ryan would agree."

"Ryan's upset. But he's a good guy. Sooner or later it'll pass. Of course, if you made a little more effort to help things along…"

"I'm trying, alright? It's not easy."

"He will forgive you."

"I hope so. But what about you?"

"What about me what?"

"What are you doing, Ian?"

"What the hell are you talking about?"

"I saw her there."

I glance at him.

"I thought you'd ended that, bro. And yet there she was today, sitting in the reserved seating. Is there something I should know?"

I swallow hard.

"Are you back in there?"

I lie down, covering my eyes with my arm.

"I was never out of it, Nick. I never will be."

24
Riley

I fiddle with my fork, pushing my Caesar salad around the plate, setting off another frustrated sigh from Kate.

"So, you're not going to talk to me, then?"

"I have nothing to say," I tell her, setting the plate and fork down on the table.

"You didn't eat your lunch," she points out and I start to regret agreeing to have something with her before going home.

"I'm worried about you, Riley."

"No need, everything's alright."

"Ray says that you were upset after the game."

"Ray should mind his own business."

"If there's something wrong, you can talk to me about it. We're friends, you know."

I give her a strained smile.

"Sometimes I don't feel like I know you at all. You're so reserved. I don't know anything about your life before you joined the theatre."

"There's nothing to talk about, Kate. My life is very boring, believe me."

"So this guy who plays for Leinster just came out of nowhere?"

Kate's phone goes off on the table, giving me a moment of peace.

"We're not done here," she threatens me before picking up.

I shouldn't have asked Ray to come with me.

Watching the game upset me. What I felt while I was there upset me. He upsets me and that can only be a bad thing.

What I feel when I'm next to him, when I think about him, when the memory of what we shared together comes back to hurt me... it's all too much, dangerous.

Wrong.

Outside of my grasp.

I look out the window of Madigan's on O'Connell Street, sighing sadly when I see right in that moment a pair of familiar-looking shoulders pass me by on the street outside.

I jump to my feet.

"Everything okay, Riley?" Kate asks, placing a hand over her phone.

I continue to watch the man walk away, getting lost in the crowd; he has his arm around a woman. He holds her closely, almost protecting her as if to say, 'she's mine, don't touch' and I'm lucky my heart doesn't flop out of my ribcage and splatter all over the lurid, sticky floor.

"Hey, what's going on?"

I sit back down and look at her, disorientated.

"Nothing, I thought it was..." I shake my head and try to sit still but I can't avoid acknowledging what's going through my mind right now. That I was this close from running up behind him and slapping him across the face.

It's unreasonable, it makes no sense: I know that. I shouldn't care who he goes out with or what he does. It shouldn't matter to me if he has a girlfriend and didn't tell me, that he deliberately tried to keep me in the dark about it when I showed up at his house. A house he probably shares with her! Or if he came to my house, if we ate together, he touched me and now he's touching someone else. Or if he beat that guy up just because he was dancing with me, as if he cared that I was next to some other man.

It shouldn't matter to me.

His life isn't my business.

He isn't mine.

But I can feel it. This terrible disappointment. This tingling in my eyes. This unbearable pain in my heart that pushes down hard, making it difficult for me to breathe.

I feel it all.

Again.

And it's all his fault.

I should have known he was a bastard, just like he told me he was. I keep telling myself this: and yet, I get up, grab my purse and run outside. I look in the street searching for the man who just walked past me and, God, there he is. I could spot him even five hundred metres away.

"Riley," Kate joins me outside. "What is going on here?"

I stop myself just in time to see her worried eyes.

"I'm sorry, it's just that I saw something, someone... and I need to sort something out."

"You're scaring me."

She's right. I'm scaring myself too. I'm afraid of my own thoughts and of what I'm about to do.

"I'll call you later, okay? I have to go now."

I kiss her cheek and start walking quickly through the crowds, unaware of the hard shoulders I'm getting as I make my way through. I'm in a trance, lost in my own madness, needing to know who that woman is, what he's doing there with her and why he's hugging her.

Why he's hugging her and not me.

I reach them in front of the bus stop. He kisses her lips before she steps onto the bus.

And then he turns. He passes me without seeing me and I stand there, frozen in the middle of the street, gasping for breath, with the terrible sensation that I'm going completely mad.

I watch his back disappear into the crowd and I feel as if I'm going to drop to the pavement in desperation.

I feel numb, crumpled, as if I've just taken a few kicks to the stomach. I'm angry, disappointed and hurt. I just chased a perfect stranger down the road, ready to cause a big scene, yell at him and give him a piece of my mind.

I can't believe it.

I was so close to doing it. Getting hysterical. Screaming. I can't hide what I'm feeling. I can't hide behind my silence. I can't find comfort in my solitude.

I was about to lose control.

I didn't lose it when Jamie would cry, holding onto me every night. When I protected him against everyone who wanted to hurt him. Not when they pulled him from my arms.

But I was ready to do it. For him.

And all because he's in my head, my body and my damn heart.

Ian is everywhere.

Ian makes me feel everything.

It's unbearable now.

I hate this labyrinth of emotion and sentimentality. I hate remembering, I hate feeling, I hate hoping and I hate what I'm feeling right now.

I hate what I want.

Him.

25
Ian

A dull thud on the door wakes me from an uneasy sleep. I sit up in the middle of my bed trying to figure out what it is, but nothing else happens. I lie back down, sleepily thinking I must have been having a nightmare, when another knock makes me jump out of bed.

I grab my jeans off the floor and slip them on quickly, going to the door. I place my hands against the cold metal and put my ear against it.

"Ian...?"

It's barely more than a whisper, but it's a call I can't avoid.

I crouch down and open the door completely.

Riley is in front of me under the pouring rain. She's shaking, her teeth are chattering from the cold and she's wrapped her arms around her chest. I don't think twice. I grab her by the shoulders and pull her to me.

I don't know why she's here. My good sense should tell me to put her in a taxi and send her home, to stop going out and looking for her. But this fucking heart never listens to anything I say.

It's always been in the palm of her hand.

She lifts her head and I lower my gaze to look at her and what I see in her eyes is something I can't stand, something I want to kiss away right this minute.

Her hands slide down my face, slowly and quivering. My legs feel like they could give way under her touch, so wanted, so longed-for.

She brushes the wound on my forehead then drops her fingertips down to my busted lip, and I almost faint at her feet. She brings her head in close to my face and when I understand what she's going to do, I grab her arm and push her away from me hard.

Her expression changes. She wrinkles her forehead in confusion then I see rage fill her eyes as she shakes free from my grip. She turns to leave but I grab her again by the wrist and spin her around to face me.

There is resentment in her eyes, discomfort and that damn loneliness that swallows me up and makes me want things I shouldn't. That has stirred up something in me ever since the night I first denied her a stupid dance.

"Why are you here?" I yell at her, angrily.

She left. She left the stadium as fast as she could and didn't look back. She showed that I'm not her player and I never will be.

She abandoned me.

"I'm stupid!" she says, freeing herself again from my grip. I grab her again with both of my hands and trap her arms. She protests, fighting and yelling and I let her get it out. Then, she looks up at me and I'm engulfed by a wave of my own desire, pulling me under cutting off my oxygen.

A desire that has worn me down to my bones and that I could die from right now.

I let her arms go and grab her face.

And then it happens.

My mouth crushes down hard on hers. Assertive, possessive.

It's a violent kiss, full of anger and blind madness.

A repressed desire full of pain.

I put my hands in her hair and pull her in forcefully, bending her into my desperation.

I slip my tongue into her mouth and invade it greedily.

I don't let her breathe.

I don't breathe either.

Her hands snake up to my hair and a shiver of arousal runs through me, devouring me completely and enticing me to press myself up to her wet body.

We're fighting.

A fight with lips, teeth and tongues.

A fight between two broken souls.

A fight I'm destined to lose.

Before I completely lose control, I back away quickly, pushing her away from me. Her lost expression breaks my heart but I can't do this. I can't have her this way.

Not if she won't be completely mine.

I close my eyes and turn from her, into the kitchen.

Please leave now, Riley.

The sound of the door closing makes me snap around. Riley approaches me in silence.

"I need this," she tells me. And then she takes my hands and places them on her hips. I squeeze her tightly. "I need it right now," she says, edging dangerously close to my body.

"You don't really want it," I say, a last-ditch attempt before I jump into a bottomless pit.

She caresses my face and speaks directly into my lips.

"I just want to forget everything, please."

And right now, all I want is to forget too.

26
Riley

I want him to take away my madness, give me back my rationality. I want him to make me forget, to block out my memories, to take everything I have left and clear out my soul.

I want him to take what can't be anything but his.

My last words seem to move him. His eyes go darker. They dig, they empty and then fill back up again.

Ian grabs my hips and lifts me up, sitting me on the kitchen counter. Then he stops, lowering his hands next to my body and hanging his head.

He's defeated. He's fighting himself just like I have been all night, before breaking down and coming here. But after believing that he could want another woman, after imagining his hands all over someone else, I really thought I was going to lose my mind.

He slowly lifts his head and when he looks at me that weight that I had on my chest lightens, allowing me to breathe again. He comes towards my face and sighs onto my lips.

I sigh too, in anticipation and pure excitement; because I want him.

He takes my bottom lip between his teeth and I let out a suffering moan that ignites his uncontrollable desire. He grabs my arse cheeks and slides me forward, to the edge of the counter, pushing his body against mine. I wrap my legs around him and squeeze, half afraid he might change his mind and try to run away from this inevitable disaster.

He and I are a mistake.

Unforgivable and destructive.

But I want to be destroyed. And I want him to be the one to do it.

"Riley..." he growls into my mouth. "God... Riley."

He rubs his face against my neck. The heat of his tongue runs over my skin, and then his teeth bite down.

Leaving their mark.

Ian is marking his territory.

I let my head fall backwards and allow him to mark me, write his name on my skin, and I feel an excitement I've never felt before flame up between my legs.

I have never felt this wanted in my life.

He climbs up my neck to my earlobe.

He bites me again.

He licks me. Hurts me.

Then cures me.

He's my destroyer and my saviour.

I turn my head slightly to welcome his lips, which capture me in a possessive and hungry kiss; I give in without hesitation.

He pulls away suddenly, and as I gasp for air, he grabs my shirt and pulls it over my head, throwing it to the floor.

He looks at me a few seconds as I watch his chest heave up and down, then he submerges his head between my breasts and squeezes them hard with his big hands.

He bites me again, this time harder.

I feel his teeth scratching me even through the fabric. My hands are in his hair, imploring him to do it again, wanting him to keep wanting me.

He grabs me by the arse again and lifts me up, keeping me pressed tightly up against him as he slides his tongue into my mouth. He carries me over to the bed and lies me down. He takes off his underwear and stands before me, completely naked.

The sight of his hard body thrills something between my legs, encouraging me to open them for him. I'm shameless, and I want to feel him inside me right now.

He lowers himself onto me and I lean into him, waiting for him to invade me with his tongue, but he pulls back and gets on his knees in front of me.

I'm afraid he's going to back away, but I won't let him.

I sit up too, and bring my hands behind my back to undo my bra. Then I let the straps fall down my arms before throwing it to the floor.

His eyes flash with desire.

"Is this really what you want?" he says panting.

I nod.

"No, Riley. I need to hear it."

"Yes. It's what I want.

You are what I want.

He throws himself on top of me, pushing me backwards, and starts kissing me again, devouring me with his lips and pinning me down with his body. His hands slide down my face and run over my skin. His mouth follows, and when he touches one of my breasts, I arch my back instinctively, offering myself to him. He takes a nipple between his teeth and stops to look me in the eyes, stopping my breath.

And then he bites me. Hard.

I yell from the pain and the pleasure as he continues to torment me with his tongue and his teeth. He fills his other hand with my other breast, taking the nipple in his fingers.

He pinches, pulls it.

He looks at me again.

He keeps me tied to him. He holds me hostage with his eyes and his body. He's telling me he can do what he wants with me. And I'm here to let him have his way.

He leaves my chest and brings both his hands to the waistband of my jeans and with one rip, pulls both the jeans and my underwear off, tossing them to the floor.

I am completely naked, splayed out on his bed.

His eyes devour every inch of my body. He

caresses my leg, lingering his way up to my inner thigh. Just brushing against me up there almost makes me shout out. He plays with his thumb on my clit, and slides a finger inside of me.

I ball up the sheets tightly in my hands and let myself go to him.

There is nothing left in my mind.

The only thing I can think of is the heat of his hand, his finger calling to me and his body that is demanding it.

"Riley... I have to have you, now," he says between his teeth before taking my hips and pushing into me powerfully and deeply.

And as he fills me with his body, I feel completely emptied of myself.

27
Ian

When I feel how wet she is with my finger, see her give herself to me, I completely lose control. I grab her and pull her into me, then fill into her with one swift thrust.

Riley goes rigid underneath me, closing her eyes and pursing her lips and I instantly regret what I have done.

"Riley…"

She opens them slowly and looks at me in embarrassment.

"I—"

"Please…" she implores me. "I'm already broken, Ian. Finish me off and take everything with you."

I close my eyes to control the pain, because right now all I want is for someone to take me away too.

I lean myself over her, balancing my elbows on the mattress.

And I push.

Her warmth raptures me, wraps itself around me and then destroys me.

I rest my head between her shoulder and her neck and bite her again as I push as deeply as I can. I feel her opening herself up completely to me.

I weigh down on her with my body, crushing her under my weight. I run a hand on her hip and caress one of her legs. Then I go back and push on her thigh, raising it up so I can thrust into her deeper.

She must be mine.

Only mine.

I push. Again – but this time, harder.

Riley digs her nails into my back and lets herself go beneath me, ready to accept me and let me take everything.

So that's what I'm doing, I'm taking all of her torment away from her body and putting it into mine.

That's what she asked me to do.

It's all she wants from me.

I pull myself up, grab her hips and plummet inside of her.

One, two, ten times.

I have to. I have to have her like this or I won't be able to watch her leave me. I have to give her what she needs then let her do it.

Hate me.

Not come back for me.

Let her kill me, finish me up and toss me aside.

I have to take it all without giving her anything back.

The time has come for her to know that I can only be an arsehole, a man she doesn't deserve: the wrong man.

And I'm here to make her understand that.

Riley grips the sheets tightly in her hands as I push inside her, angry and selfish.

I ignore her moaning, I don't listen to her breathing, I don't listen to my own body, begging me for pleasure.

I am not making love to her.

I'm just fucking her.

That's what I repeat to myself in my head as I continue to fill her up, up, up with me, and when I feel her tightening around my cock, I speed up until I hear her scream in liberation.

I let her hips go and I fall onto her and with one decisive thrust I submerge her in all of my anger.

I lie on top of her, crushing her under my weight, and pant into her neck. I should get up now and let her breathe, ask her if everything is okay, but the truth is I'm not able to move or look her in the eyes, because I'd find all the hate she feels for me right there. The hate that I feel towards myself too.

I fucked her like it was a punishment. I fucked her hard, trying to destroy every last bit of the emptiness that is consuming her. I fucked her to show her that I'm not the one she wants.

Instead the only thing I wanted was to touch her, feel her and to love her so that she felt it.

I wanted her to be mine.

Riley stirs below me and I understand that we need to face what we've just done.

I move aside as she stays there, spread-eagled on her back with her arms hanging by her sides.

We are silent for what seems like hours, with anxiety suffocating me, but Riley doesn't move a muscle. It seems like she's not even breathing.

What the hell have I done?

"I shouldn't have."

Guilt starts to eat me up inside.

"I asked you to."

"You wanted me to be this?"

"Isn't that what you are?"

She sits up and looks around for her clothes on the floor. She puts on her top, then her underwear – which is still wet.

"Aren't you the one who only knows how to take?"

I get off the bed too.

"It was... wrong. A terrible mistake. You told me so. God, I thought..."

I try to touch her but she moves away from me.

"...I thought it would be different. I thought it meant something to you," she says, her voice shaking. "I almost believed you," she shakes her head. "You'll never change."

She throws her disappointment in my face before making it to the garage door, opening it and disappearing into the night.

I fall back onto the bed with my head in my hands.

I got it all fucking wrong.

She came here for someone to desire her, to make her feel loved.

Me.

She wanted me to love her.

I've wasted the only chance I had. I've ruined everything before it could really turn into something.

I've done it again.

I've made the only woman I'm able to love run away.

28
Riley

I don't even know how I made it home. My entire body was on alert the entire time, still shocked by what I'd just gone through.

I had sex with Ian and I have no idea what I was thinking, showing up at his door and begging him to make me his.

What was I expecting? That things would be different? That he would actually care about me? That the emotion I felt running through me was real and that he felt it too? That he would be honest with me, that he had really changed?

That he felt something for me and wasn't just trying to get laid?

All bullshit. What a sham.

My entire life is a sham.

I close the door behind me and fall to the floor, resting my back against it. I hug myself and start shaking. I'm still wearing my wet clothes from the storm, but I can pick out quite distinctly his smell on me and it's enough to make me want to wretch.

I crawl to my bathroom, slithering towards the toilet. I start coughing, but nothing comes out.

I lift myself with great difficulty and get undressed before getting into the shower to wash away my shame, the pain and the solitude which now feels stronger than ever before.

I sit in the shower as the water washes over me, and I curl myself into a ball until the hot water scorches my skin. I pull myself out and wrap myself in a towel. Dripping wet, I walk to the kitchen in my bare feet, open the fridge and grab a bottle of wine.

The emptiness has returned.

I can't stand it.

I crawl under the covers, making the sheets wet, and start to drink until I'll finally just pass out.

I hear a dull thudding noise that shakes me from my stupor. I don't understand where it's coming from, maybe I'm dreaming or maybe it's just the hammering in my head.

I try to open an eye but the only thing I see is a bottle next to me that spins on the ground when I try to move, clinking noisily against two other empty bottles.

How much did I drink? I don't remember getting out of bed to get more.

I turn in my sordid sheets with great difficulty, shivering when I come into contact with the cold and I fall back into a restless and painful sleep.

Another noise, louder than the first one, almost makes my head explode, then someone is shaking me and lifting me, wrapping me in a reassuring warmth.

I feel water running over me again, someone

caressing my hair, my face and speaking to me but I can't make out any of it.

The water stops running and I feel myself wrapped up in something warm. Again, I am held tightly, someone is holding me in his arms, speaking to me sweetly.

I want to open my eyes, say something, but it's too much for my senses and it's too overwhelming. I let myself go completely, feeling so safe that I can escape for just a few minutes. Enough time to turn all of this off and imagine my life as something other than a disaster.

* * *

When I open my eyes, the shooting pain piercing my skull makes me wish I was dead. I try to move, but the grip I feel around my body and my physical weakness prevent me from getting up.

I turn my head and realise that Ian is here, on my sofa next to me, and that I'm in his arms.

I close my eyes and try to remember what happened, but the last thing that comes to mind is his body on top of mine and his invasive, painful thrusts. The feeling of emptiness that I felt when he pulled out from me.

I shiver and try to escape the absurd imagine of me and him - the throw falls suddenly to the floor, making me realise that I'm completely naked.

Ian's eyes snap open. I try to pick up the throw again, to cover myself, but when I tug at it, I discover that he's in the same condition as me.

I curl myself into a ball in a corner of the sofa, hugging my chest while Ian wakes up and rubs his face with his hand.

He sits up with his back to me, allowing me to enjoy a look at his perfect, well-defined back. Then he gets to his feet, revealing his tight glutes and muscular legs without a hint of embarrassment. My eyes go to the tattoos that cover his arms, his shoulders and the muscles that run down his abdomen.

I swallow hard and force myself to stop looking at him.

Ian moves around the apartment without saying a word. I feel my heart hammering loudly in my chest and my headache grows stronger than ever.

I cover my face with my hands trying to come up with something to say, but he comes back, and stops in front of me.

I let my hands drop and look up at him timidly. Ian is wrapped in a towel and extends his hand to me with two tablets in it. I accept them and put them in my mouth before he passes me a bottle of water. I swallow them as he sits down next to me.

"You scared me."

"That wasn't my intention, I didn't think you'd come here after..." I didn't finish the phrase, I close my eyes and swallow down my dignity.

"I shouldn't have let you just leave like that, not after what happened between us."

"You don't owe me anything."

He stands up, hurt by what I've just said. He paces the living room and then takes his head in his hands, messing up his hair.

"I shouldn't have taken advantage of you like that."

"You… what?"

He turns to face me again.

"I was wrong. You were vulnerable and scared and I—"

"You fucked me. End of story."

"That's not what I wanted to do."

"Now you're trying to tell me that you made a big sacrifice for me? That an easy lay isn't every man on the planet's fantasy?"

"What? Me, no…" he huffs and comes closer to me. He kneels down next to me and speaks calmly. "Do you think it was easy for me? I'm drowning in my own guilt."

Confused by his words and unnerved by my own thoughts, I get up from the sofa, but my head spins so much that I almost go down. I land in his arms that grab me and hold me to his warm body. The throw falls away from us, leaving me naked against him.

"Riley," he whispers into my neck. "I'm sorry, I swear to you it's not what I wanted."

His words hurt me and make me feel even more refused that before.

"You regret it." I say leaning away from him. "Just like the last time. What's the matter? I'm not enough for you?"

He grabs me by the wrist and forces me to face him.

"That night... Christ, Riley, do you have the slightest idea what I was feeling? How much it cost me to leave you there alone on my bed?"

I rest my open hands on his chest as his slide gently down my back. Then he speaks directly into my lips.

"I don't want to be a distraction from your loneliness. I don't want to be the last drop of emptiness that fills you. I don't want to be something you look for to hide away from the rest of the world."

I look up at him and the warmth I see in his eyes makes my knees weak.

"I just want you to be mine."

29
Ian

The feeling of her body against mine is enough to make me lose my lucidity, freeing my thoughts and my words.

I slept next to her, held her to me, skin on skin and breathed her in with the only hope that when she woke up, we could start from zero. That we could touch each other, taste each other slowly, one step at a time.

When she looked at me that way, when I could read the resentment in her eyes as clear as day, I felt myself sinking again. I can't lose her again, not before having truly had her.

"I want you to be mine," I tell her with fire in my veins and my heart racing a million miles an hour.

Riley leans back, afraid, and I let her. I let my words suffocate her because I know that's probably what it's doing.

A year ago, I told her I didn't want to burden myself with the weight she carries and now I'm ready to bear it for her so she can save herself.

And now I'm ready for all of it.

Riley's confused. She doesn't know where to go and she hasn't faced what's happened to her yet. She's not in full control of her life. I'm the one who's told her what I'm really feeling, what I've felt about her since that damn night I wouldn't dance with her. I shouldn't feel like this: it'll only hurt me in the end.

"I can't reason when you're in the middle of things. I lose my mind, I lose... Everything, Riley. I always lose when it comes to you. The idea is devouring me... You're destroying me. Even if I know I can't stand it, I can't do without it. And it's all your fault."

"My fault?" she stutters, confused.

I lean in close to her and she falls backwards onto the sofa.

"You show up at my house. You ask me to..." I close my eyes and inhale deeply but when I open them the view of her naked shoulders and chest before me make me lose control.

I close the gap between us and take her face in my hands, covering her mouth with mine. Riley doesn't know what to hold on to, what to do and is completely overwhelmed by me, by my fingers that are running over her, by my mouth that holds her hostage, by my desperation. I pull away from her just enough time to grab her from behind, lift her up and sit her on me.

"Ian..." she pants.

I snake my hands behind her head, grab her hair and pull her to me.

Her breasts crush against my chest, her hands anchored to my shoulders, her lips that brush against mine. I bite her and she moans in my mouth and I try to pull away my towel with the other hand – now the only thing separating us. I grab her hips, throw the towel to the floor and forcefully sit her on top of my pulsing cock.

Riley goes rigid, I feel her tensed muscles in her legs shaking.

I realise I have zero control when she's in my arms.

So, I stop myself a minute to breathe, to quiet my instincts. I rest my forehead against hers, breathing heavily and keeping a firm grip on her hips. A part of me is afraid that if I let go, she might try to escape, and I couldn't bear that.

"If this isn't what you want you have to tell me right now," I say with a heavy heart, feeling every part of my body shaking with the fear of rejection.

"I… I want…"

"What? What do you want?"

She tries to kiss me but I turn my head.

"I want… you to fuck me, Ian. Please, just fuck me and stop talking."

She whispered what she said but I feel like she just screamed it in my ear. And it makes a terrible noise.

She's just looking for a lay. Someone to sleep with her and take away all her pain. But I want to love her and give her everything.

Disappointment devours me, piece by piece, and I let it, as I grab her by the waist and push her away from me. I put a hand between our bodies and gently touch her clit with my fingers.

Riley squeezes her legs together, but I don't stop.

I slide a finger inside her and as I start to move it, she slowly relaxes. I add another finger and Riley moans right in my ear, falling against my shoulder and squeezing my arm tightly. I move my fingers in deeper and rest my thumb on her clit. Her breath on my ear, her warmth all around me, and the desire to feel her again explode in my body without control. With the other hand, I accompany her movements, pulling her towards me and holding her hip so my fingers slide in and out of her as she moves against my hand. When her breathing gets heavier, I realise she's about to come.

"Not like this Riley," I tell her pulling out my fingers. "You have to feel it. How much I want it."

I grab her hips and sit her on top of me. I squeeze her tighter and move with her hips so that she takes it, deep and painful, and lets herself be filled with my dick and nothing else.

Because I'm not the one she wants, I'm just someone to fill her for twenty minutes and then leave her even emptier than before.

I'm only doing what she wants, I tell myself, as I try not to think about the pleasure running through my own body mixed with the painful awareness that this is the only warmth I'll ever feel.

The only thing she's willing to give me.

30
Riley

When I feel him filling me so deeply, the painful pleasure erases every inhibition and I melt into his warm hands that grip my hips tightly, pulling me onto him.

Ian takes me completely.

He is fucking me, like I asked him to, even if I wasn't really sure this is what I wanted.

I wanted his hands, his mouth, his body and that warmth... *Him*. I wanted to feel him.

With a strong thrust, my body folds completely over his; my energy is gone, my head is hammering and my stomach is grumbling.

And yet, I allow him to have me this way, full of anger and selfishness. Ian projects his frustration and desire into me.

And I let him.

I take it all.

I would take anything from him.

His face slides between my breasts and I feel his beard scratching, burning my skin. His lips capture a nipple and suck at it before biting down furiously. Ian doesn't stop. He carries on biting me, sucking me and tormenting me, making me lose any sense of embarrassment I may have felt.

The only thing I feel is Ian O'Connor inside me.

It's the only thing I want to feel.

"God, Riley... it's killing me. All of this is killing me. Having you this way..." he pants against my chest making me feel, for the first time, that I am the woman he really wants.

I grab his hair with both my hands and pull him to my mouth. I want to feel his lips, his tongue, his flavour.

I want it all.

Because the same thing is killing me too.

I clash with his mouth, sliding my tongue in and he moans, sending vibrations rippling through me.

"I want you to forget about everything else," he says through his teeth as I wrap my legs around him, trapping him in my grip. "I want you to understand exactly what's happening here. I want you to see what I'm doing to you." He squeezes a nipple tightly, forcing me to look at him. "I want you to know that your body is in my hands. That it's all in my hands." He takes one in his teeth and bites it, burning me with his eyes and enjoying my agony. "I want you to think about the fact that I'm inside you, that I'm fucking you."

He slides his hands along my back until he gets to my buttocks and squeezes tightly. I move over him and take it all, feeling my excitement balloon as our sweaty bodies bump up against one another.

"I want you to understand what it means to want something so badly you wish it could kill you, because that's what you're doing to me," he growls angrily, before marking me again with his teeth.

Neck, shoulder, breast. Ian bites me everywhere, furious and breathless, and each time he does, it takes my breath away – his tongue soothes the wound he's just inflicted on me.

And then he grabs my hips and pushes down hard, before biting my earlobe and ordering me: "Come for me, Riley. Just for me."

I grab onto his shoulders and do as he tells me.

And I do it loudly and desperately as if, through my liberating screams, a part of me is killed, dispersed with the air.

Ian follows me, filling me with his hardness and his rage before stopping and letting his head fall onto my shoulder, breathless.

We stay like that for a few minutes before I try with to get off of him. My legs are quivering and my body is still rocked by tremors.

Ian doesn't let me move; he gets up, keeping me tightly in his arms, and starts towards the bathroom.

"What...?" I say in confusion.

He opens the shower door and turns on the water, then in a tone of voice that is so sweet and tender it smashes me to a million pieces he says: "Now I'm going to take care of you."

31
Ian

I let her slide slowly off of my body, resting her feet in the shower. Riley seems scared. Maybe I really did take it too far. Maybe I should have gone a bit slower, enjoyed every moment, let her know that what I wanted wasn't her body.

I don't say anything. I just caress the wet hair that falls over her shoulders and I take care of her, because she needs to be looked after. We both do.

I didn't want all this, for things to freefall out of control. It was rage, a strong desire to feel her, to have her for myself and to give myself completely to her, because I know she's the only woman I could do it for. She's the only woman I could live for.

I don't know if I'll be able to put things right, turn it around and get her to trust me, to open her heart to me and let me in.

I don't know if I'll ever get a second chance, or if she'll ever be able to see me for what I am, to see just Ian and not someone to vent her anger towards and who can fill her emptiness. To realise that behind this façade, there's an entire world to discover.

To believe in me and what we could have. I take the shampoo bottle and pour a little into my hands. I delicately massage her head as she closes her eyes and lets herself go to my touch. I soap up her body, reddened by my own bite marks, my beard scratching and the bastard that I have been once again.

I try not to think about it and to make things better as much as possible, to show her that she can have whatever she wants from me if she just asks for it.

Because I could be hers.

Completely.

If she wants me.

I rub her body with soapy hands, slowly and respectfully, and she lets me without making a sound. She's still under the spell of my hands washing over her - this time, to take care of her.

Then I rinse myself off too as she looks at me, confused, wrapping her arms around her chest.

It's such an intense and intimate moment – us, here like this – it's hard for me to wrap my head around.

I don't think I've ever experienced this kind of intimacy with anyone. It's a sensation that really undoes me; I didn't think it was possible for me to feel this way, for me to surrender to a feeling that grows devastatingly larger with every passing second, occupying my every thought and invading my every heartbeat.

I never would have believed that I could let down my guard, let myself be dragged in by someone. I never knew that my heart could swell in my chest so dominatingly, so out of control.

But it's happened and I don't know how go back, or make it stop.

32
Riley

I sit in the armchair in my bedroom, wrapped in a towel as Ian takes off the old sheets and replaces them with clean ones. I watch him moving around without embarrassment, wearing just a towel around his waist, his wet hair plastered to his forehead and a serious yet tender expression on his face that could crack my heart in two.

I bite my lip at the sight of his muscles flexing as he makes my bed. I can't take my eyes off of him or ask him what he's still doing here because I have this huge weight on my chest, crushing me.

He turns to look at me and embarrassment flushes through me.

"All done," he says coming towards me, and all of sudden, I close up, drawing my legs into my chest.

He kneels down on the carpet next to me and lifts my chin up with two fingers. "Riley..." The sound of my name on his lips is the sweetest, most tender sound I've ever heard. I close my eyes, praying I don't cry.

Ian sighs, before slipping an arm under my legs and the other one behind my shoulders and lifting me up. As I near his body I stiffen in his arms; then he rests me down on the bed and covers me with the duvet. He looks at me for a few seconds before turning to leave so I jump up and grab his hand.

Ian freezes in place, his back to me.

"S-stay," I beg him, my voice is shaking.

He turns slowly and his eyes nail me to the wall. They're so clear that I can almost see myself in them, for the first time, as I really am.

He lets go of my hand and walks around the bed. I hear the blanket moving and the mattress sink under his weight, then I feel nothing but a warmth I've waited for and wanted for so long, the kind of heat that could warm up everything it touches.

His arm wraps around my waist and he pulls me in to him. My back is pressed against his chest and I find myself holding my breath for a few seconds as I feel his erection rubbing against my buttocks.

Then his lips are on my shoulder and I shudder at the tenderness of his touch; it frightens me, because I'm starting to hope, to dream, to believe.

In him.

"I'm not going anywhere unless you ask me to," he whispers into my ear.

"You already have before. You'll do it again."

He pulls me in tighter to him as if by doing so, he could erase the words that I just said.

"I couldn't now. I'm in too deep."

His words are sweet and whispered over my still sensitive skin and my heart, which has been reduced to a pile of small fragments.

I find myself wanting something for myself. A man, this man; wanting his hands on my body, to feel him inside me and breathe the same air as him. Someone I can share my thoughts, my space and my fears with.

I've never felt this safe, wanted and protected in my life. I've never been so desperate to have the scent of a man on me.

I stroke his arm with my hand and feel him sigh heavily against my neck. He holds me tighter and then slowly rises up towards my chest and hugs me so tightly and possessively and I'm afraid of welling up again.

"Riley," he whispers again, giving me chills. "I can't stand it. I knew that if I touched you once, like this, I wouldn't be able to control myself," he continues and I feel the proof of it in his growing erection right between my legs. "I want you again," his tone is desperate and has an immediate effect on me.

I instinctively pull back my hips: an unspoken invitation to let him slide into me and take me again.

He squeezes my nipple hard between his fingers and starts playing with it, while the other hand slides between my thighs. I arch my back impatiently, hoping that he'll put an end to this madness and get inside me as quickly as possible. He slides two fingers into me and a moan escapes my lips while I close my eyes and let myself go to his touch.

He uses his knee to open my legs wide enough to feel his erection push against my clit.

"Say it – or I swear to God, I'm not going to do it, Riley."

"Ian…"

"Tell me."

"Please, I need it."

"What do you need?"

"You." And I can hardly believe the words coming out of my mouth. "I need you."

"Fuck," he says through gritted teeth as he slips into me.

I'm ready to feel him crush me, pure animal instinct, his thrusts bending me under his force, but it doesn't happen.

This time, it's different. It's all different.

He's different.

All of this sweetness, this thoughtfulness, this unexpected hope that he really can take care of me, rains down on me and makes me melt in his arms, giving me everything I need.

33
Ian

I didn't want to take her again, but then when she said those words that I no longer held much hope of ever hearing – that *I need you* – my heart took over.

I sink into her, wrapping myself in her warmth that slowly envelopes me, together with her breathing. It's enough to bring tears to my eyes, this intimacy between us. This meeting, not only of two bodies but two souls, two wounded souls that are trying to sew themselves back together.

I caress her, enjoying her body, inhaling her clean hair and holding her desperately to me.

Because that's how I feel.

I need her desperately and I need to be everything that she can breathe.

I feel her pussy contracting against my cock, wanting, needing. I kiss her skin, tasting it and committing it to memory, this, our first real time being together. This time she's not just giving me her body: she's giving herself to me and I could never have asked for anything more.

"Make love to me, Riley," I whisper in her ear. "It's all I ask for."

She turns her head and I catch her lip in my teeth. I bite it slowly, I suck it and then slip my tongue into her mouth, drinking in her moans and quenching my thirst with her passion, crashing from her body into mine.

When I break away from her, she looks at me intensely with wet eyes.

"You really want me?" she asks incredulously and I could cry at the fact that she doesn't believe she's what I really want.

I thrust deeply into her, forcing a sensual sound to escape her lips. "Can't you feel it?"

She nods.

"This is how much I want you," I bite her neck and push again. "You're beautiful, Riley," I murmur. "You turn me on," I continue, biting her earlobe and panting into it. "And this body," I hold her breast in my hand. "I can't help but want it. I want it to be mine. I've always wanted it, Riley. I've never stopped thinking about it. Not a fucking second since you came into my life."

She exhales and I feel her start to shake in my arms.

"This is the only body I've ever wanted."

Her breathing becomes heavier.

"You're the one I've always wanted," I confess to her for the first time in three years, setting aside my fear of another abandonment.

"Let yourself go."

I caress her between the legs as she moves against me and I help her get to that pleasure spot she's trying to reach – if only because I can't control myself.

When I hear her panting rapidly, I push deeper so we can enjoy the moment together.

Riley doesn't yell this time, she expresses herself in weighted sighs, making me explode into her again.

We come together and breathe together as if we were one – and I almost wish it were true.

We stay there, anchored one to another, desperately entwined because we both know that once the moment has passed, we're going to have to face the music.

I kiss her shoulder, her neck, her back. I caress her breasts tenderly because what we have between us is more than sex and instinct.

What we have shared together is love.

Riley is still in my arms as I try to communicate wordlessly with her.

We fall asleep like this, next to each other, tightly embracing and I feel life itself returning to our veins.

* * *

When I wake up, the heat coming from her body makes me sigh with emotion. I hold her to me and kiss her shoulder, sliding my hand to her stomach.

I feel her scar under my fingers. I start from down low and move up to her belly. My thumb traces her, quivering with rage and pain.

I swallow hard and close my eyes, trying to send away the thoughts that have been oppressing me for weeks now, wreaking havoc on my heart.

Riley gets up slowly. She moves in my arms and when she realises what I'm doing she pulls away from me, turning onto her back and covering herself with the duvet up to her chin.

"Riley," I say, the emotion in my voice nearly betraying me.

She shakes her head and gets up, wrapping herself in the sheet. She seems small, defenceless. My gut instinct is to run to her and hug her, make her understand that I'm here, I'm here for her, that she can tell me anything and I'm ready to take it all on.

I get up and go over to her but she hurries away to go sit in the armchair. She hugs her legs to her chest, curling up into a ball.

She's closing me out.

I kneel down before her. "Trust me," I tell her gently, trying to catch her gaze.

"I can't."

"You can. It's going to be alright, I promise you."

"I'm afraid."

"Afraid? Of what?"

She shakes her head and looks elsewhere.

"I'm afraid of you," she says in a whisper. "Afraid of wanting you so badly that I feel it coursing through my veins. The need I have to inhale you, to hear your breathing. Afraid to come out in the open and show myself for what I really am. Afraid that it's all too much, that you won't be able to accept it and that I really am that problem you'd rather not deal with."

Then she turns her head slightly and looks at me.

"Afraid that you'll break my heart again, Ian O'Connor – and that this time I won't be able to repair it."

I close my eyes and swallow the rest of my hope that I could take care of her, and love her as she deserves to be loved.

34
Riley

"Why would you say all of these things after what's happened? We made love, Riley, don't you get it? Are you aware of what's happened between us?" he says, getting to his feet.

He takes a few steps into the room before shaking his head and picking up his clothes.

"I didn't... think..."

He turns to me and chills me with a look that pours out all of his resentment.

"What didn't you think? That I would've stuck around? That I'd want to know?"

"I don't know. I was just confused, okay?"

"You *were* confused? Past tense? What about tonight, this morning... are you even aware of what we did?" he yells furiously at me.

He comes towards me and bends over me while I try to make myself smaller in front of him.

"Did you know it was me that was fucking you?"

His words hurt me and send me into a spiral of shame and embarrassment.

"What were you looking for? What did you want from me?"

"I don't know... I wasn't looking for anything. I didn't know what would happen," I mutter as my embarrassment inches up to burn my face and neck.

"You didn't know? You were the one who showed up on my doorstep!" he says waving his hands dangerously close to me.

"I just wanted…"

"Someone to screw you."

"What…?"

"You thought a night of sex with the arsehole of the week might be enough to help you turn the tide and lift you out of your sadness."

This has gone too far. My anger shoves aside the sadness, giving my tongue a shot of courage. I stand up and face him, facing his glare head-on.

"And you? You got what you wanted, didn't you? A nice lay – better, more than one. Isn't that the only thing you're capable of giving?"

My words assault him. The expression on his face changes and the resentment makes space for a different emotion, something much deeper and more ingrained, something that looks like blunt pain. A pain so overwhelming it leaves his eyes and hits me in full.

"I didn't get everything I wanted! Is this what you think I was looking for? You think it was fun for me… that it was easy? If that's all I wanted I would've taken it a year ago!"

Confused by his words, I shake my head and try to get back in touch with reality.

"I'm still here. I'm here for you."

Then he rubs his face with his heavy hands in exasperation and takes a deep breath before calming his tone and speaking again.

"I don't want your body, Riley. I've already had it and it almost killed me, slowly and painfully."

"Then what do you want, Ian?"

"I want more. I want to know what's going on inside your head, what you're hiding, what you feel, what... what it is that hurts you." He hesitates before putting on his t-shirt. He looks at me for a second and his pain melds with mine and its weight is so huge I believe it will crush me.

"I want all of it."

"I can't give that to you."

"Then I don't want anything."

He turns and leaves, slamming the door behind him.

I stay where I am, curled up on my armchair in my bedroom, trying to calm these tremors that are pulsing through me. I want to cry, honestly. Right this minute. Cry for myself, for what's been taken away from me, for what I'll never be able to have.

An incomplete life.

A wounded soul.

And now a broken heart.

I don't know which weight is heavier to bear.

35
Ian

"Wow, you've bulked up."

Ryan gets in my face as I'm trying to bench press. He helps me set down the weights and I sit up.

"Pass me that towel."

"Don't pretend you need to wipe away your sweat."

"Don't piss me off."

Ryan throws the towel at me and I could wring his neck.

"Do you always have to be such an arse?"

"I don't know, do you have to always be so highly strung?"

He's right. I am highly strung, agitated and completely out of my mind.

Riley in my arms, on top of me, close to me...

I grab the water bottle and pour it directly over my head to cool off my instincts.

"We're a bit off today."

Ryan keeps prodding me as usual, and in normal circumstances I'd ignore him – but today, just about the slightest thing could set me off.

"What are you doing here?" I say standing up and throwing down the towel.

"Coach called me."

I look at him, waiting for him to continue.

"I don't know anything else."

"I think he's in the office."

"I'm going to go and see what he wants. Will you wait for me? I don't think I'll be long."

"I've finished here. I'll get showered and wait for you in the car park."

He nods and walks off through the gym, stopping to say hello to some of the guys.

I go in the changing rooms, take off my sweat-soaked clothes and hop under the shower, hoping to wash away the thoughts of her and what I'd be willing to do to hold her close to me just one more time.

* * *

Ryan comes towards me, his face like thunder. He grabs his helmet gruffly and gets on my bike.

"How'd you get here?" I ask him, starting the engine.

"I took a cab."

"Don't you think it might be worth looking into a more practical idea like a short-term rental or having yours brought over?"

"I still don't know how long I'm going to be around."

"So, what did the coach want?" I ask cautiously leaving the UCD car park.

"I don't feel like talking about it."

"Where shall I take you, home?"

"To your place please. I need to keep my distance from Nick for a few hours."

We let ourselves in to my apartment and I throw my keys down on the counter. Ryan goes straight to the fridge looking for alcohol. He never used to touch the stuff. He grabs a bottle, opens it and then flops onto the sofa, running the cold bottle across his forehead.

I follow his lead and join him on the sofa.

"Hard day?"

"Total shit."

Perfect.

My own shit wasn't enough for me to take on – now I have to deal with his, too.

"Is it because of Nick?"

"Kind of."

"Do you want to talk about it or do I have to read your fucking mind?"

He scoffs and opens his eyes, sitting up and leaning his elbows on his legs.

"The president was there with the coach," he starts nervously, peeling the label off his bottle.

"They offered me a position."

"What?"

"Don't get too excited."

"Sorry, I'm just surprised."

"No big deal, just a spot on the bench."

"And what did you say?"

"That I'd have to think about it."

He turns and looks at me with sad eyes. It feels like I'm looking at the kid who took a beating on the field every day and then came to me at night begging me to teach him how to improve and get stronger.

"I haven't decided yet."

"But you don't have a team right now, right?"

"Not exactly. Let's just say there's a deal on the table. Someone's on their way out."

"It's a great opportunity. They're not going to ask you a third time."

"I know, but I don't think I'm ready to put down roots here just yet."

"And our family? Don't you think about them?"

"They're the only thing I'm thinking of, otherwise I'd have told them to go to hell."

"They need you. Mum's getting tired and I can't always be on-call. I do what I can, but I need you, they need you – *both* of you. Maybe if we were all nearby, we could hold off looking for another solution for a while."

"What are you talking about?"

"Dad asked me to—"

"No," he says firmly, not letting me finish. "Mum won't have it and neither will I."

"Do you think it's something I want for him?"

"I don't know, is it?"

"Don't be a dick," I say standing up in front of him.

"Maybe you're tired and don't want to take on the responsibility."

"Are you shitting me? I'm the one who stayed, Ryan, while you two ran as far away as possible."

"Didn't you want to run away, too?"

"I never did and never will."

"What a great role model you are…"

"There are things that are more important than stupid fights between brothers."

"Stupid fights?"

"Okay, maybe it's something more than that, but not so serious you have to distance yourself from your parents. Especially now that they need you."

Ryan snorts derisively and I sit back down.

"You're not a little boy anymore, Ryan. You can't keep running away. You haven't got a lifelong career in front of you. You need to decide, now. Either you accept this offer or…"

"It's over. I know."

"You could always be a model like Nick, you're not bad-looking."

"Fuck off, Ian!"

I laugh because Ryan isn't really angry: not with me at least.

"Think about it, bro. It could be a good opportunity."

"What's that? The return of your shadow?"

"You know it never was like that."

"That's what you think. You've always been the champion in the family."

"Only because I'm the only one around here who takes it seriously. I don't let everything else influence my work."

"Yeah well..."

"What's that?"

"That's all changed now, hasn't it?"

I jump to my feet to avoid answering him.

"Oh sure, we never talk about you, I forgot."

"There's nothing to say."

"Really?" he asks, stretching out the word.

I look at him threateningly. "Watch it, Ryan."

"I am. I've been where you are and I swore that I'd never do it again. Now look at you, drowning in a lake of your own shit."

I look at him, shaking my head as he waits for my reply, waiting for me to open up to him – something that will never happen, even if he tortures me.

"I lost her."

The words pour out of my mouth like a river. I throw up on my brother with three concise, confused words because I'm feeling angry, worried, a step away from losing my mind.

"I haven't got it right even once. Letting her get close to me... waiting around to see what happens... waiting for what? I should never have said no that night, fuck."

"I warned you." He points his finger at me.

"You know how things were for me then. How I used to think, how I reacted to things... you know full well that I couldn't have done anything else!"

"The only thing I know is that you acted like a selfish bastard."

"That's who I am."

"You? You don't even understand the concept of only thinking about yourself, Ian."

I run a hand through my hair.

"I spoke to Jamie a few weeks ago."

"And?"

"I wish I hadn't."

"What are you talking about?"

"I've always been missing a piece, I felt that she was hiding something from me."

"I'm not following."

"He's broken, Ryan, just like me."

"How broken?" he asks, worried.

"Something that maybe no one can fix. Not even me."

"Oh, Jesus! I had no idea! Jamie is so..."

"I know," I say, shaking my head. "I swear to you, I don't know how he does it."

"Well, you're pretty good at hiding yourself too."

"Not as much as I'd like."

We lose ourselves in the silence for a few minutes. Ryan's trying to get his head around all these new ideas and I'm trying not to be squashed under the weight I'm carrying.

"Is there something I can do? Something *we* can do?"

"You and Nick?" I ask incredulously.

"We're a family. If one of us calls, the others will come."

"Once, maybe."

"Don't change the subject, we're talking about you right now. What's the situation?"

"Bad, Ryan."

"Nothing new there."

"I slept with Riley."

"Holy shit!"

"And it was a mistake. Another one."

"She isn't—"

"She isn't ready. She doesn't trust me and I don't think she ever will. She won't let me in."

"So, now what?"

"Now it's a big fucking mess."

Ryan sighs.

"You're not going to end up like me, right, Ian? We're not already at that stage, are we?"

I slowly lift my eyes to meet his.

"Jesus Christ," he says, dropping his head into his hands.

We're well past that point.

We're past the point of no return.

36
Ian

"Damn it, Ian O'Connor! If Scott tackles you one more time, I'm gonna bench you this weekend, do you understand me?"

I pick myself up from the grass with Scott pulling me to my feet. He pats me on the shoulder and runs off with his head down.

I breathe in, bending my knees as the guys head off the field and make their way towards the gym, each going to his own machine.

"What's your problem, kid?" The coach is storming towards me, and he's not happy.

"I'm just—"

"You're just an idiot, that's what!"

Okay, that's a pretty perfect definition.

"You show up like this again and you're out, seriously. You're done for today."

I nod, absorbing the coach's wrath, and I can hear snickering over my shoulder.

All that was missing from this picture was the biggest pair of arseholes to witness it.

I turn towards the stands to see my brothers sitting there, sitting apart obviously, but at least there're here together. I move towards them as they stand up and walk down the steps.

"Jesus, Ian. I didn't remember you being so

bad. Your age must be catching up with you." Nick punches my arm and I try not to react.

"Good thing you're the big champion in the family," Ryan teases me, and Nick snickers.

"I'm glad to see you two dickheads are united in making fun of me."

"United my arse," Nick gets serious quickly.

"Then what are you two doing here together?"

"We have to talk to you."

"I'll have a shower and be right there. You guys try not to gouge each other's eyes out."

"I can't make any promises," Ryan calls as I head towards the changing rooms. I'd better avoid fucking up anything else here or they really won't let me play.

* * *

I leave the gym and head towards the car park, where my brothers are waiting for me next to my motorbike.

"Where are we going?" I ask.

"Your house."

Obviously.

"I'm coming with you," Ryan says grabbing the helmet.

Nick raises his hands and goes towards a car parked a few feet away.

"A car?" I ask Ryan.

He shrugs his shoulders and gets on the bike

behind me as I start the engine and head off for my house, towards the next impending disaster.

We go inside and my brothers start opening my fridge, oblivious to the fact that they're in my house uninvited.

"What the hell are you doing?"

"I'm hungry," Nick says, with his head in the fridge.

I scoff and push him out of the way. "You too?" I ask Ryan.

"Er…"

"Fine, I'll do it," I make a gesture for them to back off. "You can open a beer and I'll take care of the rest."

I set the plates down on the counter where my brothers are waiting impatiently. I sit next to Ryan on a stool as Nick sits opposite us, on the other side. They plough into the mushroom omelette I've just made as I sit there with my fork in the air, stomach closed and my gaze firmly on the spot where Riley was sitting a few days ago, clinging to me.

I set the fork down and rest my elbows on the counter.

"Aren't you gonna eat that?" Ryan asks, eyeing up my plate. I shake my head and he steals the plate out from under my nose. Nick claims his half with a fork.

"Big problems," he comments, as I give him the eye.

"Enormous," Ryan corrects him.

Is it possible that the only time these guys get along is when they're in it together to take me down?

"Would you please tell me what you're doing at my house?"

"And can you please tell us what's up with you?" Nick replies.

I cross my arms over my chest. "You first."

"Okay," Ryan sighs. "I need a place to stay."

My eyebrows shoot up.

"Let's say that, for the time being, I'll be around. Don't look at me like that, it's not definite, alright? But I need a place of my own, I can't live with Mum and Dad, I'm not thirteen."

I nod.

"And I can't stay here with you."

"Sounds about right."

"So..."

"I need to find you a place, right?"

"I need a place too," Nick says.

"What the fuck do you two take me for, a lettings agency?"

They both stare at me.

"And I can't see you both sharing a flat."

"Are you kidding?" Ryan says with wide eyes.

I run my hands over my face in exasperation.

Why did I make them come home? What have I done to deserve this?

"Is that all, or is there more?"

"Ah yeah, I've accepted the offer. I sign tomorrow."

I sigh – I'm not sure whether in relief or anxiety. I'll find out soon enough.

"And what's the deal with you, what's happened?" Nick asks.

"*Her*. She happened to me."

"She? She who?" he asks with fake innocence.

I slowly lift my head and look at him sideways.

"You aren't here because you need a place to stay, are you?"

Ryan pretends he doesn't understand and Nick lets go of a little grin that crosses his face.

"At least we're together."

Small consolation.

"Don't get too excited, we're just here for you."

"Well, it's something."

"What can we do?"

"I've ruined everything. There's nothing I can do to fix it."

"Even if we go and beat somebody up?" Nick says, rubbing his hands together.

"Who do you want to massacre? I'm curious."

"I could start with Ryan."

"What the hell do I have to do with it?"

"You're close by. Maybe it would help Ian

relieve some tension."

"Fuck you, Nick!"

Nick laughs. He really is an idiot. He still hasn't understood that every moment he spends with Ryan could be his last one.

"Let's get back to more serious things," Ryan says, shooting a glare at Nick before looking at me. "There must be something you can do. Something you haven't tried yet."

"I think anything I do will just make it worse."

"So, you're ready to give up by the sounds of it."

"I don't know."

"We never give up," Nick adds.

"I don't know if I have another choice."

"If you want, you can hit me."

"Why would I do that?"

"You need to get it out, you need to let all this, whatever it is, out. I'm the less important of the brothers, the one to be sacrificed."

Nick tries to cheer me up in his own way. Despite the fact that he's a total arsehole, when I need him, he's there.

I look at him gratefully.

"You know, anything for family."

37
Riley

I make it through the theatre door at two o'clock. I wasn't sure about making it in to work at all today, I feel disgusting, but we're organising a new show before Christmas and I can't sit home and let the others do all the work.

I've got a fever and sore throat that means I can't swallow – probably because of that storm, and the fact that I went to bed soaking wet and then...

Ian.

I close my eyes instinctively at the thought of him.

Okay, maybe the reason I came to work is to keep my mind on something else for a while - to think about something that doesn't hurt me, doesn't make me think about the pain that always comes back to find me, to remind me what I am and where I come from.

What the hell did I have in mind? Showing up at his house, letting him have me, the way that he took me... to think I might be able to forget about it, might be able to have someone like him, for myself.

God, am I stupid.

When I get to my office, Kate and Ray run over to see how I'm doing.

"You shouldn't have come in, Riley," Kate

says, sitting down on my desk as I flop into my chair. "You look terrible."

"Wow, thanks," I say, blowing my nose.

"I'm going to get you something hot, how does a cup of tea sound?" Ray asks.

"Thanks, tea would be perfect."

"I'll be back in a bit, but ladies, do not utter a *word* until I get back."

I look at him with an inquisitive eyebrow.

"You don't think I'm buying that story about the flu, do you?"

"Ray!" Kate chides. "Can't you see what condition she's in?"

"I see, I see," he says elusively, walking towards the door to my office.

"Oh wow… this is just what we needed today," he says as I lift my head with difficulty from my desk.

I sigh in exhaustion. "What are you doing here?"

"No, what are *you* doing here?" Jamie says, walking into my office. "With that face, you should be at home in bed."

"We told her the same thing," Ray says, jumping right into the conversation. "But she doesn't want to listen. Maybe if you…"

"Let's go, I'm taking you home right now."

"You can't tell me what to do."

"I'm your brother, of course I can."

"I'm older." I argue like an impertinent child.

"But now you need your little brother and I'm here to take care of you."

* * *

We're sitting on my bed with our plates on our laps. I'm trying to get some of this rice with shrimp down but my throat is clenched shut. I'd better make a show of it if I want that half a glass of wine Jamie promised me to convince me to come home, or I'm going to end up with my head down the toilet.

"I saw Ian the other day."

"That's obvious," I say trying to ignore his intention to strike up conversation with me.

"He's not doing so well."

"Happens," I say flatly.

"I'd even say he's devastated."

"Jamie," I stop him quickly.

"I'm worried, about him and about you."

"You're a traitor," I tell him resentfully.

"I love both of you."

My heart beats painfully in my chest.

"So, now I want to know: what the hell is going on?"

"I don't think you really want to know."

Jamie raises his eyebrow in challenge.

"Let's just skip the parts you think might upset me."

I smile against my will. Talking to Jamie has never been difficult for me.

He's not just a brother for me, he's a friend too, the best one I could have and I've never had problems talking to him about any of my relationships, serious or otherwise. But talking about Ian…

"Riley," Jamie calls my attention. "Did he do something to you?"

I shake my head.

"Okay. I had to ask, even though I don't think he's capable of hurting anyone – if he were, we wouldn't be friends and you would never have trusted him."

I bite my lip at the tension of his last words.

"I get it. Is that the problem, you don't trust him?"

I set my plate down on the side table.

Jamie shows me the bottle and I hold the glass out to him thankfully. It would appear this discussion deserves more than the promised half a glass of wine.

"He wants it all, Jamie."

"What do you mean?"

"He wants all of me."

He nods and takes a slug directly from the bottle.

"And you don't want to give him everything."

"I can't. You know that."

"Sooner or later this weight is going to crush you, Riley."

"You don't appear to enjoy talking about it with just anyone."

"Ian isn't just anyone, and we both know it."

"But he could leave, or worse, send me away," I say as the memory stings my heart. "Come on, Jamie. Ian is a champion, a well-known player on the team. What would he do with someone like me? If he knew everything, if he knew where I came from…" I shake my head at the thought. "Not everyone is ready to accept something like that, to understand it and carry the weight of it. It's immense, Jamie. It's oppressive."

"But you can't go on carrying it all by yourself. You have to face it, that's the only way you're ever going to leave it behind you."

"I'm not strong enough."

"You? Are you joking? I don't know anyone stronger than you. You've been my strength all my life. You've got it together, Riley. You're my rock."

He takes my chin in his fingers and lifts it so that I'm looking him in the eyes.

"You don't need to be scared. You never need to be scared again."

I smile gratefully at him. His support means the world to me.

"You can do it and you can be whatever you want. You're not just this, and we both know it. I'm convinced that you'll understand when the right moment comes, just as I'm sure that man feels something for you, Riley and that he's just waiting for you."

Jamie's right.

Ian feels something, something strong and frightening. The sincerity in his eyes lets me know that's true enough. His words help me to believe him. My heart even tends to agree with him.

But my mind is telling me not to do it, that I

shouldn't let myself go and let him bring everything I'm trying to bury down into the light, knowing that it will destroy him too.

38
Riley

One year earlier

He lifts the garage door, rubbing a hand over his sleep-ridden face, when he sees me there and freezes.

"Riley?"

I don't move. I don't speak. I don't breathe.

"What are you doing here so late?" he asks, worried.

"I don't know."

He shakes his head and moves aside, inviting me in. He closes the door behind us and I stand like a statue in the middle of his living room.

"Riley," he sighs and I close my eyes.

He touches my shoulder and I step away from him. I hear his breath getting heavier and the tension swells in the apartment with things unsaid and withheld emotions.

With fear.

With loneliness.

"Has something happened?"

I shake my head.

Another sigh, this time with an air of suffering.

"Come on," he says, leading me into the kitchen. "I'll make you some tea, how does that sound?"

I shake my head again.

He stands a few metres away from me,

observing me, his muscles tensed. I realise now that he's wearing jeans but that his chest is bare.

I try to breathe but it gets stuck in my throat.

"Tell me what's happened."

"Nothing's happened," I lie.

Everything's happened. It's all back, I can't tell him. Not now. I can't do it.

If I open this door it'll all be over.

I'll be over.

"You came to me."

It's not a question.

Ian is looking at me. He's digging.

He comes towards me slowly and takes me in his arms. I close my eyes and feel safe.

At home.

Ian is shaking. He feels it, too.

He strokes the whole length of my hair, and I let him. He kisses my forehead gently and I let him. He pulls me to him to feel his heartbeat and I let him.

I listen to his breathing and his silence. I listen to the reassuring sounds in this house and I start to catch my breath again.

The silence in these walls doesn't scare me. It's discreet, safe and is almost enough to offset mine.

It's the only thing I can bear to listen to.

"Hey," he says to me, moving slightly and lowering his gaze to me.

Ian is tough, impenetrable and a bit arrogant at times. But he never has been with me. Not once.

"Do you want to talk about it, Riley? I'm starting to worry about you."

"I'm fine," I say flatly.

"Don't pretend with me. You can let your guard down, I'm not going to tell anyone about it."

I lift my eyes to his.

"I'm okay now."

His gaze widens, and his lips come apart. I instinctively put my fingers to them to stop him from speaking.

If he asks me anything, if he speaks, I won't be able to resist.

His warm breath tickles my hand and my body is invaded with a hot, sweet sensation. It's weak, silent but inside of me, it's making a deafening racket.

He takes my face in his hands and I close my eyes to soak in this moment. I try to imprint it everywhere, in my eyes, in my head, in my heart. I need it desperately.

"Do you want to stay here?" he asks, guessing my intentions.

I nod and he smiles tenderly.

"Come on, you look exhausted," he says taking my hand and leading me towards the bed. I sit down and let myself fall back, lifeless. He lays down on his back next to me.

I look at his tough profile, his defined features, the curve of his nose, his full lips and his weeks-old beard that covers his face, giving him a dangerous air. I look up at the ceiling, because I can't hide what I'm feeling: it's about to explode out of me and destroy everything we have. We're about to lose what we're both defending.

I can't hold back anything.

"Riley," he whispers, and I sigh.

"Look at me," he continues, and I give in.

I turn and he does too.

"We can't go on like this," he says, and I shake.

His hand slides along my side. He hesitates a few seconds before slipping under my shirt, running his hand slowly and sensually against my skin.

I try to repress this weakness that is threatening to strangle me, to make me fall apart here and now in his bed, in his arms.

Ian is touching me. Ian has welcomed me into his house. Ian is giving me the most intimate moment of my life.

Ian is the man I want with my whole being.

He sighs into my mouth and I breathe him in before his mouth pushes against mine, soft and intimate for the length of one breath.

I try to suppress the tears. And yet they fall without my permission. They slide away, caressing my check until stopping at the corner of my mouth.

I'm crying.

And it's not from pain, anguish or desperation. I'm crying from emotion.

Ian is kissing me. He wants me.

He's running his fingers over my curves, his fingertips tracing along the lines of my bones. He rises up along my abdomen and stops under my breast.

A shiver runs down my spine.

I feel the heat, the pressure of his hand, the shape of his fingers that call to me. Desire that can't be held back.

I feel everything. I want to feel it all.

His hand stays still, almost encircling my breast. Then his thumb moves away, pushing down on my nipple.

This time I'm the one who sighs.

He starts playing around, slowly, purposefully and my body freezes. Sucks it up. Wants more. Wants it all.

I instinctively draw my body closer to him and as our breathing synchronises, Ian closes his eyes and stops moving. I touch his lips but he slides his hand away immediately and holds it against my mouth, calming my frenzy. Our accelerated breathing fills the silence.

My chest rises and falls quickly against his. I open my lips and he traces them with a finger.

I stay frozen on his bed, trying to slow down my desire for him to keep touching me. With this need, I'm afraid of feeling everything all over again.

Light, colour, sun, rain.

Desire, loneliness.

Pain.

Me.

He sighs heavily and then backs away, letting me fall back into the darkness. He turns on his side and touches my face with his hands.

"I can't do it," he utters, more to himself than

to me. "It would be a mistake. You don't really want this."

"I... I don't..." I stammer in shock.

"I can't give you what you're looking for. I can't give you anything. No emotion, security or warmth. I take and that's it. I like you, Riley, and there's no denying that I want to fuck you right now, but we'd have problems afterwards. You'd be a problem for me and I don't want to complicate my life."

He turns to me again and finishes.

"You need too many things, but all I can give you is a night of sex, maybe two, nothing more. I'm a bastard, Riley, one of the worst, and I'll never change - not even for you."

He stands up, puts his shirt on quickly and walks away from me.

"Ian," I say, making one last attempt. "Stay." I say pathetically, because I know if he walks out that door now, it'll all be over.

We'll have ended our story right here.

He shakes his head, snatches the keys off the counter, opens the garage door and closes it behind him. A few seconds later, I hear his motorbike disappear into the night, with him and all of my hopes and dreams and my useless heart.

That's how the silence returns. The most painful and oppressive kind. I can't listen to it, it hurts me too much.

I hold my hands over my ears to muffle its cry, pulsing in my eardrums. And that's when I hear it.

The most deafening sound of them all.

The sound of my heart breaking.

39
Ian

Present

I open the garage door and pull my bike out.

"You let me go."

Her voice almost gives me a stroke, making me nearly drop the bike to the ground.

She's sitting on the pavement in front of my house. Her hair flows freely over her shoulders, tousled and she's taken off her shoes, her feet bare on the concrete.

I go to her and extend my hand to her to help her stand up but she refuses, turning the other way.

"That night, at your house. You touched me, you kissed me and then you didn't want me. You really threw me a curve ball."

I take a deep breath, ready to tell her the truth about all these years and my silence, my presence, that night and my insane fear. About what I know I shouldn't have known.

But then what I see in her eyes makes me understand quite instantly that no, I can't risk losing her, not before having given it my best effort. Not before laying myself bare before her. Not before I give her the best I have to offer.

"These years of friendship, being close, moments we've spent together... They were consuming me. I couldn't even think about anything that wasn't you."

I swallow hard.

"I was ready to let you into my life, to let you dig your hands into my past and become part of me."

In her voice, I hear anger, resentment and a lot of bitterness – the same bitterness that burns my stomach now.

"And you told me you couldn't give me anything. That I was a problem you didn't want to have anything to do with. And that's exactly what I expected from you."

She looks at me again and I feel like I'm burning alive in the flames of hell.

"What I felt for you was so intense and terrifying and if I had let myself feel it, if I'd let my feelings show, all the rest of it would have followed it, don't you get it?"

I nod. My legs are shaking.

"I was confused, scared, but I knew what I wanted. I really wanted it. Despite everything. But you destroyed what was left of my heart, instead."

Fucking idiot.

"After that night, I couldn't feel anything other than my immense loneliness. I was ready to be swallowed up into nothingness. I cancelled everything, I cancelled myself too and thought that I would sit in that emptiness forever. And then I saw you. Just a few minutes at the hospital was enough for me. Just to hear your voice was enough for me to set foot in your house again, and I thought that maybe all wasn't lost, that we might be able to try again..." she whispers weakly, and I realise what a genuine bastard I've been, that I didn't consider for a moment what she might have been thinking in that situation, about her internal struggle.

"And when we were together... I panicked. I felt crushed, I didn't have enough air. It was so... it was too much. You wanted everything and you wanted it right that minute because that's how you are. You're a taker, Ian. You demand things."

"It's not like that. I'm not that man, Riley, not anymore. I could never be that man with you."

"You left me," she cuts me off.

"What?" I asked confused.

She gets up and gathers her shoes from the floor.

"You said you wouldn't have done it."

I look at her intensely because I don't know what she's talking about.

"And I believed you," she looks at me harshly for a few seconds. "I trusted you. I believed what you said and I thought you might be different," she concludes, turning and walking bare-footed away from me.

I watch her walk away, unable to speak or rationalise, or do anything at all that would demonstrate to her that I'm not a complete arsehole. Before she turns the corner, I run after her, grabbing her shoulder.

She looks at me again with the same harsh expression on her face, before I pull her to me and she hides her face in my neck.

A year ago, she begged me to stay. A year later, I'm the one begging her not to leave.

"I'm sorry," I whisper into her hair. "For everything."

She tries to wriggle away but I tighten my grip on her.

"Please don't leave like this."

She pushes me away, putting her hands on my chest and stepping back a few paces.

"You're confusing me! I don't know what to think, if it's right, if we could ever have—"

"Everything, Riley, you can have it all."

Me. You can have all of me.

"What are you looking for? What is it that you want?"

"You. I only want you."

"I don't believe you."

"You are the only thing I want. I wanted the same thing a year ago and I want it now, more than ever."

"I'm not strong enough for this. If everything were to go back to how it was, I wouldn't be able to bear it alone."

"You don't need to," I tell her, taking her hand and squeezing it slightly. "You don't have to go through anything alone, Riley."

"You don't understand. It hurts me. Everything

hurts me. It hurts to eat, to sleep, to remember. Some days it's hard for me to breathe."

"Then on those days I'll do the breathing for you," I tell her, smiling at her and letting my thumbs slide down to her cheeks.

"You don't really think that."

"I can stand anything, but only if you're with me."

"I'm a mess, Ian."

I take her face in my hands and I speak to her with my heart.

"You're *my* fucking mess."

Because that's the way it is, I always knew it had to be her. And I won't let her go anywhere until I've given it everything I've got.

She has to know who I am, what I'm willing to give and how I am able to love. She needs to understand that she can just be who she is with me, because that's all I want.

"We can start from scratch. Me and you, together. Nothing forced, no rushing things. Nothing that you aren't ready to face."

She looks at me suspiciously.

"One night, with me. You'll tell me everything you want to and I'll do the same. We'll be honest with each other. We'll be ourselves. We can try it just once. And if after that you don't want me, then I'll disappear."

I see the doubt in her eyes but I know that she's about to give in.

"Tomorrow night, I'll come by and pick you up at seven."

She thinks about it for a few more seconds before saying: "With what, that thing?" pointing to my motorbike.

I can't hold back my smile.

"You know where I live," she concludes, before turning away and walking down the street.

40
Riley

I look at myself again in the mirror as I hear him parking in the street. I take a deep breath, then exhale. I'm nervous and worked up, as if this were a first date. Let's just say that's what it is; it's useless to call it anything else.

I open the front door and Ian is standing there, proud and confident in his white shirt under a leather jacket, his unkempt beard and crooked smile.

"I'm early."

"I'm ready."

I take the keys and my bag and close the door behind me.

"Everything okay?" he asks behind me.

I nod and walk the few steps over to his motorbike. He hands me the helmet and gets on, extending his hand to me which I accept. I place mine in his, feeling its heat rising, and my heart goes wild. Now I just want to get on the bike without humiliating myself.

"Hold on tight," he says, before doing a U-turn and pulling out onto the street.

I hold onto his waist, not too tightly or too loosely. I slide my hands under his jacket, over his shirt, and I feel his muscles contract at my touch. I sit straight up against his back, grabbing onto his chest and abandoning myself to this feeling of peace, to these new healthy emotions – I'm aware it could destroy me, but I don't want to give up this opportunity, not before seriously hurting myself.

We head towards the city centre, merging into traffic on O'Connell Street. Ian turns down an alley where I see a spot for motorbike parking.

He turns off the engine and gives me his hand once again to help me get off. I take off the helmet and give it back to him before running a hand through my hair to smooth it back into place.

I look up and catch him staring at me.

"What?" I ask.

He shakes his head and puts away both of our helmets. "Nothing."

"Weren't we supposed to be honest with each other tonight?"

"Jesus, Riley, you're... you're... shit."

"That doesn't sound like a compliment."

He bursts out laughing, then he comes closer and squeezes my waist with his hands.

"I don't know how to tell you without sounding like an idiot, but you're the most real and beautiful thing I've ever seen in my life."

I lower my gaze in embarrassment.

He takes my chin in his fingers and lifts it so that we're eye to eye again.

"I just wanted you to know. But if it makes you uncomfortable, I swear I'll shut my mouth and stop talking."

I smile again as my cheeks go aflame.

He lets me go, slowly.

"Th-thanks," I stutter.

"Are you hungry?"

I nod.

"Let's go," he takes my hand.

My eyes drop to observe his gesture.

"Alright?"

"I think so."

"I swear that will be the only contact we have."

God knows why, but his words leave me with a strange, bitter disappointment.

* * *

We go into Flanagan's on O'Connell Street. Ian gives his last name at the desk and the manager is all in a fluster when he realises who he has in front of him. I smile in embarrassment while Ian signs an autograph for him, then he informs us that our table will be ready in ten minutes and suggests we sit at the bar.

We sit on some stools that are way too high for me, so much so that I struggle to clamber on, while Ian sits calmly beside me with his feet resting comfortably on the ground.

I order a glass of white wine while he gets something non-alcoholic, and we toast for no apparent reason. I swallow half a glass in one gulp under Ian's watchful eyes, making me sit a little straighter.

"I don't drink that much," I say, feeling the need to justify myself.

"I wasn't judging you."

I set the glass on the counter. "I don't have a problem."

"I didn't say you did."

"Excuse me, sir, if you'd like to follow me…" the waiter interrupts us to escort us to our table. We bring our glasses with us.

"I'll be back in a few minutes," he adds, handing us the menu.

Ian thanks him and opens his as I stop to admire him. Intensely and persistently. I look at his hands, the tattoo on his wrist, the leather bracelet that wraps around it, his muscular arms and his powerful shoulders. His face, his full mouth, that sexy beard that…

"Something wrong?" he asks, waking me from my daze.

"Er, what's that?"

"You were staring at me."

"That's not true," I lie, gluing my eyes to the menu. Ian sets his menu on the table and crosses his arms over his chest.

"Weren't we supposed to be honest with one another?"

I also set the menu down and look at him sheepishly.

"You're a really handsome guy."

He laughs so heartily that everyone turns around to look at us.

"But now I think you're a real, fucking..."

"Hey! Since when do you use these words?"

"Since I started hanging out with you," I cross my arms too.

"Oh yeah?" he flashes me a crooked smile sending my heart into palpitations.

God, that busted lip makes him even more...

"You're doing it again."

Are you serious?

"Sorry."

"Don't joke around. You can stare at me as much as you like and for as long as you please."

I'd be happy not to look at anything else for my whole life.

"Riley..." he starts, but then doesn't say anything.

My name vibrating on his lips is enough for me - full of meaning and passion and desire. His deep, penetrating eyes are enough for me. His crooked smile is enough for me.

A few withheld breaths are enough to make me understand that this won't be a one-time thing.

41
Ian

I don't finish the sentence, there's no need. I think my body is speaking clearly enough because every muscle, nerve, tendon, vein or drop of blood is tensed even more than when I'm on the field.

Being close to her is impossible without jumping on her, touching her, tasting her, having her...

One-time thing, my arse.

The waiter thankfully comes to my rescue. I order spicy chicken wings with a side of potatoes, then a grilled steak with vegetables and she orders just a Caesar salad. A pang of nerves hits me suddenly.

I try to not let it show, to seem calm and comfortable but inside, I want to smash the room to pieces.

"How's the training coming along?" she asks innocently. "You still have that busted lip and that cut on your forehead."

I touch my lip instinctively as she sighs, biting hers.

So, I'm not the only one here having problems.

"Same old shit," I say, playing it down. "It's all part of the job."

"Of course, I know."

What an arsehole. Obviously she knows.

"I was scared, when you seemed—"

"It was nothing," I cut her off. "I'm fine, I'm right here in front of you. And... I'm not going anywhere."

She smiles slightly as the waiter brings us our starters. She dresses her salad and starts playing with it but I can tell she has no intention of eating it.

"Riley?"

She looks up at me.

"I can't help worrying."

"You don't have to. I'm fine."

"That's the first lie anyone tells themselves."

"Okay. I'm not fine, but I'm better than I was. Yeah, better."

I watch her as she gathers her courage.

"Sometimes I just want to forget. It would be so much easier."

The anger goes right to my hands. I grip the edge of the table to avoid punching a wall.

"I would be different – maybe I'd even be enough for someone like you."

It's all too much. I let go of the table and extend my hand to her. I grab hers and squeeze it hard. Riley looks up quickly.

"Don't you ever think that, or say it. You're simply perfect. I don't give a damn about the past and know that it's not going to change things."

"You don't know that."

"I know what I feel when I'm with you, when you're here, when I think of you, when I think about holding you and what I felt when I was inside you."

Her face reddens all the way to her ears.

"If I hadn't been an unbelievable arsehole, if I'd had you in my house, my bed, I would never have let you go. I never would have let you leave. I wouldn't have let you feel lost and alone. I wouldn't have given you up for any reason in the world and I don't want to give you up now. I don't think I've ever wanted anything in my life the way I want you."

She looks at me with her mouth slightly open.

"Sorry," I say, taking my hand back. "I shouldn't have. I don't want you to think I'm only saying all of this because I want to get between your legs."

"Really? Isn't that what's happening here?"

"Well, clearly it is – I mean, have you seen yourself, Riley? Do you have any idea how beautiful and sexy you are? Christ, since I saw your body, since I first touched you, I can't think about much else."

She bites her lip nervously.

"We said we'd be honest. Well, that's how I feel. If that scares you, I'm ready to take a step backwards, even to go away for a while if it makes you feel better, because the only thing that matters to me is that you're okay, that you get a chance to take your life back in your hands. With or without me."

We sit in silence for a few minutes and the only thing I can hear is my heart beat beating mercilessly.

"I like you, Ian O'Connor," she says suddenly. "I like being with you."

"Is that a good thing?"

"I'm not sure yet," she replies honestly. "I'm going to need some time to figure that out, but it would be nice if you'd stick around in the meantime," she concludes looking at me hopefully.

"I told you before, Riley, I'm not going anywhere."

She smiles, taking her fork and pointing to the chicken on my plate. "Do you mind?"

I stop breathing.

I don't need to breathe anymore.

I don't think I need anything at all anymore.

"You can take anything you want."

42
Riley

Pulling up outside my house, we get off the motorbike and take off our helmets. I hand him mine, smiling as I go towards the door, searching around for my keys in my bag. When I try to put the key in the lock, I realise that my hand is shaking, then I feel his warmth on my hand, helping me open it.

I turn to him slightly. "Thank you."

"I had a good time with you tonight, Riley," he whispers coming closer to me, putting all my senses on high alert.

He kisses me gently on the cheek and I shiver with emotion.

"I'd invite you in but..."

He shakes his head. "I can't set foot in your house."

"It's not *that* bad."

"No, Riley, it's not that. Why do you think I care about the house?"

I look at him, not understanding.

"I can't come into the house with you," he says, taking a lock of my hair. "I wouldn't be able to keep my word. If I came in with you, Riley, I wouldn't be able to resist - I'd jump on you and I'd consume you with my hands, my mouth, my tongue. I'd make you mine again and again and I don't know if I'd be able to stop."

My body pushes against his instinctively. He lets go of my hair and brushes it back over my shoulder.

"But I don't want you to think that's the only reason I'm here. I want you, Riley. All of you."

"I-I don't know what I think," I stutter.

"Don't pretend with me. Don't hide what you're feeling."

"It's not that simple," I say, as he shakes his head. "I learned how to fake things years ago, I had to. It was the only way to get through those days."

"What does that mean?" he asks me wrinkling his forehead.

"I understood that I had to pretend. Always. Pretend I was fine, pretend to be intact even if I was broken inside because no one wants anything to do with half a person. No one wants to see what you really are. The truth is scary. Pain is scary."

"I'm not afraid of your pain, Riley. I'm not scared of seeing your demons. I'm ready to face them and defeat them with my bare hands. I want to be clear with you about that, I don't want you to have any doubts about it."

"It's not easy for me to believe you," I tell him truthfully.

"I know, but I'm asking you to try. Try putting some trust in me."

Seeing Ian O'Connor standing at the door of my house, in all his charm and determination, with that body calling to me, with his sweet sexy smile and the sincerity of his words: I have no choice but to believe him.

"I'd like that," I say, smiling at him.

He smiles too, then gets serious again. "I'm trying, Riley. To go slowly, to respect your space. To do what's best for you, believe me. But what more can I do if I believe that I'm the best thing for you?"

He looks at me intensely and my heart melts at his feet.

"It's damn difficult."

"I'm sorry."

He sighs in frustration. "It's okay like this. For now."

"I should go in now."

"Yeah. I have to go too. I've got training tomorrow morning."

"Goodnight then, Ian."

"Goodnight, Riley."

I close the door and rest my back against it.

I hear him start the engine and drive away, and I try to slow down my breathing.

I go in the kitchen, take off my jacket and put down my bag on a chair. I open the fridge and grab a bottle of wine. I let the cold glass sit in my hands for a moment before putting it back, deciding to make myself a cup of tea instead.

I bring the mug through to my room and set it on my nightstand. I get undressed slowly, put on my trackies and sit with my legs crossed, hugging the mug between my hands.

The house is silent, the street outside quiet. I don't hear any noise, but I can't let myself be swallowed by the emptiness.

I don't feel pain. I don't feel the need to pretend, to smile if I don't feel like smiling or to think about what to say or do.

I'm me, with all of my chaos, but with my mind firmly set in the present, standing tall, with a heart that's ready to start beating again.

43
Ian

I pull into my driveway and park my bike. I walk into my living room and almost have a heart attack on finding Nick on my sofa.

"What the hell are you doing here?"

He shakes the sleep off and sits up.

"Hey, where you been? I waited for you all night."

"I didn't know I was supposed to keep you updated on where I am at all times. What are you doing in my house?"

"I stole the keys from Ryan."

"I see you two keep picking on each other – do I need to ground you both?"

"I just needed a bit of peace. And you still haven't found me a place to stay."

"So it's my fault."

"You're the one who made us come back."

I go to the kitchen and put the kettle on to make myself a cup of tea, even if what this situation really calls for is one of those relaxing brews that Mum used to drink before going to bed. My nerves are already wound up and my body is on high alert after having been with Riley. Of course what I really needed tonight was Nick.

"So, what are you going to do?" I ask, turning

towards him.

He ruffles up his hair. "I don't know."

"What about the team?"

"They don't need me for now."

"You out too?"

"Not exactly. Let's just say they've given me some time."

"Some time."

"To do what I need to do."

"You giving up with this whole dumb modelling thing?"

"What should I do, Ian?"

"Play the game. You weren't bad."

He forces a laugh and comes to sit at the kitchen counter opposite me. He steals my mug and takes a few sips, wrinkling his nose.

"Haven't you got anything stronger than this?"

"I have training tomorrow morning."

"Oh yeah."

"Want to come with me? I don't think coach would mind."

"I don't know, it would be kind of awkward."

"It wouldn't hurt. You're getting a little chubby."

He looks at himself a minute and then goes back to drinking my tea. Why the hell is he drinking it if it's so damn disgusting?

"I don't think I need to, by this point."

"You're not going to play again?"

"I'm thirty-two, Ian."

"That's only two years older than me."

"And I've been out of the loop for a while now."

"You also still have a contract."

"A pro forma contract."

"Got it."

"I had to."

"You had other choices."

"Not after someone decided to steal my place on the team."

"Nick, come on…"

"Okay, okay. I'll knock it off."

"How's Ryan doing?"

"Why don't you ask him?"

"Because he doesn't talk about himself. He's an O'Connor."

"He's terrible. Worse off now than when he left."

I run my hand roughly through my hair. Why does nothing ever go right around here?

"How about you?"

"Huh?"

"How are you?"

"That's none of your fucking business."

He shakes his head. "You're an O'Connor too."

I really wish that were true.

* * *

Fifteen years earlier

"Here," Karen shows me to a bedroom. "This is Ryan's room."

I look around suspiciously. It's the room of a child that wants to show the world he's already a man. Posters of rock bands on one wall and muscular rugby players on the other. This guy still hasn't figured out which side he prefers.

"Ryan, say hello to Ian," she prompts gently as he lifts his hand in a small wave. "We've got an extra bed here. Nick and Ryan used to share a room before Nick moved to the other room above the garage. You know how it works, everyone wants their own space."

I don't know how it works. I didn't even have a room. I practically lived on the sofa. Our apartment had one bedroom and it belonged to my mother.

"At the end of the hallway, there's a bathroom. You'll find clean towels if you'd like to have a shower," she adds kindly. "And then," she hands me some clothes. "These are Nick's, they might be a bit big for you, but for tonight they'll do."

I nod in embarrassment.

"Well, I'll leave you to it. I'm going to make you something to eat. What would you like?"

I look at her, completely baffled, taken aback

by all the attention she's giving me.

"I don't know, eggs and bacon, or pasta, or maybe a sandwich?"

I have to hold back the knot that is trying to choke me. "Anything is okay."

"Oh," she comments uncomfortably. "Okay then, I'm off. When you're ready, just head downstairs, I'll be waiting. Take your time and if you need anything, ask Ryan."

She turns to leave the room.

"Thanks," I say through clenched teeth.

She looks at me and smiles.

She is smiling. Honestly.

A mother who smiles. I thought they were a myth.

She leaves me alone with this little kid, who's sitting on his bed with a worried look on his face and a very straight back. He looked like someone who wanted to scream 'What the hell are you doing in my house?' or 'How come I have to share my bedroom with you?'

I turn towards him as he looks me over, head to toe. I'm wearing jeans that are caked in mud and water, a hoodie and old beat-up trainers that have definitely done some damage to Mrs. O'Connor's carpet.

"So," he says, lifting his head. "You're staying here."

"Just for tonight," I say flatly.

"Yeah, right," he says raising an eyebrow.

"You're not a psychopath, are you? You're not going to cut me up with a chainsaw tonight?"

"I don't have a chainsaw with me," I say, winding him up, but he doesn't appreciate my sense of humor.

"Well, I sleep with the light on."

He wants to be a tough guy but his red cheeks betray his embarrassment.

"No problem."

"Better to be clear about it."

I nod.

"Go have your shower," he says, nodding towards the bathroom door. "You really need one."

I leave the room and walk down the hall, scrutinising the doors, trying to work out which one is the bathroom.

"It's the last one on the right," Ryan says from behind me, his arms crossed. "And you can use my shampoo," he continues in a whisper. "It's the green bottle. Don't use Nick's, whatever you do. He'll make you drink it for breakfast."

In that moment, in the bathroom doorway of a house full of strangers, surrounded by kind people who act the way they do purely because they want to, I don't know if I should cry, laugh or thank God that I've got another shot at living.

44
Riley

Present

"Riley?" Ray pops his head into my office with a smile that goes from one side of his face to the other and a smirk in his eyes. "There's someone here for you."

"For me?" I stand up and join him at the door, where the sight of his shoulders fills up my eyes in an instant.

"Do you have something to tell me?"

"Not now."

"I don't know if I can wait. Maybe I should just ask him."

"Don't you dare," I growl through my teeth.

Ray smiles broadly before turning his attention back to Ian. I hear him say that I'll be right there and then he pretends to disappear behind a column.

God, he's so obvious.

I try to compose myself, pulling the pen out from behind my ear and letting my hair fall freely on my shoulders before taking a breath and walking over to him.

"Hi," I say, shyly.

He flashes me a sexy smile. "Good morning."

All he said was 'good morning' and I'm ready

to jump in his arms.

"I hope you don't mind that I stopped by?"

"I'm glad you're here."

He hands me a paper bag.

"I got you some blueberry muffins."

"Thank you. Do you want to come into my office?"

"I'm just passing by, I'm on my way to UCD."

I nod.

"We're playing tomorrow," he says with an overly-false distracted air. "It's an important game, it's a Champions Cup qualifier."

"Yeah, Jamie told me about it on the phone. He wasn't thrilled to be on the bench for this one."

"I bet."

"But the wait's almost over, right?"

"He'll be playing again soon."

"And he'll go back to being the captain?"

"No one deserves it more than him."

"Thank you."

"For what?"

"For your support, for being his friend."

"What can I do? I love that arsehole."

I laugh, shaking my head.

"I know that the last time you were at the stadium it was a bit strange."

"I was terrified," I say honestly, and he rewards me with a broad smile.

"But I'd love to have you there," he says, full of

confidence. His eyes lock onto mine, leaving me breathless. "If you'd like to, or if you don't already have plans."

"Really?"

"What?"

"You really want me to be there?"

He takes a deep breath. "I want you there," he says with a tone that is both full of confidence and begging me at the same time.

"VIP seating?" I ask, biting my lip.

He stares at my mouth intensely and my body flushes with an unbearable heat.

"Your name is written on that seat, Riley. It's just waiting to be filled."

And I don't know why, but my heart comes alive with the idea that he's not referring just to a seat in a stadium.

45
Ian

I take a deep breath before stepping out onto the field. Today we're facing an important match: the Champions Cup qualifier, where the national coach will be making his requests for the player's roster. I'm not overflowing with hope, I realise I'm getting a bit too old to play, but the dream of seeing my own name on a national jersey never dies.

Today is a day that could have my name written down in the history books and for the occasion, I wanted my whole family to be there, dickhead brothers included.

I wanted her there too.

We huddle up before the first whistle to keep morale high and to plan our tactics. The guys are hyped up and ready to go, but no one is quite as worked up as me.

I've never had anyone there for me in the stands, someone who was really cheering for me, someone who would jump for joy with my every tackle, burst with pride at all of my accomplishments.

Of course, my family has always cheered me on, but now someone's doing it from the heart just because they want to, and not because they had to drive me to training as a kid.

We take to the field and the first thing I do is to look up at the reserved seating, where I know she'll be, because that's her place and no one else will ever sit their arse down there.

When I find her, I smile like an idiot, impaled in the middle of the field. When she stands up and makes a small gesture with her hand, my whole world stops, waiting for my heart to start up again.

How the hell did I come this far without her?

How could I think that what I had before would be enough, that I could go on as I was, without love, that I could get by just on sport, the team and my family?

How could I have been such an idiot?

"Hey," Jamie says jumping on my back and he's lucky I don't slam him to the ground. "We've got an audience today."

"The stadium's packed."

He laughs and hops off my back.

"The stadium...?"

"Fuck off, Jamie!"

"I like it," he says in my ear.

"Huh?"

"I like how you are when you're with her," he pats me on the arse. "And I like what she is when she's with you, even if you're not my idea of the perfect man."

"It's enough for me to be *her* kind of man."

"Wow, it sure took you long enough," Jamie

waves his arms in the air before going back to the bench.

He's getting back into training but hasn't yet set foot on the field. I know how much it pains him to still be sat on the bench and not be able to participate, but he needs to get better to start playing again and avoid any further injury.

I look back once more at the reserved seating section before meeting up with the other guys in the middle of the field. A few seats down from Riley, I see my favorite pair of arseholes, my mum and dad sitting between them.

They're all here for me. All the people I love. All the people I owe my life to. The ones who haven't abandoned me, that have supported me, raised me, fed me and loved me.

The only thing I want to do is make them all proud of me, because they deserve it. It can't be easy taking a hurt, angry young man with no future into your house and giving him a life, a bit of hope and the will to go on.

It's not easy at all. Just about anyone would fail in their attempt, but they did it.

The O'Connors did it.

I couldn't be prouder or more honoured to wear their name on my back.

When I hear my name called over the loudspeaker, along with my number and my image on the big screen, I raise an arm, waving to the crowd as my way of saying: yes, I'm a damn O'Connor, and now I'm going to tear you apart on this field.

46
Riley

This time, I came alone. I didn't even ask Ray to come with me. I took the afternoon off; Ian wants me here and I'm happy to do it.

I sit in my assigned seat, two spots down from a man in a Leinster jersey, complete with matching hat and scarf. As he turns his shoulders, I see the name O'Connor on the back.

I'm overwhelmed with a sense of pride.

Is it right for me to feel this way? To feel connected to him somehow?

I decide not to interrogate myself too much today, to just enjoy the game, Ian and his muscular legs running ceaselessly up and down the field. He seems so fit, strong and determined that I do feel proud to be here cheering him on.

When there's a try, the whole bench jumps to their feet and starts screaming – without expecting it, I find myself doing the same. I sit down again like all the rest of them and the man next to me smiles in satisfaction.

"That's my boy," he says and I almost feel faint.

"Yeah, okay. Let's not get carried away with the enthusiasm. There's still time for him to get railroaded like he did last time before the game's up," says the man sitting next to him.

"You don't always have to be such an arse, Nick!" another voice calls from a few seats down.

I listen in confusion at their conversation as a woman stands up and impatiently changes seats, taking the one to my right.

"You'll have to excuse them. They're like children."

I smile kindly.

"We're all here to watch Ian play," she says, pointing to him. "You see him? Number 11?"

I nod nervously.

"That's our son."

"You could try to at least pretend he isn't your favourite," one of them speaks again.

"Shut up, idiot!" the other one says, standing up threateningly. I recognise one of the faces, partially hidden by his hat.

Oh shit.

"Here we are then," says the older man, leaning towards me. "This is our family. We're the O'Connor's." he says extending his hand. "Everyone, please say hello to—"

"Riley," I say in full crisis, ready for a panic attack.

"Riley," he repeats to himself. "I might have to ask you more than once – don't take offence, my mind plays tricks on me sometimes."

"Do you guys want to shut up so we can concentrate on the game here?" the other one says, standing up and looking towards me. "Ah... hey, wait a minute. It's you."

Everyone turns to look at me.

"That's her!" The other man stands up too.

"She, who?" the mother asks, not understanding.

"Hi Riley, I'm Nick", he extends his hand too, which I accept fearing that I might have lost my mind. "I'm Ian's brother. We finally get to meet."

"F-finally?" I stutter, afraid.

"Would you please explain to me what's going on?" the mother asks looking at each of us for some clarification.

Nick has a sly smile on his face before announcing quite loudly: "That's her. She's what happened to Ian."

47
Ian

The guys celebrate our victory loudly in the changing rooms, and after such a long time, I find myself celebrating with them in my newfound enthusiasm.

"See you later at the club?" Jamie asks, euphorically. "Don't be a dick, we'll be there waiting for you."

"I might stop by."

"And bring her with you, that's an order."

Her.

I hurry to find my phone among my things. I need to hear from her, to share this moment but when I find it, there's a message from Ryan that puts a stopper on my enthusiasm.

"Get home, it's urgent."

I park the bike and jump off it as I search nervously for my keys in my pocket, but as soon as I get to the door, Nick opens it.

"What the hell happened?" I yell, passing him and making my way into the house. I go straight into the living room and her laughter blocks the breath in my chest.

Riley is sitting on my parents' sofa between my dad and Ryan.

And she's laughing.

It's not a smirk or a grin. It's not a smile. She's laughing. Seriously.

And I shake.

My legs, my arms and my hands. My whole body is shaking.

My heart is shaking.

I stand at the entrance of the living room, observing the scene with my heart beating out of control and the feeling that, for the first time in my life, I might be in the place where I belong.

Riley lifts her gaze and meets my eyes. The heat that flashes through me the moment her eyes smile at me makes me understand in an instant that I'm hopelessly in love with her, and can't do without her.

"Relax," Nick whispers in my ear.

"How...?"

"You know what Mum's like," he says, shrugging, and goes over to join them on the sofa.

"Honey, you're home!" I turn to my mother, who is smiling enthusiastically at me. "How come you've kept her hidden from us?"

"I didn't—"

"Oh, it's fine. Luckily your brothers are still good for something," she says sarcastically, before turning serious again. "It was about time, Ian. I was getting worried it might never happen!" She touches my face. "Don't let anyone else manipulate your emotions. Leave them free to breathe and you'll see that they bring you wonderful things, like this one here," she says, pointing to Riley.

I nod because I can't say anything, as she gives me a kiss before joining the others.

Riley stands up and comes towards me.

"Hi," she says shyly. "I hope you don't mind that I'm here, but your brothers are a little insane, you know? They've practically kidnapped me. I'm not sure it's entirely legal."

I grab her arm and pull her across the living room towards the front door.

"Okay, now you're scaring me too. You're not bipolar or something, are you?"

I take her face in my hands and draw her to my mouth.

"This. This is your place. Please, don't leave."

She looks at me in wonder and surprise.

"Not unless you ask me to," she whispers before I can pull her lips towards mine again.

I don't touch them. I don't suck them. I don't kiss them.

I love them.

She puts her hands in my hair and I moan into her mouth, pressing my body against hers in the living room.

She doesn't let herself be kissed by me.

She lets herself be loved.

"Er... guys?" Ryan tries to interrupt us, but we don't draw apart.

We can't.

"I just wanted to say… For Christ's sake, Ian, you could have at least waited to get out the front door!"

We don't listen to him. We're not there.

Because now I am hers.

And she is me.

48
Riley

When we sit at the table, I start to feel uncomfortable. I let myself be dragged here by Ian's brothers, who practically shoved me in a car and brought me here. I wasn't sure if Ian would appreciate the whole idea – it seemed like such an invasion of his life – but from how he kissed me before and how he's looking at me now, sitting opposite me, I don't think he minds.

Ryan and Nick are impossible. Everything they say is inappropriate. They're constantly goading one another, winding themselves up. They shoot each other dirty looks and never close their mouths, which I guess helps avoid any awkward silences at the table.

Ian's mother is sitting next to me. She filled my plate to the brim. Meatballs, roast potatoes, broccoli and corn on the cob. There are also Yorkshire puddings on the table, a salad and some salami.

I look desperately at my plate, trying my best but I'm not used to eating this much or being with this many people at dinner. The idea of hiding myself somewhere and making myself invisible starts to take root in my mind. I feel my body starting to get smaller and my hands begin to shake, ready to drop my silverware when a strong, reassuring hand comes down on mine.

"Don't worry, Riley. Karen's used to boys, you know. She always goes a bit over-the-top. Just do what I do, one bite of everything and she'll leave you alone."

Ian's dad is disarmingly sweet. A true gentleman, a father who keeps everyone under his protective wing, someone who oozes warmth and safety.

I nod, feeling a sadness growing within me: I don't know what it means to have a father figure like this.

"So," Nick says, raising his voice. "What do you do, Riley?"

"Nick," his father chides.

"What? Can't I make a bit of conversation? Get to know Ian's girlfriend?"

At the word *girlfriend*, my cheeks break out in flames.

Someone must have kicked him under the table because I see Nick jump before cursing.

"You don't have to say anything if you don't want to," his father says in my ear, and I'm not sure why, but his tone is so respectful and calming that it melts my reservations.

"I work at the Gate Theatre."

"The one on Parnell Street?" Karen asks.

"Exactly."

"I was there once with a friend. What a fabulous place."

"Yeah, it really is," I say with pride, feeling

comfortable once again.

I can talk about my work without getting nervous. And eventually, between forkfuls of food and good conversation, the time goes by pleasantly and I'm able to clear off almost half my plate.

By the time dessert and coffee comes around, I stand up to help clear the table as Ian and his brothers start talking animatedly about the game. To be more accurate, Nick and Ryan don't exactly speak to one another. It's Ian acting as the mediator and the whole thing perplexes me a bit. I'm guessing the other two can't have a great relationship.

I set the plates down on the counter in the kitchen and stop to admire the pictures on the fridge. Ian's mum joins me.

"They used to be cute once," she says, sighing. "Look at them now, insolent pigs looking for a fight."

I smile, looking at her.

"This is little Ryan," she says pointing at one of the pictures. "This is Nick. He's always been a hothead."

"What about Ian?" I ask, looking at the other pictures which seem to be the same two children I've already seen. "No baby pictures of him?"

"Oh honey," she says, squeezing a hand over her chest. "Ian came to us a long time after these pictures were taken."

I look at her, not understanding, and by my expression she realises that she's said too much.

"You didn't know."

It's not a question.

How can he ask me not to leave if he hasn't even let me in?

49
Ian

When we close the door behind us and walk down the path, I can feel that Riley is no longer with me. Something has changed her mood. I lean against my motorbike, take her hand and pull her to me.

"What is it?"

"Mmm?"

"You're acting strange. Distant. Did something happen in there?" I move my head in the direction of the house.

"No, I had a good time."

"Did they embarrass you? Were you feeling uncomfortable?"

"No, Ian. Your family are great," she says, not looking me in the eyes.

I take her chin in my fingers and she raises her eyes to mine.

"It's just so hard."

"What?"

"To understand why some people are like the ones in your family and others…"

I don't let her finish. I take her in my arms and hold her tightly. She rests her head on my chest and lets herself be help.

"Everything's fine," she whispers. "I'm just a

little sad, it'll go away."

"It doesn't have to go away," I tell her as she lifts her head to look at me. "I want you to be yourself. You can be sad when you feel it, happy when you feel it. I want you to tell me everything and trust me."

At my last words I feel her stiffen.

"Is that the problem? You don't trust me?"

"Can I?" she asks and I'm not sure I understand where this is coming from. "Can I really trust you?"

My head is telling me to tell her everything now, before it's too late. Before she hates me and really can't trust me anymore. But my heart... my heart is scared shitless.

"I'd really like you to," I tell her, resting my forehead against hers. "I really would."

Riley sighs against my lips.

"Promise me that you won't ever lie to me. That you'll be honest with me and you'll tell me what you're feeling even if it hurts me."

"Do you really want that?"

She nods.

"I want to take you to mine."

"N-now?" she mutters.

"Right now. I need to have you, Riley. I need to know that you're mine."

"Weren't we supposed to be taking things slowly?"

"I'm willing to wait, to respect your timings. I

am, I mean it. But today after seeing you in the stands cheering for me, and then seeing you in that house..."

"You're pulling out all of your charm to get me into bed?"

"Say yes."

She lets her hands run through my hair and whispers into my lips: "Take me home with you".

* * *

I open the garage door and park my bike. Riley follows, and waits in the middle of the living room as I close the door. The silence plunges down on us. Silence that means waiting, anxiety and desire.

I approach her and slip her coat off her shoulders. I toss it onto the sofa and brush her hair out of the way, uncovering her neck. I kiss it, and feel her shiver. I pull her to me from behind. My hands slide under her jumper. I caress her hips and then rise up to her breasts. Riley rests her head backwards on to my shoulder and abandons herself to my touch.

I'm scared. Seriously. I'm afraid to have her now, afraid that she really is mine and that I might not be able to hang on to her. That she could wake up tomorrow and tell me it was all a big mistake. That she could leave me during the night and I'd wake to find myself alone in a bed of pain.

"Riley," I whisper in her ear before taking her earlobe in my teeth. "I want to be everything. I want you to not be able to breathe when I'm not around. I want you to be unable to even imagine a better place than here in my arms. I want to be the centre of your fucking world and if you don't plan on sticking around, then tell me now before it's too late."

I hold her breasts tighter and she moans loudly, making my erection even harder. I play with her nipples through the fabric of her bra and my underpants are about to explode.

"Ian?"

"What?"

"Everything," she pants. "I want to feel everything."

I pull my hands back and grab her by the shoulders, spinning her around. I lift her up as she wraps her legs around my waist, squeezing them and I push her up against the wall.

I kiss her.

I breathe her in. I breathe her panting and all of her desire; I breathe her lips and her tongue, that plays sensually with mine. I breathe her in, her body that is burning up under my hands as I run my hands under her jumper again, looking for her breasts. I torment them, squeeze them, I want them. I pull away from the wall and take a few steps towards the counter where I sit her down. The memory of our first night together pounds painfully in my head, but the desire to have her again is stronger and more devastating.

I leave her mouth just to pull off her jumper

and she frantically takes off my jacket. I grab my shirt and pull it off, throwing it to the floor.

Riley sighs, her eyes full of desire. She bites her lower lip on seeing my bare chest.

Shit. I'm going to devour it.

I take it between my teeth and then suck on it anxiously, searching for the clasp to her bra. I let it slide down and toss it over my shoulder, before leaving her lips and throwing myself onto her chest, hungrily. She arches her back and puts her hands in my hair as I torment one of her nipples and press my hard erection against her legs.

Riley's moaning pushes me over the edge.

My hands run down her abdomen and when they arrive at her waist, I undo the button on her jeans, half crazed as she takes off her own shoes. She lifts her buttocks so I can pull the jeans off of her completely.

Seeing her in her wet panties, my need to lose myself in her takes control.

I touch her and she grabs onto my shoulder.

"I want to feel you," I whisper in her ear. I slide her panties to the side and slide a finger into her.

She stifles another tormented noise.

Her heat surrounds me, making me want more – much more.

"I want to taste you," I tell her, and I feel her body tingling.

I push her back on the counter so that she's propping herself up on her elbows. I look into her eyes and I can see a shadow of embarrassment tinging her desire to live in the moment.

"It's just you and me," I tell her, touching her skin with my lips. I give her little kisses all the way down until I get to her panties. I gently remove them and toss them to the floor. I caress her legs and rest them on my shoulders.

I can feel her eyes on me the moment my tongue touches her inner thigh.

"I just want to have you. All of you. I want to feel it all." I exhale against her pussy as my dick pulses between my legs.

I kiss her, slowly feeling her tingle at my touch; I slip my tongue inside her and she arches her back.

"Ian," my name comes out as a suffering sound and she instinctively tenses her legs.

I raise my eyes and let them do the talking for me. They tell her how much I want her right now, and how impatient I am to give her everything a woman like her deserves. To be the first and only man to make her understand what it means to be loved more than anything else.

And a moment later her taste is in my mouth. My tongue slides over her and I moan into her as her body quivers with desire. My hand runs over her abdomen, inviting her to lay back and just give herself to me completely. I push her legs forward and lift them. She is open before me and her taste is everywhere.

I hear her panting and quivering.

I feel her in my hands.

I continue to play with her with my teeth and my tongue, as her body resigns itself to my invasion. I let go of one of her legs so that I can feel her with my fingers too.

My tongue on her. My fingers inside her. I am overwhelmed with desire to have her now, just like this, all for me. To have her trust, her body and all that she's willing to give me.

She puts her hands in my hair and pushes me against her.

She wants more. She wants it all.

And I'm here to give it to her.

I push my fingers all the way inside as I go on sucking her swollen clit, excited by her taste and hungry for her skin.

I feel her shaking against my face and her grip on my hair tightens before she lets out a liberating yell that vibrates all over my body.

I get up quickly over her.

"I told you, Riley. I want it all," I pant, my heart racing a mile a minute, before picking her up in my arms.

I bring her to the bed, where I'm going to give myself to her completely, and love her without reservation.

50
Riley

He lays me down on the bed, my body quivering. He undoes the button on his jeans and slides them down his legs. His does the same with his underwear as I stand there, watching him, short of breath. I watch his muscles contract, the veins pop on the back of his hands, in his arms, his shoulders and his neck. I look at the tattoos that cover his side, his abs and the V-lines that run below it. He rests a knee on the mattress and comes dangerously close to me. His dark, burning eyes tell me he's ready for me, and I, in my silence pregnant with desire, respond to his request, willing to let him have his way with me.

He bends over my body, resting an elbow next to my head while his hand runs over my curves. He comes towards my mouth and runs his tongue along my lips. I can still taste myself on him and, turned on by it, I open my legs instinctively.

He slides his tongue into my mouth taking everything with him - my breath, my fear, my insecurities and my pain. Ian takes it all, but I don't feel empty.

This is exactly how I want to feel.

Desired. Wanted.

Loved.

His tongue is bossy and so are his kisses. So are

the bites he gives me and his hands that run over me. Everything about him is screaming 'you're mine', and just thinking about it, I feel the excitement growing in me like a wave lapping against my body.

Ian makes his way between my legs. He moves slowly, rubbing his cock against me.

"Do you have any idea how I felt, Riley? Feeling you this way... God, I want to do it all over," he pants against my skin as he slowly moves down to my breasts.

He circles my nipple with his tongue. He tickles it and then bites it. I arch my back, and once again reach for his hair. Another bite and I'm pulling on his hair again, invaded by pleasure. He takes me between his lips and looks dangerously at me.

"I want to know what you like," he whispers seductively against my chest. "Tell me what you like, Riley," he comes back up towards my face to capture my lips in a kiss and take my breath away.

Then he grabs my shoulders and squeezes, me then rolls over onto his back, pulling me on top of him. He runs his thumb along my lip, then speaks again.

"I'm here for you. Tell me what you want."

He grabs me by the hips and sits me on top of his hard erection.

I let out a cry.

"Do you like it like this?"

I nod.

"You have to tell me, Riley. Do you want me to take you like this?" he says moving his hips against me.

"Yes," I cry.

I feel him pushing inside me as I grab onto his body.

"God…" he says between his teeth, pulling me down onto him, hard.

"Now take everything you want, Riley."

His request helps me let go, to ride him without inhibition. I move over him. Ian's big hands caress the length of my back, glistening with sweat. He pauses on my butt cheeks, moving in a rhythm that allows me to set the tempo.

The feeling of having this power over him liberates me from every reservation I take his shoulders, inviting him to come closer to me.

"Is this how you want me, like this?" he asks me, embarrassing me. "It's me, Riley. Don't hide from me." He tightens his grip on my bottom. "Look at me. Don't leave me."

I put my hands in his hair and pull him to my mouth.

"I'm here," I tell him, speaking against his lips before capturing them with my teeth.

Ian moans and I tighten my grip on his hair. He pants against my skin and I feel his beard rubbing against me. Then he bares down on me, taking one of my nipples in his mouth. I throw my head back and continue to move, sitting on top of him, helped along by his hands pushing against my hips as the heat rises quickly between my legs, ready to be rocked by another wave of pleasure.

He rises to whisper in my ear. "Come for me."

And I do it.

I yell his name. I cry out and break myself onto him.

Ian yells a few seconds later, squeezing me tightly, with his face in my neck.

And he breaks himself onto me.

We stay as we are for a few minutes, lost in breathing against one another, then we put ourselves back together.

I'm inside him and he's inside me.

Ian stretches out, bringing me with him. I lie on top of him as he caresses my back with his fingertips running along my spine. Then he lets me slide off of him so that I am now under him and he covers me completely.

"Tell me that everything's okay," he says seriously. "Tell me that this time no one's going to run away or regret this or lose their mind over it."

I look at him and smile. "None of those things are going to happen."

He exhales and caresses my face with his hand.

"Riley Murray, you're breathtaking, you know that?"

My heart swells in my chest,

"You're not so bad yourself."

He laughs, rolling onto his back and bringing me with him. I lie down and stretch out alongside him, resting my head on his chest. I caress his pecs, his shoulders and his arms. I hear him sigh every time I change the movement.

"Do you want to know what I really like?"

He turns his head to look at me better. I raise my gaze and let myself be taken in by the warmth in his eyes.

"This. You and me."

He exhales deeply as if he had been holding his breath this whole time.

"I'm begging you, please don't leave me in the middle of the night."

And in this moment, with his eyes as sweet and melancholy as I've ever seen, Ian O'Connor takes my heart and I know he'll never give it back.

51
Ian

I turn myself on the bed, stretching out my right arm and when I feel the cold sheet there, I sit up right away.

My heart beats wildly in my chest and the agony of solitude rushes at me.

I take my head in my hands and close my eyes with the hope that I'm just having a nightmare, that I'll wake up soon and find her clinging to me just as we had fallen asleep together a few hours earlier.

A noise coming from the kitchen stirs me. I jump off my bed with shaking legs and a racing heart.

God. I see her.

She's still here. Riley is standing there. In my kitchen. In my house. In my life.

She's moving around the space, taking two cups and opening the fridge. She's wearing a shirt. *My shirt.*

I go to her, trying to calm my breathing down.

"Hey," I say but she doesn't turn around.

I move her hair and bite her neck. "What are you wearing?" I ask into her ear.

"I found this shirt on the armchair, hope you don't mind."

"I do mind."

She tries to turn to me but I hold her firmly in place. "I don't like how it looks on you."

I slowly unbutton it and let it slide off of her, slipping from her shoulders, and I see her shiver.

"There we go," I say, touching her shoulder. "That's it. I prefer you like this."

She laughs. The sound of her laugh fills my entire world.

"You prefer me with nothing on."

"No." I place my hands on the counter, trapping her. "I prefer you with me on."

I rub my hard dick against her butt.

"Ian..." the sound vibrates sensually on her lips.

"Tell me how I survived before, without all of this."

I squish her against the counter, my erection pulsing.

"Tell me that I won't have to do without it."

"Never again," she says, before pushing her hips backwards, an invitation I don't resist a second more.

I grab her by the hips and a second later I'm inside her again. A deep thrust and she welcomes me in a tight grip. I extend myself over her and overwhelm her with my body, which seems to have been designed just to hold hers. My hands slide down her arms, looking for hers. I block her against the counter and push. I bite her shoulder, then her neck and then let go of her hand and I take her face, pulling it towards me. I lick her lips before suffocating her moans with my mouth. Her cry mixes with my breathing. I push inside her, I push against her body. I grab her breasts and hold them as I penetrate her again and again.

I feel her completely in my hands, I feel her running through my veins, my soul and my heart.

Riley is everywhere.

I let her merge into me as I continue to push inside her and take what she's willing to give me. I rub her clit with my fingers and my name escapes her lips.

"Ian..."

"What?" I breathe on her neck.

"Don't stop."

"I wasn't going to."

I go on touching her and moving inside her with long, deep thrusts that make her arch her back towards me. I lift her up and hold her to my chest. I want to feel her skin, her heat, her shivering, her desire. On me.

Her body crushes against mine, her hips going against my thrusts, her pussy tightening around my cock.

Her. Mine.

I feel her quivering against my hand and I accelerate my movements until I feel my dick explode with pleasure as her screams melt together with mine.

I fall onto her, leaning on her sweaty back, still shaking from the orgasm that almost bent me in two. I lift myself slowly, keeping her pulled against me. I hug her to my body tightly to show her how desperate I am to have her next to me, always.

When she turns to look at me with her red cheeks and messed up hair. I feel overwhelmed with tenderness. I lift her and take her in my arms, bringing her back to my bed. I lay her down and I kiss her. Slowly, sweetly and desperately. Then, I pull away from her and caress her face. Riley bites her lip. And damn it, she shouldn't have done that.

I suck it in my mouth instinctively between my teeth before letting it go.

"Stay here," I tell her. "Don't move."

"Where are you going?"

"To make breakfast, and we'll eat it here, in bed."

She smiles cheekily. "I like eating in bed with you."

I smile back.

"I like eating you."

52
Riley

I put the phone down and take a sip of coffee. It's eleven a.m. and I'm already exhausted. After all night with Ian, I hardly have the energy to breathe.

He brought me back home, I took a quick shower and then I ran to the theatre, late and a little dazed after having the best sex of my life.

He really wanted me. He wanted my body, my mind and my soul. My breathing and my moaning. He wanted me to want it as badly as he did, and to let myself go to him, in every way.

With him, it's different.

Ian is different.

He's strong, proud, ridiculously sexy and passionate.

Ian takes everything. But he gives it all back to me.

I don't think I've ever felt so desired, so desperately wanted. I felt like the centre of his world and I have to admit that I like being there.

My mobile rings on my desk. I look at the number and smile happily.

"Hi," I greet him.

"Hi. How's your day going?"

"Full and stressful. How about yours?"

"Sweaty, with lots of exercise." I flush with warmth. "I'm at the gym, I just took a minute to call you."

I smile even wider.

"I've got plans tonight, a dinner I have to go to. Do you want to come with me?" he asks hopefully.

"I'd like that," I reply, without hesitation.

"Great. I'll swing by and pick you up at seven."

"Perfect."

"We're going to borrow Nick's car."

"The car? How come?"

"It's a gala dinner."

"Oh," I say, a bit shocked.

"Is that okay with you?"

"Er, yeah."

"Okay, see you tonight."

"See you."

"Oh, and Riley?" he adds before hanging up. "Last night? I can't stop thinking about it."

I smile as I end the call, feeling emotional and anxious because I was just invited to a gala dinner and God knows I don't have anything to wear.

I need to take a break, to run to Grafton Street and I need Ray. Right now.

* * *

Ian gets out of the car and walks around to the opposite side. He opens the door and takes my hand. I accept it and set my high heel on the tarmac. He helps me out, pulling me towards him.

"God, Riley," he sighs heavily, closing his eyes.

"What is it?"

"Have you seen yourself, by any chance? How the hell am I going to make it until the end of the night?"

"I d-don't understand," I stutter.

"Do you have any idea how stunning you are?"

A knot forms in my throat.

"You're just... you."

I think I could burst into tears.

He rests his forehead against mine and breathes in next to my lips. His hot breath gets lost in the cold night air but it does manage to warm up my nerves.

"Are you ready?"

I nod and bite my lip.

"Hell no," he says, sighing heavily. "Don't do that. Not tonight."

"What?"

"What you just did."

I look at him, not understanding.

"Don't bite it, Riley or I might not be able to answer for myself."

My legs quiver and a heat radiating from down below makes its way north.

It's going to be a long night.

* * *

When we get to the hall at the Sheraton, two well-dressed men take our coats and another leads the way through to the dining hall. I follow Ian, holding tightly onto his hand. I'm nervous and out of place – I've never been to anything like this before.

Before entering the room, Ian bends down and comes close to my ear.

"Everything's going to be fine. Just don't let go of my hand, okay?"

The doors fly open and we're hit full-on with the music, the flashes of photographers and people pushing forward wanting to shake Ian's hand and tell him how much he's appreciated.

Overwhelmed by the situation and feeling exposed, I freeze at the doorway, stopping Ian in his stride.

He stops and turns to me, worried.

"What's wrong?"

"I wasn't expecting all this."

He gives me a crooked smile. "It's nothing, just a bunch of crap."

"A bunch of crap?"

"I have to be here."

"I've never been to anything close to this, Ian. I feel so uncomfortable."

Ian pulls me to him.

"This is exactly your place, okay? Trust me."

He slides his hand down my bare back and my body responds to his touch. "I want you with me."

"Hey! There's the star of the moment! You're keeping us waiting," a familiar voice says from behind us.

Ian sighs and breaks away from me.

"Hi dickhead," he greets his brother Nick. "Who invited you?"

"Good one…" he says, letting his gaze fall on me. "Holy shit," he exclaims, running a hand through his hair. "Everyone will have something interesting to talk about tonight."

"Shut your mouth," Ian growls menacingly.

"Riley, you're—"

"Knock it off!"

"I just wanted to give her a compliment."

"Don't."

"I see we're already at the cuddling and hugging stage," Ryan says joining us. "Riley…" he says by way of greeting, bowing to me.

"Do both of you really need to be here?" he asks with fake harshness.

Ryan shrugs. "Are you kidding me? We're family. We had to be here."

"Are they all here?" I ask, looking around.

Nick and Ryan look at me as Ian replies: "My parents couldn't be here tonight. My dad's not in great shape."

"Oh," I say bringing my hand to my mouth. "I

hope he'll be better soon," I continue, sincerely sorry about it.

Ian nods without replying to me and his mood changes a bit.

"O'Connor!"

We all turn around.

"Jesus, mate. It was about time! I was starting to lose hope."

"Fuck off, Jamie."

"Hey! Not in front of my sister."

Jamie comes over to me, takes me in his arms and lifts me up.

"I'm happy to see you here, even if it took Ian O'Connor to convince you."

"Don't be jealous," I tell him as he sets me down.

"I'm not. Okay, maybe I am a bit. Just promise that when you come to the next match you'll look at me too."

"Maybe…"

Jamie exhales deeply before leaning over and whispering in my ear. "You okay?"

I nod.

"Stay calm, it's just one night. And as long as you stay with Ian, everything'll be fine. Alright? Enjoy this moment." He pulls away from me and takes my hands. "You really can't imagine how amazing it is for me to finally see you here."

I feel the emotion closing my throat but try to keep it cool.

"I'm about to make a comeback," Jamie says. "The doctor gave me the green light."

"Oh Jamie, that's fantastic!" I hug him tightly.

"I couldn't stand sitting on the bench any more without kicking their arses."

"Cut it out, okay?" Ian interrupts.

Jamie smiles again, truly happy.

"Come on, let's go," he says to Ian. It's time for the group photo. I'll have him back to you in just a few minutes, Riley."

"No problem, Ian, I'll take care of her," Nick puts a hand on my back, inviting me to follow him.

"I'd rather she went with Ryan," Ian says, glaring at him, coldly.

"Don't be an idiot, Ian."

"I'm not. How about you?"

They look at each other a few seconds before Ryan grabs my hand. "Come on Riley, let's go find a seat."

I follow him as Ian nods in the direction of a round table with ten people at it. Ryan pulls out the chair for me and helps me to sit down. I look at the table and pick up the little notecard resting next to my glass.

Riley Murray.

It's my name. I smile spontaneously.

Ryan leans in to my ear. "They're going to announce the teams soon."

"W-what?"

"The official draft."

"I don't get it."

"The national team, Riley. Ian got called up to represent Six Nations."

I sit there with my mouth gaping open, completely incredulous as Ryan grins at me.

"Didn't he tell you?"

I shake my head.

"He's an O'Connor," he says, sipping at the champagne that has just been served. Then he looks at me seriously. "Don't hurt him, Riley. Okay? Just... don't do it."

I open my mouth to reply but someone grabs a microphone, setting the evening off and announcing one by one the names of the players on the team. I sit there with my eyes on the stage waiting to make eye contact with him. I'm short of breath and straining my eyes.

When he sets foot on stage, he looks out towards the banquet hall and I feel a sense of pride together with something else. Something that maybe shouldn't be there, but is.

Ian stands proudly in his perfectly-fitted tuxedo with a look in his eye, a sexy smile firmly planted on his face that's enough to make my legs quiver.

And when his eyes find mine, burning me with their warmth, I understand that for the first time in my life I am exactly where I am supposed to be.

53
Ian

When I go to sit down after the official presentation, the group photos, and going through a receiving line shaking hands and patting backs, I find Riley talking animatedly with Ryan.

I stop for a minute to watch them, and hope it might be the first step for him to stop hating the world, for him to maybe start trusting people again – especially the female half of the population.

Riley notices me standing over Ryan's shoulder, so I join them taking my place next to her on the opposite side.

"Everything okay?" I touch her hand.

"Why didn't you tell me?"

I shrug. "It wasn't such a big deal."

"What? You're kidding!"

I take a sip of champagne.

"Ian, it's amazing. I'm so proud of you."

And I don't know why, but after hearing it from her lips, I start to feel the same way.

The night is long, full of good food, alcohol, conversation and some frustration, seeing as I now have Nick sitting next to me and Ryan three seats down.

They've barely exchanged two words all night, and when they did it was to threaten one another. It's giving me a headache. I wonder if they'll ever give it a rest.

"So, you're the oldest," Riley says to Nick curiously. "Do you play, too?"

"He used to play," Ryan interrupts, chugging the rest of his drink.

"Doesn't seem like you're in a better position than I am."

"It's better to be on the bench than not to play at all."

"Look, I'm still on the team."

"Sure Nick, let's go with that."

Nick gets to his feet, but I gesture for him to stay calm. He sighs and sits back down, throwing back another glass of wine.

My bow tie is starting to choke me, so much that I want to just take it off altogether – along with this bloody tux – because I've had just about enough of this dinner, my brothers, people hounding me and not being able to feel Riley's skin against mine.

The background music starts up, inviting people to dance, taking advantage of a pause between courses. Riley places a hand on mine, waiting for me to lead her to the floor.

"You know I don't dance."

In her eyes I see the reflection of the night we met and my stomach starts burning.

"I'll dance with you, Riley," Nick interrupts.

"Don't even think about it."

"I just asked her to dance, Ian," Nick replies seriously. "I'm not what you think I am. I'm much more than that."

Feeling guilty for how I attacked him, I nod as he stands up and offers Riley his hand.

"May I?"

She accepts and stands up, confused by our conversation, and follows him onto the floor. I keep an eye on them to make sure that Nick keeps his hands to himself or I swear I'm going to kill him with my own.

"Are you sure about this?" Ryan asks over my shoulder.

"I think it's time to trust him a bit, don't you?"

"Are you serious?"

"Nick made a mistake."

"A mistake…"

"People screw up, Ryan. But life goes on and we hope to be forgiven."

"Are you still talking about me and Nick?"

I don't answer him.

"You're going to lose her."

I sigh in resignation. "I know."

Ryan decides not to push it any further and I decide to let go of the weight I'm carrying for a second and to concentrate only on what's happening on the dance floor.

Nick takes Riley in his arms and I squeeze my

glass tightly in my hands.

Nick puts his hand on her bare back and I feel something dangerous bubbling up in me.

Nick spins her and makes her laugh.

"You're an idiot," Ryan says to my shoulders. "What the fuck are you still doing here? You don't want to make the same mistake twice."

Fuck, no.

I storm over to the dance floor. Riley freezes when she sees me, while the music keeps going. Nick realises something's wrong and turns around.

"Listen, I was just—"

"It's not about you. It's about me."

Nick gives me a crooked smile and bows to her bending his arm at his waist and giving me her hand.

I take it and pull her in to me, as she slams up against my chest.

"I thought you didn't dance," she smiles cheekily, running her hands slowly down my chest.

"I let you go once before. I'm not going to make the same mistake."

"Well, at this point I could say you've repaid me your debt."

"I'll always be in debt to you."

I don't believe that an entire lifetime would be enough for her to forgive me, for me to pay her back and give her what she deserves.

I caress her bare back. "Have I already told you

that I don't like this dress?"

She looks at me with one eyebrow raised.

"Nope. In fact, I think I'm going to take it off as soon as we get home."

"Home?"

"Do you think I'm letting you go anywhere? Do you think I'd be able to drop you off at your apartment with a goodnight kiss and then go home alone with my dick as hard as marble and a head full of perverse fantasies?"

She stifles a laugh.

"I'll tell you what's going to happen. As soon as this song ends, I'm going to take you away from here. I'm going to take this outfit off of you with my teeth and then I'm going to do the same thing with your underwear. I'm going to lay you down in the middle of my bed and I'm going to taste you again."

I rub her back and touch her earlobe as she quivers under my fingers.

"And then I'm going to have you sit on top of me and you'll feel very clearly how much I want you. Until you've had enough of me."

"And what if I haven't had enough of you?"

"I was really hoping you wouldn't."

The song ends and I do exactly what I told her I would. I take her away from there immediately. I don't say goodbye to anyone. We get in the car and head home. I don't let her set her foot down. My mouth is already on her. I take off her outfit with my teeth, and then her bra and panties and I lay her down on my bed. I kiss her, I bite her, I lick her as she pulls my hair begging me for more.

She yells.

Jesus Christ, does she yell.

And then she yells again, as she sits on me and takes what she wants. And then she yells again, when I turn the situation around and I suffocate her with my body. And she keeps yelling in my head when she falls asleep on top of me. Her hair on my chest, our legs entwined and our hearts inside one another's.

54
Riley

"There's someone here for you."

Ray pops his head into the store cupboard while I'm trying to drag out some Christmas decorations.

"For me?" I ask, a big box in my hands.

"She's waiting for you in your office," he says mysteriously before disappearing.

I bring the box with me – it had to go to the entrance anyway. It's almost Christmas, and even though we'll be closed for a few days, the theatre should be decorated properly. I'm not crazy about Christmas, I don't have any amazing memories, but people like a holiday atmosphere and I do what I can to keep the place up to expectations.

"Karen? What are you doing here?"

"I was in town and thought I'd stop by and say hi."

"Good, I'm glad." I set the box on the desk and brush my hands on my jeans. She hugs me affectionately, then she lets go.

"Have a seat," I say, pointing to a chair. "Can I get you something to drink?"

"Oh no, thanks, I'm just passing by..."

I sit down across from her.

"I love this place," she says, looking around.

"I do too."

"It seems like just the place for you."

I smile. "Thank you."

"Do you like what you do?"

"Very much," I light up. "Sometimes I still can't believe I work here. I got lucky."

"I'm sure you deserve it, dear, and even more."

"That's kind of you to say."

"I know what I feel and what I hear. Ian never would have set eyes on you if it weren't like that."

Her words are embarrassing, but at the same time leave me inexplicably happy.

"To be honest with you, I also stopped by to ask you something."

"Sure thing, what is it?"

"What are you doing for Christmas?"

Her question catches me off guard.

"Er, I really…"

"Will you be spending it with your family?" she asks cautiously.

I take a deep breath. "We're alone, it's just me and my brother."

Compassion shadows her face.

"I'm fine, Karen," I reassure her. "It happened a long time ago."

"I'm sorry, dear."

"It's in the past."

"The past never stays in the past. It's part of us and follows us right until the end."

I lower my eyes.

"I'm sorry, I didn't mean to upset you."

"You haven't."

"So...?"

"I don't know, Karen. Thank you for the kind offer, but I'm not sure it's the right thing to do."

"I'd be really happy to have you with us - and I know Ian would be even happier." She smiles, knowing she's said the right thing.

"I'll think about it."

"You can bring your brother."

"He's not crazy about Christmas. He prefers to just let it go by, unacknowledged."

"Oh, poor guy."

"We've been doing it that way for years."

"I understand, but I'd like you to try something different this year. I'd like you to spend it with the *family*. With us."

I barely hold back the tears as Karen squeezes my hand tightly.

"I'd better get going."

"Did you come to town by yourself?"

"Yes, I took the bus in. Nick's at home with his father so it's nice to get out. It's best not to leave him alone. We never know how his days are going to turn out."

I look at her wrinkling my forehead.

"Well, I'm off – hope to see you at Christmas then."

I walk her towards the exit. I hug her and then open the door and let her out. I go back to my office, confused by our conversation and with the growing sensation that I hardly know anything about Ian.

This situation is making me very uncomfortable.

* * *

"So, will you come?" Ian asks me later, as we're sitting on my bed.

He came over after training with two shopping bags full of stuff to eat. He cooked for me. Chicken tenders with mushrooms and baked potatoes. And then he brought two slices of lemon cheesecake. I limited myself to preparing the tea which we're sipping now, leant against the pillows.

"Would you like me to?" I ask, looking up at him.

"Are you seriously asking me that?"

"I don't want it to seem like too much."

"Don't talk crap."

"It's your family, Ian. I have nothing to do with them."

"You do have something to do with them, Riley, always."

"Jamie prefers not to celebrate, anyway. I think he's going to meet up with a few other players who aren't going home for Christmas."

"You can't be alone."

"I like your family, it's just that…"

"Come with me, Riley. I want you there."

I sigh.

"Two days with the O'Connors. We could even stay there and sleep in my old bedroom," he whispers suggestively in my ear.

"We can't do it in your parents' house, Ian."

"Oh yes we can. Of course we can."

He takes the mug out of my hand and sets it on the nightstand. Then he comes back to capture my lips in a passionate, boiling kiss before letting his hand fall between my thighs.

Oh yes, we can.

Of course we can.

55
Ian

"You're all wound up."

"No, I'm fine."

"Riley…"

"Okay, maybe a bit."

"But you've already been here."

"I know, it's stupid of me, but Christmas always puts me in a bad mood."

I squeeze her hand and kiss her forehead.

"I'm sorry."

"It's not your fault."

She rests her head on my chest and I inhale deeply through her hair. "It'll go well, you'll see."

The door opens behind us.

"You're here," Ryan greets us.

From the look on his face, I can tell he must be in a really bad mood. I break away from her and go inside. Ryan grabs my arm at the door.

"It's not a good day today."

I nod, clenching my jaw, and go in the house, taking off my jacket and helping Riley with her coat. We head to the kitchen where my mum is fiddling with the oven.

"Hey guys, it's great to see you," she says, hugging Riley. "Both of you."

"Where's Dad?" I ask right away, worried

about what Ryan said.

Mum looks at me with sad eyes that make me want to put my fist through a wall.

"He's in the living room."

I leave Riley to chat with my mum and go through to the living room. Dad is sitting in an armchair, reading the sports pages of the newspaper. When he notices me, he lifts his eyes in confusion. I sit in front of him in silence, waiting to see what kind of turn today's going to take. He goes back to looking at the newspaper and after a few seconds says: "Do you follow rugby?"

I clench my fists.

"Every now and again."

"Leinster is doing well this year."

"Yeah," I say, smiling bitterly.

"Both in the Pro12 and in the Champions Cup. I think they've qualified for—"

"The quarter finals," I say, helping him.

"Sunday they're going to play against Zebre. Ha, those poor Italians – they have no idea what they're up against."

I smile.

"They've got this player, the one that just got called up to the national team. Number... er, 11, yes, number 11. What's his name?"

I open my mouth to answer him, but the air gets blocked in my lungs.

"Ian O'Connor," says her voice from behind me, as her hand runs slowly down my arm. "His name is Ian O'Connor," Riley repeats as I grab her hand with all the desperation in my heart.

* * *

"The house is simply stunning, Karen," Riley admires the tree that dominates the living room, reaching from floor to ceiling.

"Thanks, dear," my mother hands her a glass of wine and smiles before going to check up on my father.

I go over to her anxiously, aware that I need to say something, to explain and apologise for not having told her about my family's problems. I hold her tightly around the waist and rest my chin on her shoulder.

"I should have told you."

"Would you have? If I hadn't come and figured it out for myself, would you have told me sooner or later?"

"I don't know," I say honestly.

"I'm sure you have your reasons for not telling me but I'd be happy knowing you trusted me."

"It's not that easy."

"It's not easy for me either, trusting someone. But I'm giving it a try."

"It's just that they're my problems. I'm not ready to share them yet."

Riley stiffens in my arms.

"And it seems like you haven't been completely

honest with me, have you?"

She pulls away from me to look me in the eyes.

"Well, maybe this thing between us isn't the greatest idea, Ian," she says seriously. "We're both closed in behind our walls and I don't let you in and you don't let me in. There are no windows or doors. I just wonder sometimes what we're doing," she concludes, before leaving me standing there.

I look at my father in the armchair and my mother next to him. She speaks to him, caresses him and reassures him – and he lets her. Despite his confusion, he trusts her even if he doesn't know who she is at times. He trusts her blindly. Maybe their love is stronger than any illness. Stronger than anything.

And maybe what Riley and I feel for each other looks nothing like this.

Maybe it doesn't look like love at all.

56
Riley

The mood at the table is tense, not at all like the last time we were gathered here. Everyone is trying to force a bit of cheer and some conversation, a few laughs. Ian doesn't raise his eyes. He's sitting opposite me but he feels further away than ever, as if he's keeping me at a distance – or as if he's just realised that this thing we have isn't wasn't what we thought it was.

I sigh, disheartened as I try to eat a few bites of turkey but my stomach is so full it hurts me terribly, enough to make me feel nauseated.

A loving hand rests gently on my arm.

"Excuse me dear, could you remind me what your name is?"

"I'm Riley," I tell him kindly.

"Riley," he repeats to himself as if he were trying to connect me to something in his mind. "And why are you here?"

"Karen invited me."

He smiles upon hearing his wife's name. "And are you a friend of the boys?"

"I'm Ian's friend."

He looks his children over and then returns his eyes to me.

"You know," he says starting back up to eat.

"Ian came to us when he was 15 years old. He was angry, hurt and suspicious. He wouldn't let anyone get close to him." Without realising, he raises his voice. "They advised us against taking on a boy like him because the wounds in his heart were too deep."

I can barely hold back the tears that threaten to choke me.

"But I – we," he corrects himself, looking at Karen who isn't holding back anything, "We did it. We knew his rage wasn't directed at us, and that his hard shell wasn't because he was bad... I don't know if I'm explaining this well."

"You are," I say taking his hand in mine.

"He was just a boy then, but he's become a man now."

I can feel Ian's eyes on me. I can feel how upset he is, his anguish and his desire to jump across the table and put a stop to the conversation. But I also feel his pain and his need for it to come to light.

"He's been through a lot," he says, shaking his head and drying his eyes. "And no one noticed him, what he was going through. He was left alone in the world and for days at a time lived under the steps at the stadium outside the school. Who knows how long it had been since he had eaten something," he says innocently, shaking his head. "We had our two boys, you see," he points to Nick and Ryan, who aren't doing a very good job of masking their emotions. "But we didn't consider it even for a minute. A look between

Karen and I was enough and our decision was made."

I look at Karen, who is holding Ryan and Nick's hands.

"When Nick brought him home to us that night, cold, scared and lost, something in my heart broke."

That same thing is breaking mine right now.

"He didn't have anything, and we—"

"And they gave me everything," Ian interrupts. "They fed me, took care of me, dressed me and sent me to school. They allowed me to play rugby, to have a house, a family and a life," he says calmly and raising his eyes to look at mine. "They gave me what I needed and a lot more."

I'm tied to him, to his eyes and everything he's telling me without saying a word.

His torment and his pain, that feels a lot like mine.

His desire to open up and his fear of being abandoned again.

His immense heart that is always trying to hide away, instead of letting it show, even though he doesn't realise it.

I stay tied to him, to what I'm feeling, to what I want.

I want Ian O'Connor.

Always.

57
Ian

When I close my bedroom door behind me, I find Riley looking out the window.

"Hey," she says, turning to me. "Everything okay down there?"

"I put the kids to bed. Hopefully they won't try to suffocate each other in their sleep."

She smiles sadly at me and looks outside again. "I think it's going to snow," she says after a few minutes of silence.

I go towards the window and set my hands on her shoulders. "That would be nice. A white Christmas."

"It would be nice," she echoes, sighing.

"Riley, about what happened…"

She shakes her head and walks away, going to sit on the bed. I let my arms fall by my sides and ball my fists, staying where I am.

"It's not easy for me to talk about it," I start, aware of the fact that it's now or never. If I don't do it now, I will seriously lose her.

I asked her to trust me and not to hide from me, and here I am doing the opposite.

"I came to this house when I was fifteen and it was Nick who brought me to them. We went to the same school and were on the same rugby team."

"Why did he bring you here?"

"He'd gone back to the field after training – he'd forgotten his jersey in the changing rooms," I sigh painfully. "He found me under the stairs. I was trying to stay out of the rain. He didn't think about it for a second, he took my arm and brought me to his house."

I feel her eyes on me but I don't have the courage to turn and look at her.

"I was living with my mother in a flat in Ballymount. Small, mouldy and claustrophobic. I came here to school in Santry. I took the bus when I could and walked when I couldn't afford to."

"And your father?"

"I never knew him."

I hear her sigh.

"My mum had different men," I say, gritting my teeth. "But none of them ever stuck around for very long. Until she met Mike. He and I didn't get along too well. You could even say when he was there, I preferred not to go home."

"Was he violent?" she asks, the fear in her voice palpable.

"No," I shake my head. "Just allergic to children. My mother always looked for men she could lean on, men who gave her nothing - but she depended on them. It's just that she wanted someone to be with her at all times. I wasn't enough for her." I say feeling a knot in my throat. "When Mike left her too, she just gave up. She wouldn't do anything all day and stayed in bed. She was depressed, unresponsive. She drank. I tried to help her, to do what I could, but I was just a kid, you know? I was going to school, I had to study, I did the food shopping, the cooking and was trying to get both of us by on welfare."

"Then what happened?"

"One day I woke up and she wasn't there. She'd left with him. In the middle of the night. She abandoned me. I stayed there alone for a few weeks, until the owner of the building noticed she wasn't there anymore. I was left with no mother, no house, nothing. The night Nick found me was the fifth night I'd slept at the stadium. No one noticed me except for him." I smile despite myself. "Nick's a bright guy, a lot brighter than people think, himself included. His family accepted me into their home without knowing anything about me. They gave me everything, Riley. But most of all, they loved me and helped me to trust people again."

I turn to her.

"When you were telling me your story that night on your sofa... I felt everything. I felt it all. Your loneliness was already mine. Your soul was already chained to mine. That night, Riley, you took my heart. I saw you for what you were and what you were trying to hide from me, because I saw myself in you. I saw and felt all of it, as if it were happening to me. It was a tie between us. Something that you only feel once in a lifetime. I knew it from the first day. I always knew you were special. You were the only person that could give me what I was always missing. But I was scared that I would never be enough for you and that one day you would leave me. I couldn't have gone through that again. And that's what would have happened if that night…" he shakes his head. "I was convinced that you would've left me. Everyone leaves, it's just a question of when. The day I walked into this house, I decided that I would stay alone. It was my choice, you know? I had to defend myself then, had to defend myself against you. But you seeped everywhere like a spilled glass of water, and I couldn't avoid it. You were dangerous and I had to protect myself, so I let you go before it was too late for me; I swore to myself that I wouldn't ever get in so deep again. But when I saw you again… everything came charging back. What I felt for you, my fears…" I say gritting my teeth trying not to give in. "If I hadn't had the O'Connors, what would my life have been? They adopted me. I was almost 17 when they gave me their name. Can you believe it? They took in a perfect stranger – a potentially dangerous boy who was angry at the world. Who would have done that? And now my father doesn't even recognise me half the time—"

She stands up from the bed and throws herself into my arms. I hold her up as she wraps her legs around my hips. I bury my face into her hair and breathe in deeply.

She's still here.

"You've become a wonderful man, Ian O'Connor," she tells me, squeezing me tightly. "Your family is proud of you and I'm even more proud."

"Don't go, please. I couldn't bear it."

And she kisses me. Sweetly.

She takes my lips in hers and gives them life. She loves them. She puts her hands in my hair and pulls me to her and the kiss becomes more passionate.

Her tongue in my mouth, her hands on me and her…

Her. Everywhere.

58
Riley

He squeezes my hips and pulls me to him.

"Make love to me."

He looks at me with frightened eyes.

"All I'm asking you is to make love to me," I tell him, already short of breath, my heart beating wildly in my chest.

He brings me towards his bed without tearing his gaze away from mine. I unbutton his shirt slowly, then let it slide down his arms. I run my fingers along his skin and he watches intently. I scratch his back with my nails before he pushes me to the mattress and presses his body onto me.

I wrap my legs around his hips and feel his stiffness through his jeans. I let myself moan a little as his tongue runs along my neck before catching my lips in one of those kisses that takes your breath away.

He unbuttons my shirt, looking me in the eyes. There's a sweetness there that's tinged with his desire - two emotions are battling it out inside him. On one side, there's his desire to have me, and on the other, his will to feel and taste everything along the way.

He sighs onto my breasts. He caresses them with his face, lips and tongue before taking my bra off and using his hands on me.

He doesn't bite. He doesn't mark his territory.

There's no need.

He lets his hands slide down my abdomen and stops at the button on my jeans, opening them with an unnatural slowness before sliding them off of my legs. I lift myself up to undo his button and when we're both completely naked, he lays over me again, breathing onto my lips.

He caresses my thighs and slides his finger inside me.

"Ian," I exhale his name.

"Riley," he whispers against my skin.

He moves inside me as he continues to hold my gaze, transmitting everything he feels for me in this moment.

Desire, passion... and love.

Ian is loving me.

He's giving me everything he has.

And I want to give it all back to him.

The first wave of pleasure bends me in two. Ian has to suffocate my yell with his hand so that the entire house doesn't hear us. When my breathing becomes regular again, he removes his hand and we both laugh.

And then he loves me, again and again.

Ian O'Connor loves me.

And I... I love him.

We wake up in the morning with a lightness in our hearts. I am on my stomach with my hands under the pillow as Ian caresses my back with his fingertips.

I keep my eyes closed, enjoying this moment of pure intimacy, his delicate touch and the shivers it leaves along my spine, as he slides up the same spine leaving a trail of wet kisses.

He ducks under the covers and grabs me by the hips, turning me to face him. He holds me by the buttocks as he draws me to his mouth. I feel his breath and grip the sheets tightly the moment his tongue enters me.

His movements are slow and deep, his teeth biting and his mouth calling to me.

Ian moans and my entire body quivers. Ian breathes and my mind races. Ian loves me and I let myself be loved by him.

Heat rises in me and I pant, waiting for the pleasure to strike me again.

His hand runs slowly over my skin and I bend at the orgasm exploding between my legs, unable to suffocate a yell that vibrates through the room. I slowly loosen my grip on the sheets and cover my face with my hands.

Ian comes back up my body, kissing every centimetre before popping out from under the covers with a cheeky smile. He comes to my face and captures my lips with his teeth.

"Good morning," he says with a face I'd like to smack.

I look at him with a raised eyebrow.

"What?" he asks with fake innocence.

"I definitely woke up the whole house."

He laughs, enjoying it, before giving me another kiss. Then he stands there, looking at me for a few seconds before I realise why he's concerned.

"I'll do it," I tell him, stroking his beard.

His face lights up hopefully.

"I don't want to force you to tell me about something that hurts you, Riley. But I'm sure that it will help you: I'm here now, and you won't have to go through anything alone."

I smile, grateful to him. "I know."

He slides out of bed and stands up, goes to the window completely naked. I bite my lip, trying to control my desire for him to take me again.

Then he turns to me and extends his hand.

"Come and see."

I get up too, also naked but confident as his eyes devour me. I go to him and look out the window. The ground is covered in snow.

"Oh my God, It's beautiful!" I say, observing the white blanket that covers everything.

"Really and truly," he whispers onto my skin before sliding something around my neck.

"What?" I look down.

"This way, everyone will know that number 11 is yours," he murmurs into my ear.

I turn and he sits on the windowsill.

I take the chain he gave me, the number '11' charm in my hands, moved by the gesture.

"Merry Christmas, Riley," he says, kissing me.

"You got me a present," I say feeling stupid and childish, "But I..." he stops me with his mouth.

"This is the best present you could give me. You and me in this house together..."

I wrap my arms around his neck and my legs around his waist.

"Mine?"

"Hell, yes," he exhales deeply against my neck before biting it.

I'm naked, exposed in front of the window: and couldn't care less. The only thing that matters is the look in his eyes the minute I grab his erection tightly in my hands. I squeeze it and feel it pulsing.

I rest my back up against the cold window as I let him inside me. I let myself be invaded by him, by his body and by the love that he is willing to give me.

Because Ian O'Connor gives.

He gives himself.

And I want all of it.

And only with him.

As I fix my hair into a ponytail in front of the mirror, Ian surprises me by hugging me from behind with his strong arms.

"Are you ready?"

"For what?" I ask, turning to him.

"To go kill my brothers."

Everyone is awake downstairs. Ian's mother has made breakfast which everyone is shovelling down, before running outside like crazed children. We all put on hats and coats, boots and gloves and head outside.

The light that greets us is blinding. There's a blanket of white clearing the air, the sky is clear too and so are our hearts.

Nick pelts Ian in the back of the neck with a snowball. Furious, he runs after him, ready to knock some sense into him.

I laugh at the scene. I laugh because I'm happy. I laugh because Ian O'Connor is wonderful and he's mine.

"Don't ruin everything," Ryan says coming closer to me.

"That's not the plan."

"Women always say that."

"Are you mad at me by any chance?" I ask him, because that's sure what it feels like.

"Not yet, and I hope I won't have to be in the future, either."

Ryan walks off, and leaves me with a strange feeling inside.

I'm annoyed at being accused of something; but then Ian raises his eyes and gives me a goofy grin before hitting me mercilessly with a snowball.

No, Ian O'Connor. That's something you should *never* do.

59
Ian

"Did you have a good Christmas?" Jamie sits next to me on the bench.

"I don't think you want to know all the details."

"Jesus, no! I might be open-minded, but I don't want all the details about you and my sister."

I shake my head and stand up to tie my shoes.

"I spoke to her on the phone today."

"Yeah, and…?"

"She was happy, Ian. So happy I wanted to throw up. I haven't heard her like that since… no, what am I saying? I've never heard her like that, ever."

I smile at the idea of Riley finally being happy.

"Have you spoken?" Jamie asks cautiously.

"Er, yes. Sometimes we talk, too," I say, poking fun to take off the dramatic edge.

He looks at me with an eyebrow raised.

"Not exactly," I say getting serious. "She's not ready, but she's promised that she will."

"Do you believe her?"

"Don't have much choice."

"Haven't you tried to bring it up?"

"I don't want to force her. I told her I'd wait and give her the time she needs so she can start to trust me. I don't want to ruin everything."

"Well, that's something. She's not someone to trust people easily."

"I know. Having her trust means everything to me."

"I'm begging you, no more bullshit, okay?"

"That's old news."

"Yeah, but you're still the same person."

"What's your point, Jamie?"

He holds his hands up, defensively. "Don't get pissed off. I just wanted to have a little chat."

"Well, mate, you are starting to piss me off."

"Well, if it helps, you can kick someone's arse out there on the field…"

"Not necessary."

"So, is it serious between you guys?"

"Are you really asking me that? Do you have any idea how much I've kept pushed down inside me all these years?"

"I know, man. Better than anyone else, just like I know she was doing the same."

I close my eyes instinctively.

"Can I ask you a question?"

He shrugs.

"How… How do you do it, Jamie? How can you be the way you are?"

He looks at me seriously for a second and then gives me half a smile.

"You want to know the truth? It's because of

her, mate. She pulled me out of it. She stood by me, she fought for me. She was my strength – and then rugby took care of everything else."

I don't know what to say. I don't see how it's possible for those guys to still be on their feet. I had the O'Connor family, my brothers. Jamie and Riley only had each other.

"I feel suffocated, Jamie. I wish there was some way to talk about it with her, so that she could just let it all go..."

"I know."

I sigh in resignation.

"We're in the same boat: let's try not to drown her."

"Hey dickhead," Nick interrupts our discussion. "You haven't had too much turkey, have you?"

"Who the hell let you in here? Don't you know this is a reserved area? The team meets up in here."

He shrugs with his usual devil-may-care attitude.

"There are no locked doors in my world."

Self-absorbed bastard.

"I just came to tell you that we're all here. Me, the arsehole and Riley."

Just hearing her name, my stomach does a few somersaults.

"They're waiting for me in the bleachers. Mum and Dad stayed home. They're a bit tired out after

Christmas."

"Not hard to believe, with you two hanging around."

"Speaking of that, I wanted to let you know I might have found a place."

"It was about time."

"Nothing fancy, just an apartment in Northwood."

"In Northwood?" I look at him, narrowing my eyes.

"Yeah," he says a bit uncomfortable. "I wanted to stick around close to home."

"Seems like a good idea."

He nods with a serious expression.

"Your being around is important. I can't make miracles, but if we all do our part, it'll make a difference."

"Hope so," he says, sighing heavily. "I move in in January but I have to take care of a few things first. I'll be gone for a few days."

"What is it, another photo shoot?" I say making fun of him.

"Fuck off, Ian!" he turns and starts to leave.

"Hey, Nick!" I stop him. I dig around in my bag in search of something then turn back to him.

"Could you give this to Riley?" I hand him my keys.

"Oh shit," Jamie declares. "This is serious."

"Shut up!" I say scoffing, before turning my attention back to Nick.

"Tell her I'll be waiting for her. *At home.*"
"Are you sure about that?"
"I've never been so sure of anything in my life."

60
Riley

Nick drops me off outside Ian's apartment. After having cheered him on like a rabid fan, I find myself here, holding the keys to his house, ready to leap into the darkness – or, rather, ready to leap into his arms.

I lift the garage door with some difficulty then close it behind me. I take my jacket off and look around with both my heart and my stomach upside-down, feeling very emotional and a bit anxious because he wants me here. He really wants me in his life. He wants me in his family, in the stands and in his bed. He wants me in his past and his present and I want to be all of his future.

I didn't think I'd really be able to do it, to feel emotions without the past influencing my every breath. I still don't really feel like myself, but I feel like I am able to build something new and healthy. I know I'm still in pieces, as if I've been run over by a lorry, leaving my body a shell full of dust, but I'm still here.

I'm broken, but still in one piece.

I imagine it'll take Ian a while to get home so I decide to make myself a cup of coffee and maybe read the online show timetable to see what's planned for the New Year. We've also got a new show coming up, something important, and I want to check out our competition.

I grab my coffee and wander about the house looking for a computer - I think I saw one in Ian's room a few nights ago. I walk around the bed and find it on the desk. I sit down on the stool and open it up. I turn it on, and after a few seconds the screen saver appears. As I'm about to press the button for the internet my eyes fall onto a file on the desktop.

'Fucking Bastard' is its name.

I bite my lip and drum my fingers nervously on the table. I know I shouldn't open it, that it would be an invasion of his privacy, but something pushes me to do it.

I click on it with my fingers shaking and the folder opens.

My heart beats wildly and my throat is so parched that I can't get down even a sip of my coffee, but my fingers and my eyes move of their own accord, spurred on by a sensation stemming directly from my stomach.

Fucking Bastard. It thunders in my head, strong, so strong it could fracture my skull. I look over the content frantically, every sentence that I read showing me that this is exactly what I think it is.

Photos, information, research.

My life.

My entire life in a folder on Ian's computer, and now flashing in my face.

But it's not seeing my past before me that hurts. It's not reliving the emotions again, like this, and all in one place.

The garage door closing makes me jump up, but I don't turn around. I hear him coming towards me. Heavy steps, suffering steps.

Guilty steps.

"Please, let me explain."

I shake my head, overwhelmed.

"It's not what it looks like."

I get up, knocking over the stool as Ian reaches his hand out to me.

"Don't come near me!"

"Just let me speak, okay?"

"Tell me how long you've known."

"Don't be like this, Riley."

"When you slept with me…" I say, shaking.

Ian is frozen, not moving.

"You knew it then, didn't you?"

His jaw clenches.

"My God," I bring a hand to my mouth. "You pitied me."

"What? No!"

"You slept with me because you pitied me."

"No!"

"Don't lie to me!" I say pointing my finger at him.

"I swear to you, Riley."

"Now I understand everything." I let my head

fall into my hands. "Your rejection a year ago and your sudden interest now."

"Fuck, no!"

"What were you trying to do, put me back together?"

"My God, Riley…"

"Maybe my brother convinced you. Maybe you guys are in on this together."

"You're upset, you're not thinking this through… you're making a mistake."

"I don't believe you! I don't believe a single word that comes out of your mouth! How… how could I have trusted you?! All that bullshit, all those words. It was all a load of crap, all of it!"

"You can't really believe that, Riley."

"I don't believe anything," I say in resignation. "Starting today, you're back to being that fucking bastard, Ian O'Connor. The only one there is."

61
Ian

I'm frozen in place, my hands knotted into fists, short of breath and wanting to bang my head against the wall until it splits in two.

"Riley," I say, moving close to her as she takes two steps backwards.

She crosses her arms and hides, like she always has. We're back to square one.

"How many other things have you lied to me about?"

"It's not that simple."

"Well, why don't you explain it to me then?"

I try to grab her arm but I stop the moment I realise that Riley has already decided. She's already issued the sentence and all I can do now is ask how much time is left before she puts the key in the door and walks out on me.

By this point, there's no sense in lying about it. Riley's feet are already out of the house. Out of my life.

"I've known for weeks."

She is silent.

I hear her breath, her confusion and her guilt, but I don't feel her heart.

"Jamie spoke to me about it. He was worried about you, he told me you've never faced it, that you've refused therapy, that you keep pretending it didn't happen."

"He was in on it, then."

"No, he has nothing to do with it. He thought he was helping you."

"Yeah sure, making you pity me!"

"Stop saying that."

"And Jamie's little chat with you wasn't enough for you? You wanted all the gory details?"

"Please, don't be like this…"

"Those photos," she says pointing at the computer.

The photos of her face after the assault.

"They're the hardest to bear. I can't imagine what you went through," I say, before choking on my own tears.

"No," she says, shaking her head. "You don't know, Ian O'Connor. You don't know what it means to live in fear. You don't know what it means to not sleep at night just to make sure you and your brother make it to the next morning. You don't know what it means to pretend that everything is fine, that all that shit will go away some day to calm your little brother, who is scared to death just hearing the sound of his father's voice. You don't know what it means to hide in your own house."

"Not like this, Riley," I beg her.

"What is it? You wanted to know it all but you don't want me to be the one to tell you?"

"I don't want you to do it right now. You're upset, you're—"

"I'm perfectly fine." She lifts her head. "I always have been, or Jamie and I wouldn't be here right now."

She's doing it again. She's building a wall between us. Between her and the world, between her and her feelings.

"Jamie was so…" she sighs. "Jamie is wonderful, he always has been. A good boy, kind, sensitive. Jamie is the only reason for me to live. And I would have done anything for him. My dad had a lot of problems, but his biggest one was his son."

I rest my hand on the counter to help prop me up because I can't do this. I'm falling apart as she stands before me, showing me the strength, once again, that I'll never have.

"Our mother left. Another man. She abandoned her children without looking back. Jamie was three years old," she says, controlling her rage. "She left us with him. Maybe she had no idea what would have happened or maybe she did: it's not something I think about," she says bitterly.

"Our father didn't take it well. He had a bad temper – always did – but this pushed him over the edge, and day by day it got worse. He was an unreasonable hothead, was prone to fits of rage that put the fear of God in us," she says inhaling deeply.

"Never ever a kind word, no affection or hugs.

Just indifference. But Jamie and I were able to get by – he was my world and I could have gone my whole life like that just to watch him grow up. But he was insecure, fragile... He was just a kid that needed to find his path, while my father wanted to raise a tough guy just like him. A bastard. He started taking out all his rage on my brother when he was just eleven years old. Beating him, a lot..." she says, barely keeping it together. "I tried to protect him, to redirect his anger at me, to get in the middle. Sometimes it worked, and Jamie would escape and lock himself in his room as my father took it out on me, and other times..." she says shaking, but stays standing. "According to our father, Jamie was a kid who needed to be shown the right way to grow up. But Jamie was perfect – my dad was the only problem."

"That's enough, Riley, please. None of this is useful now."

"I need to!" she yells, on the edge of the abyss.

I lean over the counter, taking my head in my hands. I was the one who provoked her and set the timer. All I can do now is to sit back and wait for the explosion.

"Jamie cried every night. And if he heard..." she brings her hand to her mouth. "So, I brought him to my room, I pushed the dresser in front of the door and then I held him and kept him safe until he fell asleep. I told him all kinds of stories about how his life would be, about what we'd do when we were finally free, all the wonderful things that would happen to us. I promised him every day that I would take him away from there, and that he'd have the future he deserved. We just had to hang tight a little while longer until I could take care of him. We learned how to hide our bruises, the visible ones as well as the ones only we could see and feel. We learned to pretend, to how keep going, to stay on our feet even if we didn't have the energy. We learned how to survive," she says proudly.

"That damn day, my father saw Jamie leaving a local coffee shop. He was holding a boy's hand. His fury was uncontrollable."

"That's enough," I try to take her hand, but she wants nothing to do with me.

"God, Ian... I could hear the bones crushing under his fists," she says with tears in her eyes; but they don't fall. "I couldn't see anymore, I put myself in the middle and his rage fell on me. I yelled for Jamie to run away, to call for help and I don't remember anything else after that, apart from the pain. I woke up in the hospital two days later. They told me that my father pushed me down the stairs and that I landed on the bottom step. I had a broken arm, bruises, and this," she says, raising her shirt to show me her scar. "An internal hemorrhage. I was saved by a miracle. They took out my spleen."

Right now, the only thing I want to do is hug her but she won't let me near her.

"The worst part of it was that it was the week

before my eighteenth birthday and I could have left without looking back. I had left school, I had already been working for two years and I had a second job my dad didn't know about. I was saving my money just to escape, but things didn't go to plan," she comments bitterly.

"The first time my dad hit Jamie, I tried to call for help. They came to our house and asked my dad all sorts of questions and my father went insane. He hit both of us, he threatened us and locked us in the basement for three days. All it did was make things worse, and no one helped us. So, we tried to stick it out until we could finally leave. You probably think I was stupid, that I should have insisted and asked for help again…"

"No Riley, I don't think that."

"They put Jamie in an institution, Ian. I was in the hospital and they took him away. That's how they helped us," her voice is quivering. "It took me a year and a half to get him out. Do you have any idea what his life was like?" she is yelling again. "That bastard took everything from him and then the system took him away from me!"

"Calm down, Riley. It's all past now. Jamie is fine, you…"

"And me? You want to know how I got along while all that was going on, Ian?"

I close my eyes.

I can't do this. I can't stand it.

"You want to know what I am, Ian?"

"Please," I beg her.

"Homeless, that's what I am. With no family, no house, no money, no dignity, nothing. Invisible to the world. Someone who lives on the street and off the charity of others. Someone who lives in fear and emptiness!"

Riley is yelling again, she's all worked up, on the verge of a nervous breakdown.

"You don't know what it means not to sleep. To always have one eye open in fear that someone might hurt you. Not to eat, unless it was someone else's leftovers. To hide yourself, always. Do you have any idea what it means not to exist to the rest of the world, Ian?"

"Calm down, Riley." I grab her by the shoulders but she can't stay still.

"Calm down? Are you kidding?!"

She tries to squirm out of my grasp but I hold on tighter.

"For everything, Riley. I'm sorry, for all of it."

"You can't imagine the things I've seen," she brings her hand to her mouth. "The things I put up with. The only thing that kept me alive was Jamie. The only thing that gave me the energy to not let go. And seeing the man that he is today helps to go on now. That's the truth, Ian. Did you like my version of it? Do you feel better now?"

"I feel like shit."

She takes advantage of my momentary weakness to break away from my grasp. She takes a few steps back and looks at me. Her eyes are full of unbearable pain. Resentment, hurt pride.

Hate.

She hates me.

"Why dig into it? What were you looking for? You wanted to know more about it?"

"Yes. Fuck yes, Riley!" I yell, also exhausted. "I wanted to know everything because a part of me knew you would never tell me."

"You didn't trust me."

"That's not it…"

"Then what?" she asks, determined.

By this point, she's not afraid of anything.

Not even the truth.

"I wanted to know what happened to him. I wanted to find him.",

"Why?" she asks, but I'm confident she's already reached the answer in her head.

"I wanted to be sure that he would never hurt you again. He would never touch you again."

She brings her hand to her mouth in horror.

"What were you going to do?" she says.

In her voice I feel the accusation, the doubt.

The end.

"I wanted to kill him with my bare hands."

Riley sits back down on the stool.

"You would be capable of—"

"You have no idea what I would be willing to do for you," I tell her with my chest ablaze.

"Are you crazy? How could you even consider

something like that?"

"Don't you get it?! I can't get those images out of my head, your face, the blood, the bruises... I can't bear it! I can't imagine what you..." I cut myself short.

I've said the worst thing I could possibly say.

The silence falls over us.

The pain falls on us.

The end falls on us.

"I knew that you wouldn't have done it," she says, her voice distant. "I always knew it."

I see it. I feel it.

Her heart.

In a million pieces.

62
Riley

I can't feel anything.//
I can't feel my arms, my legs, my body.//
I can't feel my breathing. I can't feel my heart.//
It stopped, or maybe shattered.//
Millions of fragments, which my father is still trampling; or maybe, now, it's Ian.

"That's not what I meant."

I don't look at him. I can't.

"All I meant was… it's too much for one person. No one is that strong. Not even you. And I wanted to help you, I wanted to protect you. In any way."

A flash of nausea threatens to choke me.

"When I found out about it, I did the first thing that came to mind. I went looking for him. And I hired a private investigator. But it wasn't easy. I didn't know that you had—"

"Changed our last name. We did that when Jamie first started to be successful. I didn't want them digging into our past, didn't want anyone to find out. I lived like a shadow for all these years, in fear that someone would connect him to me. He was underage when all this happened. The information is inaccessible, while mine… I just wanted to protect him."

"I understand. You... you did it, you protected him. You risked everything just for him. And I wanted to do something for you. I thought that knowing what I did, if you were to bring it up first, it would be a point in my favour, to face it better prepared. I swear to you, I didn't want to lie to you or hurt you."

His words are lost in my confusion, my spite and in my own stupidity.

By this point, none of this makes any sense.

We don't make any sense.

We're one big, destructive lie.

Ian finds the courage to come closer to me. He kneels down in front of me and tries to take my hands, but I pull them away sharply.

"Don't."

He tries to grab my waist.

"Don't. Don't you ever touch me again!"

I slither away from his attempt to hold me and head quickly towards the garage door. His hand hits the metal hard, blocking my escape.

We're back to the starting point.

"What am I? Your charity case?"

"No, not at all."

"All that crap about trust, respect... God, I was such an idiot!"

I turn to him, my anger building. "Do you feel better now?"

"What do you mean?"

"Now you've done your good deed?"

"What the fuck is that supposed to mean?" he says, raising his voice.

"Bring the poor little girl with no family to your house. Make her believe something that isn't real, give her hope, make her believe that a man like you could really..." I stop to control my voice. "Sleep with me... I should have known. I certainly don't fit the bill of the sort of woman you usually go out with. I'm a problem, the kind you don't want anything to do with."

"Riley, I'm begging you..."

"Do you know why I came to your house that night?"

He shakes his head in resignation.

"My father." She says through gritted teeth. "He was ill. He called me from jail. He wanted to see me."

"What...?"

"And I accepted."

"You went to him?!" His tone is furious.

I nod.

"He wanted to ask for forgiveness. To free himself before he died." I smile bitterly. "And it was... it was like seeing everything all over again. I was confused, overwhelmed. I was destroyed, and I ran to you like an idiot." I close my eyes, trying to control my emotions. "You were the first person I thought of. I was afraid, and I thought being here with you..."

"I wish you'd told me."

"It was a mistake."

"I – Riley, *I'm* the one who made a mistake. If I had known that…"

"What? You would've slept with me then?"

"That's not what I'm saying."

"That's exactly what you're saying. What was it, a big gesture of compassion and pity?"

"What are you talking about?"

"How much did it cost you to screw me?"

"Jesus Christ, Riley, is that what you think?"

"How much did it cost you to pretend, Ian?"

"You're out of your mind right now. It all seems so wrong at the moment…"

"It is all wrong! *We're* wrong! This thing…"

"No, Riley… you are the only thing I've ever done right in my life."

He sets his other hand on the metal. Both of his hands are now at the side of my head.

"How can you say things like that?" I ask him, finding just enough energy to speak. "What am I for you? Something you think you need to fix? Someone to show how big a heart you have?"

"It's not like that, I swear to you."

"Well, I hope it was worth it. Did you at least enjoy yourself a bit?"

"For fuck's sake, Riley!"

"You know what it meant to me to think that I was loved…"

"You are!"

"You can't imagine what it was like for me to think that you really wanted me, in your bed, in your life. Me... just me."

"And you don't know what it meant for me to have you," he breathes onto my neck.

"You're nothing more than a fucking bastard, Ian O'Connor."

He punches the metal next to my head and I try to make myself as small as possible.

"Christ, no! Do you think I'd be able to take you with me, that I would have loved you so..." his hand touches my face and I close my eyes instinctively. "Riley, I'm—"

"Don't you dare!" I yell in his face. "Don't you dare say it!"

"Please..."

"Let me go."

"I can't," he says, closing his eyes and coming dangerously close to me. "I can't forget," he whispers on my lips.

"Let me out of here!" my voice is filled with fury.

"Please, don't disappear from my life." His is full of desperation.

"I'm already gone, and I wish I'd never been a part of it."

63

Ian

I let her go. I let her lift up the garage door and slam it behind her so hard that the windows and the walls shook.

I let Riley leave my life in the same way she came it, messing up my whole world.

I fall to the ground and punch the metal repeatedly. I let the emptiness consume me and have its way with me. I have nothing else. I'll never have anything else, not if she takes it all away with her.

I went behind her back. I just wanted to know everything and know it right away. I wanted to fix things, fix her life, to give her what she never had. Give her security, protection and love.

But I chose the wrong way.

I only thought of myself and not about how she might take my gesture.

And yet, I knew it was a question of time, that the truth would eventually come out, that I should have told her right away. Maybe she would have hated me or maybe she would have understood. Or maybe we wouldn't have come together as we did and I wouldn't be here, left to bleed after she's abandoned me.

It hurts more and more. Even though I'm not a little kid anymore. Even though I've grown up, and should have learned by now that these things happen, no one is safe.

And it gets worse every time.

To be rejected, set aside.

Left alone.

I drag myself into the apartment, reliving our shared moments here, the places where she smiled at me, where she ate with me, where she sat. Where we made love.

Her scent surrounding me. Her taste in my head.

And her, in my fucking heart.

How could I have believed it, to have thought that there was something out there just for me?

I wasn't born for this, to have something healthy in my hands – love, a woman, a life, a future.

I've never had anything.

Not a family, not affection or warmth. I shared my mother with pain and suffering; with men who partly satisfied her needs, but never gave her anything.

I came into a family that wasn't mine; it was never mine, despite how much they've tried to make me feel welcome.

And now I'm in love with a woman I've hurt, who I lied to because I wanted to show her the good side of me. I thought she could love me and let me be the world to her.

I fought the demons of her past, believing they

were the only things that separated us – but I never thought for a second that the only thing that could really hurt us were lies, secrets and fear.

My fear.

I was so busy destroying hers that I let mine take over, hiding everything I should have told her at the beginning.

And now, all I have is an empty house.

I look around and an uncontrollable anger assails me. I want to break everything, the whole world, with my bare hands.

I grab a stool and slam it against the counter repeatedly. I'm going to destroy this whole fucking house.

All of it. I want to destroy myself too.

64
Riley

I fall asleep after a bottle of wine or two. I pass out on the floor and get up only at dawn, woken by the sounds on the road. I get onto my knees and try to stand up, but my head is spinning and I land splayed out on my bed.

I haven't cried. Not one tear.

He'll have nothing from me.

He won't even have my pain.

I feel a hammering in my head that's reverberating all over my body. I lift my head from the mattress and try to figure out what's going on.

These sounds aren't coming from my head.

I get up and approach the door. I put my ear to it.

"Riley..."

I close my eyes. I'm not listening.

"Open this damn door."

I can't breathe.

"I'm coming in anyway."

"Go away," I try, but I know he won't listen to me, just like I know he'll find a way in no matter whether I want him to or not.

I open the lock and the door slams open, almost knocking me over.

Ian comes into my apartment and closes the

door behind him. I step back, afraid of the expression on his face. I squash myself against the wall as he nails me to the wall with his hard stare.

"You left," he thunders.

"You seriously thought I'd stick around after...?"

"You left!" he repeats, and this time his voice is desperate. "You left me alone. After having told me all those things... All I wanted was to hold you and keep you close to me, and instead you walked out on me."

He lets his hands slide down the wall and it's only then that I notice they're all cut up.

"What...?"

"I destroyed everything."

I look at him, frightened.

"I had to. I can't remember. I can't think. I can't... without you."

"You're out of control, Ian."

He moves away from me and I start to breathe again.

"I shouldn't have, but I did. I shouldn't have let you in my house that afternoon. I shouldn't have let you dig up everything I was trying to push down. I shouldn't have let you back into my life!"

He steps back a few paces and touches his face.

"I shouldn't have waited all this time. You should have been mine from the first night at that party. I shouldn't have let you believe for a minute that I didn't want you, but I was hurt and scared. I didn't think I could do it, don't you get it? So, I waited. I waited for the feelings to go away. Waited for you to get out of my head. I had to keep you away from me, Riley. You... you would have destroyed me."

He paces around, his hands in his hair.

"Every time I left your house a part of me died because the only thing I wanted to do was stay." He brings his hand to his mouth. "And when I thought that one day someone else could have you, could take you away from me forever... You were killing me, Riley. All of that shit was killing me. To breathe next to you, to smile at you, talk to you, to not be able to touch you...I knew that if I did it once, I wouldn't be able to stop. But how could I? How? How could I know? Not even my mother wanted me, Riley! How could I know that you wanted me? To tell you everything... Lying to you like that, that night when you were ready to let yourself go in my arms... that was the most difficult thing I've ever done."

"You're delirious, Ian. You're out of your mind."

"I had done it. You were out of my life, I was sure of it. I was convinced. Poor sod," he laughs bitterly. "But then I understood, when I saw you in the hospital. When you were at my house. After I was here that first time, after you smiled at me that night. You hadn't done that in so long and when you did it again..." he sighs, "...my whole world shook."

"I don't believe you. I don't know why I've even let you set foot in my house."

He turns again and speaks to me.

"The more I tried to ignore what my heart was telling me, the louder it yelled. The more I tried to kid myself that it was just a fling, the more my soul was searching for yours. The more I tried with all of my might not to fall in love with you... the more I went crazy at the idea of never being able to love you."

"I don't want to listen to you, it's all just lies!"

He grabs me by the wrist and pulls me to him.

"I slept with you because I was dying to have you. And I fell in love with you because my heart, Riley, recognised you right away. I knew that I could only love you, for the rest of my life. And I wanted you... I still want you," he lets go of my arm and caresses my face, speaking right against my lips.

"I want it all – your pain, your fears, your past because it's all a part of you. I just want you."

It's too much.

I can't handle this.

I need to breathe.

I look down, because I can't tell him what I need to while looking him in the eyes.

"I'm sorry, Ian – but I could never love a man like you."

The door slams hard behind him and I know that this really is the last time.

65
Ian

"Get up!"

A pillow lands on my head.

"I said get up!"

I open one eye and then close it right away. No. Not my arsehole brother, not now."

"Move your arse."

"Fuck off, Ryan."

"You haven't been to the gym or been home in days. I'm worried about you."

"I'm sick."

He sits on the bed and hits me again with a pillow that feels about as soft as a brick.

"Are you crazy?!" I yell, hearing my skull explode.

"You can't just give up on everything."

"Mind your own business."

"You can't do all this just for a woman."

"Are you being serious?"

"You can't make the same mistake I did, I won't let you."

I sit on the edge of the bed while Ryan hands me a cup of coffee.

"Do you even know what day it is?"

"Do you think I give a shit?"

Ryan sighs in frustration. "I warned you. You should have listened to me. If you really cared about her so much, you should have told her the truth right away."

"I don't need one of your 'I told you so's'."

"You never need anything," he says through gritted teeth.

"I wish that was true."

I stand up, and he mirrors me.

"What happened to this house?" he asks alluding to the damage that lies everywhere, the broken furniture, the smashed glass.

"Come on, I'll give you a hand cleaning up."

"What's the point? She's not coming back. I'm alone again."

"You landed on your feet once, you'll do it again. Like me. Are we or are we not O'Connors?"

I give a tight smile.

"It'll pass," he says, putting a hand on my shoulder.

"Has it passed for you?"

"In some ways; you need to go on."

"She doesn't love me, Ryan."

"I know how that feels."

"How do you get by? How do you go on, knowing that your heart won't work like it did before, that your life won't ever be complete?"

"You just survive. And you cling on to what's left. Rugby, the team, your family."

It seems like I've gone back in time, but now our roles are reversed.

"I wish that could be enough."

"I'd like to tell you that one day it won't hurt so much, that you'll find someone else and all of this will be an old memory for you, but I'm not so sure. But you've been through it once, and you found your way out of it."

"It's different this time."

"What makes you think so?"

"I just know."

"What do you think about having a shower now? Or have you smashed that up too?"

"I think it's still standing."

Only because it doesn't remind me of her.

"Make yourself presentable, I'll start picking up."

"Thanks, Ryan."

He shrugs. "You're my brother."

"You know that's not true."

"You always have been."

I nod, avoiding a response because I can barely keep it together. I could go back to breaking things like a sobbing, pathetic little boy, but none of those options seem sensible to me.

I get under the shower and let the water clear my thoughts.

Riley doesn't want me. Riley doesn't love me. Riley has abandoned me.

Just like they all do.

I let myself be manipulated and destroyed by a pair of sad eyes and a body that seems tailor-made for me.

I feel like an idiot for thinking I could have her, love her. But no one can be held down, even if you beg them to stay.

I'll never make that mistake again. I never want to feel that pain again, even if this time it's worse.

It's all-consuming. It's like a massacre.

This time it was different. This time I really believed in it.

66
Riley

"You could have stayed home for a few days. You're not looking so hot."

"It's just the flu," I justify to Kate. "And the New Year show's coming up. It's important."

"So's your health."

"A little bit of fever never killed anyone."

Kate looks at me, perplexed. I can tell she wants to say more, but the topic has become taboo between us. No one will say the words 'Ian O'Connor'.

"Here," Ray comes into my office, bringing me a cup of tea. "You have to try and get this down."

"My stomach is in knots," I say turning my face the other way.

Ray sighs in frustration and places the tea on my desk before leaving me alone. I try sitting at the computer, but my headache and constant nausea don't help. I look at the tea and think, maybe a sip wouldn't hurt, but as soon as I put the mug to my lips I'm overcome with another wave of nausea.

I cover my mouth and run to the bathroom, kneeling down in front of the toilet, but the only thing that comes out are a few choking coughs. I'm not surprised, I haven't eaten in days.

I lift myself up as best I can and go back to

where I was, with the intention of going home and trying not to think about the weight I've got on my heart.

I get in a taxi after having promised Ray that I'll jump right in bed and that I'll call him if I need anything. He even offered to stay over so I didn't have to spend the night alone, but I don't want to ruin anyone's plans tonight, especially his. He's started going out recently with a guy who's really got his life together – the kind of guy that doesn't lie to you or leave you with an empty heart.

At home, I get undressed and put on a tracksuit, planning to crawl back under the covers and die of starvation, but someone knocks on my door so I'm forced to postpone my plans.

I know it's not him. He'd never come back after what I told him.

I slowly open the door and stick my nose out when two familiar eyes surprise me.

"Hi Riley."

"Ryan?"

"I dropped by to see how you were doing."

"If he sent you here—"

"I'm not here for him, I'm here for you. Can I come in?"

I let him in, but as soon as I do, Jamie's guilty smile hits me.

"You're a traitor Ryan O'Connor! You're all the same." I turn and try to go back to bed quickly but I no longer have the energy, not even to get angry.

"Are you ill?" Jamie's questions follow me, as he takes my arm.

"Just a bit of flu."

"You could have called me, I'd have come over."

I look at him sideways.

"I know that you love me," he smiles tenderly.

"You're a traitor, too."

"Come on, I'll put you to bed."

I accept, even though all I want to do right now is slap him silly but I'm too weak to act out.

He tucks me in and stands there, watching me. "I'm sorry."

"It's not enough," I say crossing my arms.

Then I look at Ryan. "You know, don't you?"

Ryan shrugs. "He only told me because he was in pieces. He needed to vent."

"He was in pieces?" I say furiously.

Jamie takes my hand, forcing me to look at him. "He still is, even now."

I bite my lip hard and start shaking.

"I didn't want to betray your trust – or his."

"I really doubt that…"

"You shouldn't," Ryan says, interrupting our discussion. "My brother has a lot of flaws, but lying isn't one of them."

I sink back into my pillows and into my discomfort. I don't like that my life is being discussed by a group.

"Is it true?" Ryan continues.

"What?"

"What you told him."

I sigh. "It doesn't matter anymore."

"It does matter."

"Ian and I weren't meant to be together. It was a mistake, right from the start."

"I agree with you," he says honestly. "And I think it's a load of bullshit – but that's my opinion. My brother seems to think otherwise."

"Your brother lied to me."

"He really fucked things up."

"He hurt me."

"I'm sorry about that. I know how it feels."

"He's not who I thought he was."

"I don't imagine he is. People never are," he says bitterly. "And he doesn't believe in people, never has. Sometimes he doesn't even believe in himself. He seems like a rock but I assure you, Ian's just a little pebble in the middle of a big sea."

I breathe slowly in fear that the pain will take me away with it.

"I don't like you, Riley."

"Wow, thanks."

"Don't take it personally, it's not your fault, I just don't believe in women. But he believed in you – he still does believe in you and I'm his brother and I love him. I think what's good for him is you."

I bite my lip, anxious.

"You don't know much about him, do you?"

"I know about his mother and the situation with your father," I say uncertainly.

"And do you know what he's done for us over the years? What he does for our family? How he takes care of my parents while Nick and I are busy hating each other? How he helped me?"

I shake my head.

"Can I tell you about it?"

"I won't change my mind about him."

"Maybe not, but before saying that he's not the person you thought he was, you should know what kind of person he really is."

67
Ian

I'm back to living my life, back to the routine I had before her.

I take all my emotion out in the gym, on the field when I can, but I'm still a disaster. The coach keeps threatening to bench me, and I just take it and bury it because I don't know what else to do.

Not even sport has the same meaning for me that it once did.

Sitting on the bench and looking ahead of me, Jamie comes to sit by my side.

"Okay, I pretended for a while, but now I have to tell you what I have to say," Jamie starts with a low, serious voice. "This is just a warning, but it could become permanent."

"You can do what you want, Jamie."

"The problem is, I don't want to. The team doesn't want to. Neither do the coach or the president, for God's sake."

I shrug.

"In two weeks, we're going to begin training for the Nationals, Ian. Do you really want to throw this all away? How hard have you worked to be here? How long have you waited for the call?"

"My whole life," I say through gritted teeth.

"Exactly. And now you're throwing it all in the

shitter."

"It's just a shitty time."

"Think about your family, your father."

I close my eyes suddenly.

"How are things going at home?"

"There are good days and terrible ones."

He puts his hand on my shoulder. "Have you seen her?"

I shake my head.

"Mmm?"

"Okay, yes. I've seen her passing by."

"Someone told me you go to Parnell street every day."

"What?!" I say, jumping to my feet a little too quickly. "Who the hell…?"

But there's no need for him to tell me.

Fucking Ryan. Now I really would like that chainsaw.

"He's worried about you. We all are."

"No need. I'm all grown up and I don't need anyone checking up on me or giving me pep talks."

"That's true," he says standing up. "You don't need it. You don't need anything, do you?"

"Nope."

"She's not well. Again. She's really angry with me but she'll get over it. She can't keep it up forever."

"We shouldn't have gone behind her back. I

shouldn't have."

"I know, and I feel responsible. I want to fix things somehow."

"I don't think it's possible to fix anything. She hates me, Jamie. She doesn't want me."

"Both of those points are laughable."

"She made it very clear. She could never be in love with someone like me."

"And you believed it? I didn't think you were that gullible."

"I don't know what to believe right now."

"In yourself," he says seriously. "You have to believe in yourself and you'll see that things'll work out."

"I'm not so sure of that."

"Have faith, okay? Give her some time to come to terms with it, you'll see that she'll be reasonable, will be ready to clear things up. In the meantime, try not to let yourself go too much and don't give up all hope. You're not the giving up kind."

"Well, it would appear that I'm not that tough."

"You really are. Now, let's get ready, training awaits."

He smiles as he walks away from me, leaving the changing room and heading to the gym.

I stay on the bench, staring into the emptiness that I'm waiting to pass, so that I can start to concentrate on my life again.

So that I can start working out and training seriously, so that I can focus my mind on the championship, the national team. So that I can think about my family. So that I can think about me.

I have to go back, rewind the tape. Erase. Forget.

I won't let any other woman get so close to me. I won't look beyond the physical. Won't dig into their hearts. Won't let them take everything and leave me with fuck all.

No one will ever do it again.

* * *

She opens the glass door and goes down the stairs slowly, bundled up in her coat, closed away in her hiding place. Just like every other day.

She doesn't look around, doesn't notice anything, doesn't hear anything. Exactly like me.

She walks distractedly down the street and crosses at the traffic light, going almost the entire way down O'Connell Street. She stops outside the window of a Starbucks.

She waits there.

Then she continues down the street, going into Kylemore.

Just like she does every day.

She disappears into the crowd, then I see her sitting at a table, alone in the most secluded corner of the place.

She endlessly stirs her drink, staring at her cup. Then she stops and rests her spoon on the table.

Just like she does every day.

She doesn't drink it. She doesn't lift her eyes. She doesn't breathe.

Exactly like me.

She sits there for an hour doing nothing but surviving me.

I stay outside for an hour doing nothing but surviving her.

When she leaves the building, she heads back towards Parnell Street, to the theatre, as I hide away like a delinquent and keep watching her, spying on her: feeling her even if she can't feel me.

Like every other fucking day.

I watch her walk away slowly, weaving between the crowd, as I feel my heart getting smaller and smaller every minute.

I follow her steps towards Parnell Street, grab my motorbike and I jump on, ready to face another day of pretending that everything's fine, that I'm fine, that nothing's happened. That I'm not slowly dying.

Like every fucking other day.

Exactly like her.

68
Riley

"You're still not well."

"It's just hanging on a bit."

"I haven't seen you eat in days, Riley."

"It's this damn virus."

"Have you been to a doctor?"

I look at him sideways.

"You should," Ray tells me, sitting on my bed and biting into his sandwich.

"Don't you have a life?"

"I like being here."

"To torment me."

"If you like…"

I try to smile but my stomach protests and suggests that maybe it would be better to defer.

"Aren't you drinking, either?"

"I'm sick."

"Er…"

"What?"

"Are you sure it's the flu?"

"Oh, come on, Ray!"

He raises his hands and doesn't push it.

"And no news?"

I glare at him.

"You know I follow the team."

"So?"

"He's missed three games. They haven't called him up."

"That means nothing."

"He's their best player, in every sense."

"Ray."

"It's true, he always plays from the first minute."

"Maybe he got hurt."

"They would have said so, dear. A journalist tried to ask him some questions after the last match but the press is keeping quiet about him. It would appear that his spot on the national team is on the line."

I shake my head. "That can't be my fault."

"No, certainly not, maybe he's had other problems."

His reflection brings me back to what Ryan had said.

"What is it?"

"Nothing," I lie.

"Something you don't want to tell me."

"It's private."

"Er…"

"I don't want to talk about it. It's not about me."

"You don't have to explain anything to me if you don't want to."

And his words take me back in time a few

years.

"Have you at least spoken to your brother?"

"He's not in my good books at the moment."

"Don't talk shit."

"This whole thing is partly his fault, too."

"I'm sure that he did what he did for your own good."

"Well, there are better ways of helping someone," I say angrily, crossing my arms.

Ray raises his hands in a good faith gesture before looking at me with those eyes full of compassion that make me want to scream at him.

"You should call a doctor, Riley. Seriously."

"I will, I promise."

"Today?"

"Today."

"Good," he says before looking at his watch. "I'd better get back to the theatre. Somebody has to work."

"Thanks for coming round."

"Of course, sweetie," he says, giving me a hug and going towards the door, but the minute he opens it he exclaims: "Oh, holy shit!"

A round of laughter explodes.

"Er, Riley? You've got company."

I look up in time to see Nick fill out the doorframe of my bedroom.

"Oh, Jesus, you O'Connor brothers never let anything go, do you?"

Nick smiles, deeply satisfied. "Never."

"Can I leave you in his hands?" Ray asks looking him over shamelessly from head to toe.

I wave him away and sit back down. I hear the door close and I sigh in frustration. I know I'm not going to be able to get away from any of them.

"Wow, we're not doing so great," he says sarcastically, sitting on my bed and invading my space.

"Why are you here, Nick?"

"I have to take off for a few days: but before I do, I wanted to speak to you. I'm worried about Ian. I don't want him to end up like me."

"I don't get it."

"Alone, a cynical arsehole."

I snort with derision.

"He was never like me. He's always managed to do good things. He's nowhere near as tough as he pretends to be," he says, smiling and shaking his head. "He's got a big heart, Riley. He never would have hurt you intentionally. Ian's not capable of that, believe me."

"I don't know. The truth is that I just don't trust him," I say, as I slide out of bed but my head is spinning, pushing me back down.

"You're really rough," he comments.

"I just—" I can't finish the sentence because a sharp pain in my stomach bends me in two.

"Riley," Nick helps me to lie down again. "How long have you felt like this? Don't you think we should call a doctor?"

"A week," I reply, trying to take deep breaths. "Maybe two."

Nick takes the phone out of his pocket. "I'm calling someone."

"No, there's no..." but another fit makes me shout.

My body goes tense, the pain expands and then, nothing.

69
Ian

I set down all my stuff on the belt and walk through the security gate. I gather up my things and stuff them back in my bag, which I sling over my shoulder, following the guys over to the gate. People are looking at us, recognising us. We definitely don't go unnoticed and with our jerseys on, even an idiot could figure it out.

I try to ignore the looks I'm getting, but I feel their eyes on me – for the first time, it bothers me. I don't want anyone looking at me. I don't want them reading my eyes and understand how I'm feeling. I don't want my pain to be put on display. It's private and it should stay that way.

We sit down and wait to be called for boarding. Jamie is sitting next to me: he won't leave me alone even for a second. Maybe he thinks I'm going to change my mind and refuse to leave.

He had to convince me, almost by force, to come along on this trip. The coach already told me he wasn't going to call me, at least not at the beginning, but he'd keep an eye on me to make sure I didn't screw anything else up. I had to let myself be seen, or I really would have given up my position on the team.

Mum called. Ryan called. Nick called; but I didn't answer any of their calls. I don't want to hear or see anyone.

I need to concentrate, be closed off in my own world, thinking about sport because it's the only thing that doesn't hurt me right now.

The phone rings again in my jacket and I pick it up angrily, planning to throw it against the wall. I could just turn it off, but my way seems more efficient and definitive. But then a voice announces over the load speaker that it's time to board so I do turn it off, having decided to ignore everyone at least until I get back home.

They can do without me for three days. My arsehole brothers will have to deal with it.

I get in line with Jamie – who is starting to get on my nerves – close at my heels, ready to forget everything else.

* * *

When I get back to my apartment three days later even more angry and stressed, I decide to turn on my phone again.

Mum, Ryan, Nick. And then Nick again. Nick, Nick, Nick, Nick.

A terrible doubt crosses my mind. I call him right away and wait nervously for an answer but the phone rings with no answer. I'm weighed down by the worst possible situation when I call my parents' house and my mother answers after only three rings.

"Mum?"

"Ian! You're back!"

"Are you okay? Dad, Ryan, Nick?"

"Yes, we're all fine."

I breathe a sigh of relief.

"Is Nick there by any chance? I can't find him."

"No, Ian. Nick's out. I haven't seen him in three days."

"Okay. I'm trying to get in touch with him. I'll call you later, okay?"

"Oh, don't worry. He's probably up to his old shenanigans."

"Say hi to Dad for me."

I hang up, but an anxiety hangs over me.

I look over all the calls I've received which are almost exclusively from Nick with one exception. Riley.

I catch my breath in my throat.

Two minutes later I'm on my bike.

* * *

I slow down about a hundred metres from her door to stop next to the pavement. Riley is huddled up in her coat walking slowly. There's a man next to her, one I know too well, a fucking prick that I'll kill with my own hands – this time, no one'll save him.

He carries her shopping. He smiles at her. He brushes her hair away from her face. She looks down timidly, awkwardly. The rage bubbles up like a wave, knocking me senseless.

I speed up and stop right in from of her door as he opens it and holds it for her. I get off my bike, throw down my helmet and grab his shoulders.

"You're a fucking bastard!" I scream in his face, before throwing the first punch at his nose, which should put an end to his modelling career – and hopefully to his life.

Nick doesn't fall down, he holds himself up against the door, touching the point where I hit him. Then he looks at me furiously.

"What the hell is wrong with you?!" he yells, straightening up.

I jump at the collar of his jacket, lifting him up off the ground with a strength I didn't know I had - but before I can throw him against a wall, someone grabs my arm.

"What the hell are you doing?!" Riley asks, panting.

"I'm going to kill him, that's what."

"Let him go!"

Of course she's defending him.

"I can't."

She looks at me, afraid.

"I can't let anyone take you away from me."

70
Riley

"You don't fucking get it!" Nick comes back to life and frees himself from Ian's grip.

"I should've seen this coming!" Ian yells at Nick. "I should've known what to expect from you."

"I can't believe this," Nick says. "Do you really think I'd do that to you?"

"It wouldn't be the first time."

"This can't be happening." Nick says, backing away nervously. "I was just trying to give you a hand, for God's sake."

"A hand? Who were you helping, exactly? Let's hear it..."

"You, you dick!"

"Me?" Ian laughs hysterically. "And how's that? By screwing my girlfriend?"

"What?"

"Isn't that what's happening, Riley? Haven't you already found someone else?" he turns to me, spewing all of his rage.

"Are you serious?!" I yell furiously.

"My brother, Riley, how could you? How you both?!"

"You... you... Go away, Ian. Get out of my life right now." I go into the house, trying to close the door behind me, but Ian sticks his foot in the doorway, blocking it. Then he slams it, coming in to my apartment, followed by Nick.

"What was I to you?"

Nick grabs him by the shoulder and pulls him away from me.

"Calm down!"

"Are we already at this point?" he yells.

"Can't you see that you're scaring her?"

Ian looks at me and when he realises that I'm shaking the edge in his eyes vanishes, replaced with guilt.

"How could I?" I whisper to myself overwhelmed. "How could I have fallen in love with you?" I say it while holding his gaze. I say it without any other emotion breaking through, even though I'm crumbling on the inside. I tell him with pain in my heart.

Silence falls over my apartment. Silence which is broken only by our uneven breathing.

Ian doesn't react, he stands in front of me looking at me without really seeing me, as if his mind were elsewhere.

"I am an idiot," I comment out loud. "How could I have believed that behind your tough guy façade there was something else?" I step dangerously close to him. "How could I believe that you weren't a liar, a bastard?" I say, backing him up against a wall. "Believe that you were different?" He lets himself be crushed by me. "How could I believe that you felt...?" but I can't go on because my tears close up my throat. He'll have no more from me.

"There's nothing going on between us, Ian. I was just giving her a hand." Nick tries to calm us down and bring us back some peace. "You didn't answer my calls, I even tried calling you on her phone, but you ignored it. I never would have done that and she…" he looks at me smiling. "She wouldn't have either."

He puts a hand on his back but Ian doesn't look at him.

"I hope you'll clear things up now and get back to your old self."

Then he comes over to me and gives me a kiss on the cheek. I see Ian's hands ball into fists.

"I'm sure it'll work out," he says. "He seems like a tough guy but in the end he's just a teddy bear."

I smile slightly too.

"Call me if you need me," he adds, before leaving my apartment.

Ian and I stand in silence, backs against the walls on opposite sides of the room.

"My brother, Nick…"

"If you have a trust issue with your brother, you need to talk to him, not to me."

"Why was he here?"

"Are you really asking me that?"

"I don't know what I'm doing."

"You don't know me at all, Ian. How could

you even think that I..."?

He runs his hand over his face.

"He came by to talk to me about you."

"About me?"

"And then..."

"Then what? Did he put his hands on you? Did he do something? Tell me he didn't touch you or I will kill him and no one will run to save him."

He speaks right next to me, panting. His arms are tense along his sides, his jaw is contracted, his muscles flexed, his eyes dark and lost.

And then, Ian O'Connor simply breaks down.

Like an avalanche of snow.

He falls and rolls down the mountain, stopping one pace from my heart.

"I couldn't stand it, Riley," he says, shaking. "I couldn't stand someone else touching you," he continues, closing his eyes. "I can't lose... You."

71
Ian

She bites her lip and starts to shake.

I suddenly grab her face in my hands. Just touching her throws me down into the deepest, most terrifying abyss.

I pull back instantly.

"I can't touch you," I tell her honestly. "I couldn't even think straight, I could never let you go."

And then she's the one to touch me. Her hands slide slowly down my face.

"Well then don't. Don't let me go." She says, her eyes full of sincerity. Eyes in which her soul shines with all of her sweetness, her strength, her pain and her fear.

"I don't know how it happened, or when, I don't know how to tell you the exact moment my heart started beating again, but it did: just for you."

My knees go weak in her grasp, but she holds me.

"You don't know anything about me."

"I know what matters. I know that you're a good man with a big heart. That you love your family more than anything on earth. That you stayed here when everyone else left, to defend what you had. I know you love your brothers, even if you insist they're a thorn in your side. I know that you're fun, cheeky and impulsive, but you have a tenderness that comes out only when it's necessary: and when it does, there's a warmth that could heat the entire world."

I drop my gaze because I can no longer hold my head. I can't fight what I hear.

"I know you thought you were doing the right thing, that you thought you were helping me. I know that when you realised your mistake you were overwhelmed with guilt. I know that you suffered for it, that people have hurt you and that you're afraid that I will too."

"You don't understand. I can't stand it. Not if it's you doing it."

"Ian..."

"I couldn't watch you leave me again. My heart just couldn't take it. I need something that's all mine, Riley. Mine alone. Something that stays, someone who will be with me for the rest of my life. Always. Not someone who takes off at the first problem, someone who turns their back on me and leaves me alone with nothing in my hands and an empty heart. I need..."

She stops my monologue, squeezing my hands. I look at her and then my heart melts in her fingers.

"I am yours," she says. I feel the knot in my throat, my eyes burning and my heart pounding.

"I am yours, Ian," she repeats, as the first tear falls.

I leave her hands and caress her face, drying the

tear with my thumb.

"You're crying, Riley. You're crying."

She nods as her tears turn into sobs.

"God Riley…" I pull in towards her lips. "Tell me again,"

"Yours, Ian. *Only yours.*"

And a second later my lips are on her face. I kiss her tears and gently breathe in her skin. I kiss her eyes, her cheeks and then put my lips on hers, afraid that this impossible dream may vanish before me.

But then her legs give way, and she falls into my arms.

"Riley what's wrong?"

I lift her, bring her to the bedroom and set her on the bed. I touch her face and another wave of tears arrives, ready to drown me.

"What's happening? What is it? Tell me."

She takes my hands and places them on her belly. A bolt of lightning stops my heart.

"We… we're yours."

72
Riley

He looks at me, not making a sound.

"Us." I squeeze his hands, still on my stomach. "Something that's just ours," I say before a sob can break my voice. "I'm sorry."

"You're sorry? For what?"

"I didn't know."

"Everything's alright, Riley. Everything's okay. I'm here, okay?"

"Are you mad? Upset? Is this too much for you?"

Her voice is quivering. "Do you have any idea how I feel right now? Do you know how much I fucking love you?"

"Ian, I…"

"Shh," he squeezes me tighter. "You don't have to say anything. Just tell me you'll stay. Because I love you, Riley. I love you so much it hurts my heart. I love you so much I can't sleep at night and can't think of anything else. I've loved you from that first damn night, always. I have loved you every fucking day…"

I lift my eyes.

"I can handle anything except losing you."

"You won't lose me," I whisper through my tears.

"You're here, with me... You're the best thing that has ever happened to me. You're the only thing I've ever had in my hands..."

Ian holds me tightly to his chest. I take in his scent like it's a drug, my medicine, and let him cradle me, kiss me. Take everything away and give me himself back.

He lies down next to me and I curl up in his arms.

"Are you okay? Is everything alright?"

"We're both fine." Saying it out loud fills me with emotion.

He hugs me, resting my back against him. Then he puts his hands under my sweatshirt and gently touches my skin.

"My... my own child..." his voice breaks.

His control breaks.

Ian O'Connor breaks.

But I'm here to help get him back on his feet.

I let my hands rub his as I hear him crying over my shoulder. His tears wet my skin and penetrate my heart, quenching it and letting it bloom again with hope and love.

"Stay here," he kisses my neck. "Stay here with me."

I look up. His eyes are tired, immense and swollen.

"Both of you."

I touch his beard and another tear falls.

"I love you Riley. I love you so much I'd break

apart the entire world just to put it back together for you, brick by brick, with my own hands."

"Ian…"

"You… you…" he whispers, grasping onto me desperately. "I can't believe it… a family…"

"Our family."

"No one will touch you again, I swear to you. No one will ever hurt you. You don't need to hide. You won't be alone. I'm here now. I'll always be here. No one is leaving. I'm your family, Riley. You and… you both are."

And that's all it takes for me to break down.

And I cry, all night.

I cry without saying a word. I cry without strength or voice.

I cry all the tears I've been holding back my whole life.

I cry for all the years I spent in fear.

I cry for the pain that I still feel and always will. I cry for what I lost and what I'll never get back.

And he kisses me, taking away my breath and everything else, and giving me himself in its place.

It's the only thing I want.

73
Ian

"What are you doing?"

Riley shows up in the kitchen. Her eyes are still swollen and her face tells me that she's barely slept. I didn't close my eyes all night, worrying about her, about me, about this child and what I almost lost.

I spent the night holding her, hoping she'd calm down, and she only fell asleep from exhaustion around dawn.

"I'm making breakfast."

"Oh," she says, embarrassed.

"Someone has to cook to stop this family going hungry."

"This family," she repeats quietly.

"My family," I say with pride. "Go back to bed, I'll be there soon."

"We can eat here."

"Nah, I like seeing you lying down."

"O'Connor," she chides, crossing her arms as I laugh at her tone.

"Not necessarily in that sense."

Riley goes back to the room smiling, and I finish making breakfast. I take two plates of eggs on toast and bring them to her.

"Are you hungry?"

I sit in front of her and watch her eat. Okay, eat is a big word – I watch her try.

"Don't you feel well?"

"It's just nausea."

"I'm sorry."

She smiles. "It's okay."

"Can I do anything to make you feel better?"

"You could be less perfect."

I laugh, dropping my plate.

"I'm not perfect."

"You seem pretty perfect to me."

"Okay then, let's see... I'm grumpy, even when I speak."

She laughs, shaking her head.

"I'm unreasonable and a bit of an arsehole. I'm a hothead and I have two hopeless brothers."

"Okay, you've given me a clear picture," she stops me.

My laughter cuts short the moment the words rise up in me and leave my lips.

"Stay with me, Riley. Every day and every night. Let me love you and show you that I am capable of giving a lot... giving you everything. And I will. For you. For you both. Because I've never given anyone what I'm willing to give you now. I've always been yours, even when I didn't know you. Let me take care of my family from the start, because you're my whole life now. All I want is to have you with me and make sure that no one touches you or makes you suffer, that no one tries to take you away from me in any way."

"What are you trying to tell me?"

"I want you to move in with me. Today. Or we can find another place, somewhere you like."

"Don't you think we're rushing things a bit?"

I take her hands and bring them to my heart.

"Can you feel that?"

She nods just slightly as my heart beats wildly against her palm.

"That's what you've done to me. You've given me everything I needed and now I want to do the same. I want to give you a house, a place where you'll feel loved every fucking day. A place where you don't have to hide, where you can be whatever you want to be. A place where I can see you as you really are and you can see me, always. Because I swear, I'll never hold back again. I want to give you my life and my heart... Well, to be honest, you've already got it. It's yours. Your name is written on it and I've used permanent ink."

I smile before biting my lip.

"It'll be fine. I'm not going anywhere and I won't lie to you again. I'll breathe in all of your tears and your smiles and I'll always find you when you try to hide, because my heart will know where you are. You just have to trust me, Riley. Will you do it?"

She takes my hands and brings them to her heart.

Yes, she will.
Hell yes, she will.

Epilogue
Ian

I always struggle in the morning.

When I open my eyes, the first thing I do is reach out my right arm to make sure that she's there, she's real and she's sleeping next to me.

Sometimes I wake up really early, before dawn. I turn onto my side and rest my head on her arm.

And I look at her.

I look at her sleeping peacefully. Sometimes she makes faces and other times she smiles and when she does, I don't know why, but I imagine that she's dreaming of me.

Sometimes she snores, but I've never told her. I'm sure she'd deny it and be get angry over it – although, I have to confess, I like pissing her off just to make it up to her, possibly horizontally. But I don't enjoy playing with fire too much, at least not at this point.

She's tiny, it's true. But she knows how to defend herself.

I usually wake up much earlier than she does. I make breakfast which I leave warmed up in the kitchen before going to training. I kiss her lightly on the lips and she smiles – I've never understood if she's still sleeping at that point or if she's semi-conscious. I do know that one time I forgot to do it because I was in a hurry to get to the gym and she wouldn't talk to me for two days.

I say hello to him… or her. We still don't know.

I kiss her stomach and wish them both a good day, with a heart swollen with love and a commitment to do my very best by both of them so that they can both be proud of me.

We've been in the new house for about a month. We live in Santry, my parents' neighbourhood. When I suggested finding a house instead of raising a child in a garage, she was shocked. To be honest, she didn't want a house like this one. She'd have preferred something small and anonymous – something simple and basic – but it was time for a change. Time to look forward and forget about my stupid preconceptions, to give them both what they deserve.

I mean, I have to spend the money I earn somehow.

What better way than on them?

My family deserves a real house, with a back garden *and* a front garden, with two floors and a big, bright kitchen where I can cook for them. A dining room where we can eat with the family and a bedroom where – well, I don't have to explain that.

We live here because I want to stay close to my parents, to make sure they're alright. Riley has a big heart and loves them almost as much as I do, so she agreed to the idea right away.

I can't abandon them, they've given me everything and I will continue to be there for them.

Unfortunately, my brothers live in the same area – obviously in opposite ends of town.

Ryan got a small but nice place to rent in Parklands, while Nick is staying in a loft in Northwood. It's too big and too quiet for one person, but it's Nick, and he always has to show off what he's got.

It's convenient living in Santry. It's just fifteen minutes by bus for Riley to get to work. Her stop in the city is just a hundred metres from the theatre. Living so close to my family, Riley will never be alone, even when I'm away for matches.

For now, she comes with me wherever I go, but in a few months the pregnancy will become harder and she'll have to give up some of these trips. I'll definitely miss her being there, but I know that when I get home I'll find her waiting, because Riley's not about to abandon me.

It took me a while to truly believe that.

Yes, I'm a grown man, but past wounds are always there, ready to remind me who I am, where I come from and what I've been through.

For years I denied everything to everyone. For years, I've kept my distance from everything that scared me and managed to keep going, but it nearly destroyed me – and almost brought her down with me.

I'll never be able to forgive myself for rejecting her, for denying her all I will never be able to give back to her, the things she's lost.

I can't erase the shadow of her past, but I'm here now to help her face it step by step, and help her to come out of her shell every once in a while. To help her feel everything, to enjoy the little victories, to get over the sad times and to believe.

This is my place, next to her, and no one could ever take it.

And Riley... well, she's beautiful, sweet, tormented but strong. She is who she is and I love every little part of her, even the painful parts.

She is the woman who tied me to her with a stupid debt that I could never pay back. She is the one who woke up one morning screaming like a madman at my house. She always saw me for what I was. She unknowingly saves my life, every day, because she saved me from losing myself and denying myself to the world.

At times, I wonder where my mother is, how she found the courage to leave me and not look back. I'm still not a father, but I feel an unconditional love for this child that will never go away. How can a person not feel something so strong, how could you forget that it's a part of you? How could you leave it, alone, with no safety, no future?

I'll never find the answer and I won't know how things really went – a part of me will always suffer for that. But the time has come to put it behind me and think about the future.

I take a sip of my coffee as I look out the window overlooking the garden, that's just starting to flower. Dad helped Riley plant some rose bushes, and comes round to cut the grass when he can. Even though I'm perfectly capable of doing it myself, he insists on coming and I let him because he has good intentions. He loves giving back, and making himself useful to the family.

He adores Riley as if she had always been his daughter. She's the only one he talks to when he's having one of his moments, other than my mother.

Maybe sensitive people just recognise that trait in one another. Maybe it binds them somehow with strangers. Perhaps Dad feels the need to reassure her and make her feel special, even though half the time he has no idea who she is. And maybe Riley feels the need to be there for him, because she knows what it means to be alone, to feel left out and not know where to go.

I'm happy about their relationship. And the one she's got with my mother too. I'm a little less thrilled about how well she gets on with my brothers and how they all gang up on me together. I just want her to be happy, see her laugh, because when I see her laughing I know that I'm doing the right thing, that I'm the right person.

The only one who will love her more than anything else in the world, someone who's all hers.

Forever.

Riley

A horn beeps incessantly outside my house. I open the door in just enough time to flip him off then go back inside to put my things in my bag, ready to go.

I look around a moment and smile at our little hiding place, my refuge, ours, where the only thing we hide from are Ian's brothers who are always in our space.

But I know he doesn't really mind, even though he makes a big fuss about it. And I care even less than he does.

After all these years, I finally have a family. A family that listens to me, that loves me and always stands by me. A family I don't hide from.

I'm no longer alone thanks to the O'Connors, and I never will be. And in a few months, our family will grow.

I still can't believe it. It's something I wasn't expecting. I had the flu, and the antibiotics I was taking cancelled out the effect of my birth control pill: so we have this little miracle now.

The pregnancy is going well, the child is healthy.

After the fear of the initial cramps that sent Nick out of his mind, I started to really believe it and thanks to Ian and his love I'm confident that we can finally have it all: all the things we've dreamt of and never thought possible.

I'll never forget the past. What Jamie and I went through, the years that were stolen from us and the fear of not making it.

It's part of me, like a brand – even though I tried to hide it in the deepest of places. But when I look in the mirror at night before going to bed, I still feel like the same person, a young girl who was shivering in the cold one winter night, swearing to her brother that they'd have a better life. A life he now has, which I will always be grateful for.

And now I've got my chance too. After all these years, I can finally breathe. I can be and feel anything I want.

I can just be the disaster that I am. Because I know that someone loves me for what I have been and what I am now. Someone who feels exactly like I do.

The only thing that worries me now is Ian's fear. I still feel it in his gestures, his looks, as if I could vanish before his eyes in an instant.

I reassure him every morning when he watches me sleeping, because I know he needs that. So, I pretend to sleep. It's the only thing I'm still faking.

I pretend I don't notice his eyes on me, that I don't hear his sighs and sometimes a few tears as well.

Ian O'Connor is a tough man who's impenetrable for many, but not for me.

For me, he's just Ian: the man who faced his

fears and changed his life for love. And for that love, he changed mine too.

Ian is the man who has always loved me, even when I was in pieces, even when there was nothing in me to love. He's the only person who's always seen me, despite the fact that I tried to hide myself as best I could.

He searched for me, he uncovered me and made me step into the light. If I tried to hide again, he'd find me, because he knows where to look.

I open the door, set the alarm and head to the car, where I find Nick waiting.

"You took long enough."

"Hi to you too, Nick."

He makes a face that is completely meaningless because I know he's not really upset.

"Where's Ryan?"

He shrugs and turns on the radio.

We cross the neighbourhood and head towards the city, passing into south Dublin in the direction of Aviva Stadium.

I'm as excited as a little girl and a bit nervous, too - so much so that Ian voiced his concern at my coming to the game, but it's his first match on the national team and I want to be there. Jamie will be at his side, he'll start from the bench but I know he is as emotional as Ian is, and is happy to have him once again by his side on this new adventure.

We sit in our places and find Ryan there waiting for us. I take off my jacket to show off my brand-new jersey. My national team shirt with his name on back.

O'Connor.

I also have the scarf and hat, and my face is painted Ireland's colours.

I'm here. Cheering on *my* player.

I'm sure that Jamie will turn up his nose a bit when he finds out, and he'll pretend to be offended and jealous, but I know he's happy for me. For us.

I get up nervously to search the field, trying to calm the restlessness that I have in watching him play, run, win. Because Ian O'Connor is a winner and no one can say otherwise.

And he's *my* winner.

"What's up, Riley? Can you sit down? You're making me nervous."

I turn towards Ryan and give him the finger.

"My brother is a terrible influence on you," he comments sarcastically.

"Maybe the problem is how much time I spend with you," I reply in the same tone of voice, crossing my arms.

"You won't even fit into that jersey pretty soon," he says pointing at my stomach.

"Oh, fu—"

"Hey, children," Nick calls us to order. "The team is taking the field."

I sit back, immediately forgetting about Ryan and Nick and everyone else in the stadium.

Because now, the only thing that exists is Ian and his most important game yet.

The big screen shows us images of the team as the announcer introduces them one by one.

When they say his name, I jump to my feet like a lunatic, waving my arms.

Ian lifts his gaze and smiles.

For me.

I know full well that he hasn't heard me, or seen me – but he feels me.

Because Ian and I feel each other.

He knows I'm here and I know he feels my presence, as if we were one person.

Because we live for one another.

I live for Ian O'Connor.

And he lives for me.

Printed in Great Britain
by Amazon